"What are you doing?"

Lindsey brushed her knuckles against Walker's cheek, whose stubble felt wickedly sexy to her, and whispered, "You really are working too many weekends if you don't know what I'm doing."

Walker reached for her hand, ostensibly to stop whatever wonderful something she was doing to his face, but he managed only to take her hand in his. Once he'd done so, he seemed unable to turn it loose.

"Lindsey—"

Her fingers entwined with his.

"—this is not—"

She leaned forward.

"—a good idea."

Her breath fanned against his mouth milliseconds before her lips brushed his.

Walker moaned, then told himself to stop this . . . while he still could.

Dear Reader,

Welcome to Silhouette **Special Edition**... welcome to romance. Each month, Silhouette **Special Edition** publishes six novels with you in mind—stories of love and life, tales that you can identify with—romance with that little "something special" added in.

This month, Silhouette **Special Edition** is full of special treats for you. We're hosting Nora Roberts's third book in her exciting THE CALHOUN WOMEN series—*For the Love of Lilah.* Each line at Silhouette Books has published one book of the series. Next month look for *Suzanna's Surrender* in the Silhouette Intimate Moments line!

Silhouette **Special Edition** readers are also looking forward to the second book in the compelling SONNY'S GIRLS series, *Don't Look Back* by Celeste Hamilton. These poignant tales are sure to be keepers! Don't miss the third installment next month, *Longer Than...* by Erica Spindler.

Rounding out August are warm, wonderful stories by veteran authors Sondra Stanford, Karen Keast and Victoria Pade, as well as Kim Cates's wonderful debut book, *The Wishing Tree.*

In each Silhouette **Special Edition**, we're dedicated to bringing you the romances that you dream about— the type of stories that delight as well as bring a tear to the eye. And that's what Silhouette **Special Edition** is all about—special books by special authors for special readers!

I hope you enjoy this book and all of the stories to come.

Sincerely,

Tara Gavin
Senior Editor

KAREN KEAST
The Surprise of His Life

Silhouette Special Edition

Published by Silhouette Books New York

America's Publisher of Contemporary Romance

SILHOUETTE BOOKS
300 East 42nd St., New York, N.Y. 10017

THE SURPRISE OF HIS LIFE

ISBN: 0-373-09688-7

First Silhouette Books printing August 1991

Printed in the U.S.A.

Books by Karen Keast

Silhouette Special Edition

Once Burned #435
One Lavender Evening #469
A Tender Silence #536
Night Spice #614
The Surprise of His Life #688

KAREN KEAST,

a nature lover whose observant eye is evident in her writing, says if she were a season, she'd be autumn. The Louisiana resident admits to being a workaholic, a perfectionist and an introvert. Author of more than a dozen romances and two short stories, she likens writing a novel to running a marathon, noting that the same determination and endurance are necessary to overcome the seeming impossibility of the task and the many obstacles along the way. Still, happily married for over two decades, she is thrilled to have the opportunity to write about the "joy, pain, exhilaration and sheer mania of love" and to be able to bring two lovers together eternally through her writing.

Chapter One

His goddaughter was all grown up, Walker Carr thought as he watched the young woman walk down the deplaning ramp of Houston's Hobby Airport. Actually, he amended, at twenty-three she had technically been a woman for several years. Which had certainly been the case some eighteen months ago, the last time he had seen her. That fact of maturity accepted, she was now nonetheless...different. It might have something to do with the way her short blond curls had given way to a long silky-looking, shoulder-length mane. It might have something to do with the way youthful angles had given way to adult curves. It might have something to do with the innately sensual sway of her hips within the folds of the tailored steel-gray slacks. Whatever the indefinable something was, it made the stuffed teddy bear, which he'd impulsively bought minutes before at an airport gift shop for Lindsey to add to her collection, ridiculously inappropriate.

He knew, too, that given the circumstances—her return to Galveston was under less than ideal conditions—his pleasure at seeing her was probably as inappropriate as the bear, but the truth was that he was glad to see her. He guessed he hadn't realized just how much he'd missed her…and her fun-loving disposition. The truth was that no one he knew got quite so much joy out of living, no one got more ounce-for-ounce happiness out of waking up in the morning, no one had such a close personal relationship with a smile.

As always when he thought of her happy-go-lucky nature, he wondered what had made her flee on the eve of her wedding eighteen months before. What could have happened of such a magnitude that it had not only driven her from Galveston, but also from the United States?

All wondering came to an abrupt halt as Lindsey Ellison's blue-gray eyes connected with Walker's. She smiled, waved and started toward the tall familiar figure of her godfather. Walker smiled, waved and started toward Lindsey. In seconds she was in his arms. Over the years, she'd been there countless times. However, Walker could never remember her holding on this tightly before. But then, never before had she needed comforting from someone other than her parents. That in mind—though he wondered if perhaps he needed comforting, too—he tightened his arms. Neither felt pressured into speaking.

Finally, Lindsey pulled back and said, "Thanks for meeting me. I wasn't ready to face Mother or Dad."

"No problem. You know I'm always there if you need me."

By tacit agreement, they had started walking in the direction of the baggage-claim area. At Walker's remark, Lindsey glanced over at him and, for a fraction of a heartbeat, he had the oddest feeling that the smile at her lips was bittersweet, yet her words were perfectly normal when she spoke. So normal that he forgot the odd feeling.

"Yeah, I know," she said. Another smile materialized, this one as genuine as a flawless, sparkling gemstone. She nodded toward the teddy bear he held. "Is that for me? Or did you buy it for yourself?"

Walker grinned—primarily because there was no way not to when Lindsey flashed her pearly whites. It had always been that way, even in the days when the pearly whites had been enmeshed in silver braces.

"It's for you," he said, handing it to her. His smile faded as he added, "But maybe you're too old for teddy bears."

Lindsey stroked the nutmeg-brown fur on the bear's head and stared down into black button eyes, as if woman and beast were already best friends. "One is never too old for teddy bears." She looked up at Walker. "Thanks. He's adorable."

Walker nodded, inordinately pleased that she was pleased.

"How was your flight?" he asked as they moved on through the crowded terminal. A man, possibly trying to make a tight connection, ran past. Instinctively, Walker curved his arm about Lindsey's waist. He was aware of the smallness of that waist and of the gentle rhythm of the hips beneath. Those sensations, coupled with the memory of her in his arms—the memory of soft rounded breasts and fragrant skin—confirmed his first observation. Lindsey was no longer a child. Not by any stretch of anyone's wild imagination.

"Long," she responded to his question.

"When did you leave London?"

Threading back her blond hair in a weary gesture, she said, "Days ago, it seems like, but I guess it was only Friday morning." It was now almost five o'clock Saturday afternoon.

"Have you been able to rest any?"

"No," she answered, and Walker knew that her inability to rest had more to do with her troubled heart than with the inconvenience of travel. He knew, too, that both of them were avoiding the subject most on their minds.

They chose to ignore it a little longer. In fact, they ignored it the remainder of the walk to the baggage-claim area. Once the car keys had been fished from the front pocket of Walker's jeans, once Lindsey's suitcases had been stored in the trunk, once the car was headed in the direction of Galveston, Lindsey braved a question.

"How's Mother?"

Walker bent forward, adjusting the air conditioning from moderate to high in an attempt to regulate the harsh August heat. He then looked over in Lindsey's direction. Not mincing words, he said, "As well as can be expected. I think she's still in a state of shock."

"Yeah, well, I can identify with that," Lindsey responded, not bothering to mask her sarcasm.

Walker was aware that their conversation sounded as though there had been a death. It was his guess that a death would have been easier for Lindsey to cope with. Well, maybe not to cope with, but it would have sure been darned easier for her to understand. And maybe for him, too.

"What happened?" Lindsey asked. Walker could hear the pain in her voice. It took a bite out of his heart.

"You know as much as I do," he said, which was to say precious little, he thought. Except that his two best friends—Bunny and Dean Ellison—were hurting. And that he didn't know what in hell to do about it. All he knew was that he had to find a way to stand by each of them even though they were standing in opposition of each other. He could imagine the war of feelings, the battle of divided loyalties, raging inside Lindsey. Even though he must surely be experiencing only a fraction of what she was, he very definitely felt like a combat casualty.

"What goes through someone's thought processes to make him want a divorce after almost twenty-five years of marriage?"

Walker could tell that Lindsey expected him to have some enlightened insight into another man's thinking. He didn't, though. He hadn't the least notion why Dean had asked for a divorce. He hadn't the least notion how, or why, a good marriage had soured. "I don't know, hon," he replied. "I just don't know."

"Mother thinks he's having a mid-life crisis," Lindsey said, obviously hoping that Walker would agree.

"That's possible."

"She thinks that he thinks he's getting old."

Walker could relate to that. At forty-seven, he definitely had days—mornings mostly—when he felt older than old. On those occasions, he felt as though he'd been ridden hard and put up wet. On those occasions his bum knee throbbed with pain. He'd shattered the kneecap during his less-than-illustrious pro football career, the career that had lasted half a season or until an ugly, mean defensive back had decided to pulverize him. Yeah, he knew what it was like to feel old. And in a way that surpassed the physical reality.

He'd been increasingly feeling his age ever since his wife's death almost eight years before. It had been so unexpected—a bout with a virus that doctors hadn't even been able to identify. Before he'd known what was happening, Phyllis was dead...and he'd been left to finish raising their son, who was a year older than Lindsey. All in all, the death had diminished him in some way he couldn't explain, but could feel deep in his heart. It was as though the flame of life still burned within him, but it was no longer bright. Instead, it only simmered, sending him through the motions of living without any real interest. God only knew he'd never have made it without Dean and Bunny Ellison!

For that matter, Dean and Bunny had been a part of his life for as far back as he could remember. He and Dean had been friends for forever. They'd gone to the same Galveston high school, where both had played football, then on to the same college, where they had repeated their football performance. Following that, both had served in Vietnam. Afterward, Dean had started an offshore oil company, while he'd played out his short-lived football career. After his knee injury, Dean had hired him on and, ultimately, had made him an equal partner in the business. They worked well together, with him being primarily in charge of the Galveston office, while Dean, who'd long had his pilot's license, assumed responsibility for the offshore operations. Somewhere along the way—when he had been twenty-two to be precise, Dean within a year of him—each had married. The wives had rounded out a perfect foursome. They'd seen each other through thick and thin—through the birth of the Carrs' son, through the birth of the Ellisons' daughter, through the heartbreak of Phyllis Carr's death.

"What do you think?"

Walker glanced up, at the same time angling the air-conditioning vent away from his achy knee.

"Do you think it could be this mid-life crisis thing?" Lindsey asked, now bluntly seeking his opinion.

Walker repeated what he'd said before. "That's possible." At Lindsey's crestfallen look—she'd wanted him to wholeheartedly support her mother's theory—he added, "Lindsey, just give him a little time and a little space. Sometimes they're all a man needs to get his perspective back."

Lindsey started to say something, then decided against it. Instead, she eased back into the corner of the car, clutching the teddy bear to her. For the first time since he'd seen her deplaning, Walker thought she looked youthful. Vulnerably youthful. He longed to ease her pain, but he just didn't have the power. Any more than he'd had the power to ease his own eight years before. Any more than he had the power to ease his own now.

"How's Adam?" Lindsey asked.

The mention of his son, who lived and worked in Houston, brought a smile to Walker's lips. "He's gonna be a new papa any day now."

Lindsey smiled. "Is he about to freak out?"

"Actually, I think it's Grace about to freak out. Adam calls her a dozen times a day and watches her like a prison guard every minute he's home. The other night she got up to go to the bathroom and Adam was dressed when she came out—dressed and hollering that he couldn't find the car keys, which turns out were in his hand. Oh, and his jeans were on wrong side out."

Lindsey laughed. The sound reminded Walker of something pretty and lyrical. "I know he'll want to see you before you go back," he said.

"I, uh, I may not be going back."

The news took Walker totally by surprise. The look he gave her said so.

She shrugged. "I'm not quite sure what I'm going to do," she explained. "Technically, I've just taken a leave of absence—vacation time I had coming, plus my accumulated sick days. I'm to let them know later what I decide."

"But I thought you liked your job." Following the breakup of her engagement, she'd taken a secretarial job at a London-based American company. Walker knew, via her mother, that Lindsey not only enjoyed the work, but also enjoyed being in England.

"Oh, I do. It's a great job, I work for nice people, but—" she shrugged again "—it may be time for a change."

"What would you do?"

"Go to Paris, maybe. Or Hong Kong. Maybe even Timbuktu." Lindsey smiled, her pink-glossed lips curving upward. "Who knows, I might even stay in Galveston for a while."

A troubling thought occurred to Walker. "Lindsey, you're not staying because of what's going on between your parents, are you? Because I know they wouldn't want—"

"That isn't the reason I'd be staying," she interjected. The lips that had been smiling straightened into a serious line.

Walker waited for her to elaborate, but she didn't. She just allowed her gaze to hold his—one second, two seconds, just a little longer than was normally expected. Walker had the same odd feeling he'd experienced at the airport, the one that said he was missing some point.

Suddenly Lindsey smiled, shattering the odd feeling, leaving only a comfortable normalcy in its place. "Who knows? Maybe I won't stay, after all. Want to run off to Timbuktu with me?"

Run off to Timbuktu? The strange thing was, Walker reflected, there were times, particularly of late, when running off, starting over, doing something totally frivolous, even foolish, had its appeal. Maybe there was something to this mid-life crisis thing. Maybe the crazies did set in somewhere between yesterday's dreams and today's realization that dreams were for the young. Maybe the same thing, only magnified, had happened to his friend.

"C'mon, I'll bet you know a dozen guys who'd have their bags packed in a New York minute and be on a plane with you to Timbuktu...or anywhere else, for that matter."

"That's the problem. There're too many. I can't decide. Why, only last week Prince Charles begged for the chance to accompany me, but I told him that he just couldn't do that to the princess. I finally made him see that Jolly Ole England needed him and that he just couldn't go around shirking his royal responsibilities."

Walker grinned. "How noble of you."

"Yeah, I thought so, and me not even a countryman."

Walker's grin grew, then faded. "There's no one special?"

Lindsey's smile stayed in place, but a cloud of some emotion—regret?—streaked across her gray-blue eyes. "Let's just put it this way. I'll be going to Timbuktu alone. That is, if I can't talk you into going." On the heels of that, without even the slightest pause, suggesting that if she didn't blurt it out, she wouldn't be able to say it at all, she asked, "Is there another woman?"

The question needed no clarification. Walker knew she was talking about her father.

"To my knowledge, no."

"Would you tell me if there was?"

Walker pondered the question. It was a tough one. He had loyalties binding him to all three members of the Ellison family. What would he do if Dean had confided in him personally, privately?

"I don't know," Walker answered honestly. "But I can tell you in all honesty that Dean hasn't mentioned another woman to me." Of course, he hadn't forewarned him about the divorce, either, which maybe meant that Dean was sensitively aware of just how caught in the middle he was.

Relief of the most profound nature washed across Lindsey. Walker could actually see her muscles relaxing, could actually hear her silent "Thank God." Like a vase that had been emptied of all negativity, he saw her filling up with a new optimism.

"Well, then," she said, "I'm just going to have to talk some sense into Dad."

"Lindsey..." Walker hesitated, searching for just the right way to phrase what he felt he had to say. He decided that there was no easy way, no right way. "Lindsey, hon, what goes on between a man and a woman is personal. It's not the kind of thing that a third party, even someone who loves them, can mediate. It's not the kind of hurt that another party can heal."

"I know," Lindsey said, "but it won't hurt to talk to Dad, will it?"

"Of course not, but—"

"I'll just talk to him and, if it helps, it helps. If it doesn't, it doesn't."

Despite his warning, despite her statement to the contrary, Walker sensed that Lindsey thought she could "fix" her parents' broken marriage. He recognized her attitude for what it was—the optimism, even the cocky naïveté, of youth. He sighed silently, wishing he could loan her some of his maturity. But he couldn't. Maturity was something that was earned, oftentimes hard earned. All he could do was offer her a shoulder to cry on if things didn't work out the way she wanted.

Galveston.

Salt-scented air. Honey-colored beaches. Mile after mile of seawall built to protect the city from mean-spirited storms. And in no place did it storm quite as it did in Galveston. London had dank, dark weather, with drizzly rain and smoky fog, but Galveston was queen of the downpour, king of the wroth wind. There was something symbolic about the timing of her return, Lindsey thought as the car sped across the causeway linking island to mainland. Something symbolic about the storm brewing in her heart. She could never remember feeling so tempest-tossed. No, that wasn't true. She could remember a time, eighteen months ago, when she'd felt more than tempest-tossed. She'd felt completely lost at sea. But then, she'd had the anchor of her parents. Now that anchor was being compromised.

She glanced over at the man sitting beside her. When her eyes had first connected with his at the airport, she had felt a sense of profound relief. She had felt safe. Just the way she'd always felt safe with Walker. It would be so easy to lean on him now, when her heart was troubled over her parents. Was leaning on him something she wanted to do? Was leaning on him something she dared do? The truth was, she suspected, leaning on him was something she had little control over. It was just something she seemed to do instinctively. Looking back to a year and a half before, why hadn't she seen the emotional storm coming? Why hadn't she known from the beginning that events had been taken out of her control?

"What do you mean you think we ought to postpone getting married?"

The question had been asked by a confused, soon-to-be, as of the following day at 2:00 p.m., bridegroom. Lindsey could still remember the puzzled expression on Ken Larey's face...and how the expression had suddenly turned to a grin.

"Oh, I get it. This is a joke, right? A little after-the-rehearsal-dinner humor. Come here, you little tease," the tall, handsome, as-sweet-as-a-teddy-bear guy had said.

Her heart breaking, Lindsey had evaded his embrace by putting the sofa between them. Minutes before, they'd arrived back at Ken's apartment, which, as of the next day, would be *their* apartment. "I'm serious, Ken."

He'd momentarily looked startled that his arms were empty—and that she was standing somewhere other than beside him. "You're serious about wanting to postpone the wedding?" Before she could answer, he smiled. "You've just got cold feet, sweetheart. That happens. It doesn't mean a thing. Tomorrow you'll feel—"

"No, I won't. I mean, this is not a frivolous case of cold feet. I wish it were, but it isn't."

A frown, a prelude to impatience, furrowed Ken's forehead. "Then what exactly is it?"

"I...I don't know. I just think we should postpone the wedding. Until we're both sure."

"I *am* sure, Lindsey. I thought you were, too."

"I am. I mean, I was. I mean..." She had sighed, laid her hand on the back of the sofa and closed her eyes— closed her eyes to contain the tears.

"The next thing I know," Ken had added, "you'll be telling me there's someone else." He'd made the remark as though it were the very last option to consider, for how could there be anyone else when the two of them had gone together for over a year and had been practically inseparable the whole time?

Lindsey had said nothing.

"There, uh, there isn't anyone else, is there?" This time, uncertainty underscored his voice.

Still, Lindsey had said nothing.

"Is there someone else?" Ken had asked point-blank.

For as long as she lived, Lindsey would remember that question. She'd remember the verbalizing of something that she hadn't had the guts to put into words. Not even in some secret place in her heart. But to be fair to herself, the question had never occurred to her until earlier that very evening. Until the wedding rehearsal itself. When it did occur, as some errant feeling in her heart, she'd been terrified at the realization. Terrified, mortified, helplessly lost on the sea of new emotions, new emotions that she had no name for.

She'd also always remember the tears that had slid from her closed eyes and down her cheeks, the hurt look on Ken Larey's face when she had opened her eyes, the voicing of the question that she knew he would inevitably ask.

"Who?"

She hadn't given him a name, though. Nor had she given it to anyone else. In fact, she'd told her parents—everyone, except Ken, to whom she felt she owed nothing short of honesty—that she'd simply, regrettably, had a change of heart and that she needed to get away for a while, to better sort through her feelings. A friend of a friend of a friend had found her a job out of the country. For that she would always be grateful.

The time away had worked its healing magic. Muddied waters had cleared. Feelings had fallen into place. A name for the feelings had been found. Or rather, she'd stopped fighting the name she'd known all along was the only name that applied. That name was *love*. She was in love. It was that simple.

She was uncertain when her heart had made the commitment, but she knew the exact moment when she had been forced to confront the fact that something was going on with her emotions. She had wondered countless times what would have happened if she hadn't chosen to flaunt custom. If she had let someone stand in for her at the rehearsal, as was tradition, if she'd let her maid of honor walk down the aisle in her place, would she now happily be Mrs. Kenneth Larey?

"That's bad luck," Millie Moore, the petite maid of honor who was Lindsey's best friend and former college roommate, had said.

Lindsey remembered saying that nothing even resembling bad luck could touch her the weekend of her wedding. Later, she would think that she had been wrong, though she couldn't really call what had happened bad luck. Maybe it had even been good luck—good luck with bad timing.

"Besides," Lindsey had added, "we already have a stand-in, and one is enough to satisfy convention."

With that, she had looped her arm through Walker's. Since her father had been delayed on a rig, he'd telephoned Walker at the last minute and had requested that his buddy, and Lindsey's godfather, take his place during the rehearsal.

"Are you ready to give me away?" she had asked, smiling up at Walker.

He had smiled back. And she had thought how very special his smile was, how it seemed to light up his whole face, how it always seemed to light up her heart. But then, Walker, like a bright night star, had always managed to light up her world.

She literally could not recall a time when he was not part of her life. He'd been at her birth—or so she'd been told—and he'd been at every major event since. He'd taught her to water-ski, he'd pitched her balls at the same time he'd pitched balls to his son, he'd given her a teddy bear every Christmas since she'd begun collecting them, which had been somewhere around the age of ten. He'd been her pal, just the way Phyllis had been not only her godmother, but also her friend.

When Phyllis had died so suddenly, at the time that Lindsey was an impressionable sixteen, Lindsey had been devastated. She'd also witnessed Walker's devastation. Which had been complete and total. While her friends had fantasized of teenage idols—Eddie Van Halen, Rod Stewart, Billy Joel—Lindsey had romanticized about one day finding a man who would love her with the same depth of feeling with which Walker had loved his wife. He became the ideal by which all other males were judged. Critically judged. That Ken Larey had measured up had been little short of a miracle. That miracle man, the best man at his side, had awaited Lindsey at the altar that eventful rehearsal night.

"All right," Lindsey remembered the minister saying, "the maid of honor—come on, young lady," he'd said, motioning for Millie to start down the aisle "—will approach the altar." She had, pretending she was carrying a bouquet.

"Nervous?" Walker had whispered to Lindsey.

"A little," she'd whispered back.

He had tightened his hold on her arm, just enough to reassure her. "Just remember that no one's ever died from repeating the marriage vows."

Lindsey had smiled and she could have sworn that Walker had started to, as well. His smile never materialized, however. Instead, he'd turned deadly serious.

"Look, I probably won't have time to say this tomorrow—you're going to have everything on your mind but me—so I want to say it now. I wish you all the happiness in the world, hon. You know that, don't you?"

Lindsey had nodded. She did know that he wished her well. Just the way that she wished him well. She even wished that he could find someone to be happy with again, though the truth was that, out of the few women he'd dated over the years, none had really been worthy of him. At least in her humble opinion.

"And, listen," Walker had added, a grin now slipping to his lips as he jerked his head in the direction of the front of the church, "if this Kenneth guy doesn't treat you right, you just let me know, you hear? And I'll kick his rear into the middle of next week."

The image of a booted Ken sailing through time caused Lindsey to giggle. At the same time, Walker had leaned forward and brushed his lips against her cheek.

In that moment, a curious thing had happened. Looking back, with the supposed objectivity of hindsight, Lindsey realized that that hadn't been the first time he'd kissed her. Far from it. Always a demonstrative person, he'd never been stingy with expressing his feelings. No, his kissing her had not been new. It was her reaction to that kiss that had been totally foreign. And frightening.

From out of literally nowhere had come the realization that she wondered what his lips would feel like pressed against hers. No, it was more than wondering. She actually longed for his kiss. A real kiss. A man-woman kiss. Not a well-wish kiss given by a godfather to his goddaughter on the eve of her wedding.

The inappropriateness of her response had not escaped her. In fact, she'd been more than aware of its gravity. The man whom she'd pledged to marry was waiting for her at the altar, to rehearse the vows that would bind them together for the rest of their lives, and here she was wondering what another man's kiss would be like. And the man hadn't been just any ordinary man. He'd been her godfather. A man old enough to be her father!

The revelation had upset Lindsey as nothing else in her life ever had.

"Okay," the minister had stated, "now the 'Wedding March' will begin, and the bride and her father—" here he motioned for Lindsey and Walker "—will make their way to the front of the church."

"Ready?" Walker had whispered.

"Y-yes," Lindsey had stammered. Somehow she'd struggled through the remainder of the rehearsal. She'd struggled through the rehearsal dinner. She'd struggled through the difficult, and heartbreaking, talk with Ken. And then had begun the real struggle, the long months that it had taken her to sort through her feelings.

"Lindsey?"

But at least she was now armed with the truth....

"Lindsey?"

For whatever good that would do her.

"Lindsey?"

She glanced up as her name penetrated her consciousness. The car had stopped in front of her parents' home. Walker was watching her with a look that said he'd called her name before and had gotten no response.

"I'm sorry," she said. "I guess I was elsewhere."

Even as she spoke, she couldn't keep her eyes, her hungry eyes, from feasting on him once again. Just the way she had at the airport. For the most part, his hair was still jet-black, but she thought that there were a few more gray hairs frosting the temples than the last time she'd seen him. He was still incredibly handsome, though, with piercing brown eyes that peered from beneath thick ebony lashes. His skin still shone gold from the sun, telling her that, while he might spend a lot of time in the office, he still managed his fair share of hot hours out on the rigs with her father. And his lips... well, they still haunted her with their masculine strength and sensual curves.

What would he think if he knew why she'd called off her wedding? What would he think if he knew that she'd spent endless hours searching her soul for answers to the hardest questions she'd ever been forced to ask? What would he think if he knew that she still wondered what his lips would feel like on hers?

Startled?

Shocked?

Appalled?

Probably all of the above, though she had the hardest time dealing with the latter. Would he be appalled that the woman he thought of as his daughter thought of him as so much more? Could the truth easily destroy every good thing that they shared?

Maybe.

But she'd decided that it was a chance worth taking. She'd unquestionably come home at this point because of the marital problems her parents were having, but the truth was that she'd come home for another reason, as well. She'd come home because she had some unfinished business with the man sitting beside her.

Chapter Two

Home was just as Lindsey remembered it—a pretty cream-colored brick house with shutters the blue of a robin's egg. Her father's fishing boat stood in the driveway with a tarpaulin over it, while her mother's climbing roses, planted the year they'd moved into the house, nearly twenty years ago now, crept lazily up a lattice. The white wrought-iron lawn furniture, a small table and two chairs, rested beneath the drooping boughs of the aged oak tree in the front yard. The furniture needed a fresh coat of paint, a fact her mother pointed out to her father on a regular basis, though it never seemed to do much good. It was always something he'd take care of the next day, the next week, the next month.

In contrast, however, the mowing of the grass was something that was never postponed. A passion with her father, he kept the yard immaculately cut and trimmed. Which was precisely how it looked now. It was as though he'd mowed it as per usual over the weekend, then had gotten up Monday morning and had calmly asked, over breakfast, for a divorce. Not for a separation, which seemed to Lindsey to be the logical intermediary step, but for a divorce. Final and irrevocable.

Yes, Lindsey thought as she opened the car door, everything looked the same. In reality, though, nothing was, and she experienced a reaction she hadn't experienced since hearing of the divorce. She felt anger. Anger at her parents for what they were doing to her. How dare they threaten the stability of her world! Even as the dark emotion crushed her heart, she realized how self-centered she was being. Because of that, because Walker was standing before her, waiting for her to get out of the car, she brushed the thought away.

"Ready?" he asked.

"Yeah," she said, pushing from the seat. The heat immediately assailed her, making the long-sleeved white cotton blouse she wore more than uncomfortable. Then again, maybe she was uncomfortable because of what she knew lay ahead of her.

"I'll get your suitcases," Walker called over his shoulder as he headed for the rear of the car.

"Thanks," Lindsey answered, starting for the house. She saw her mother peek from a window, and in seconds the front door was thrown wide.

If the house was just as Lindsey remembered, her mother was not. Her short blond hair, every strand of which was always impeccably in place, looked mussed, as though it had not been seriously combed in a while, or as if restless fingers had wreaked havoc with any recent attempt. She, likewise, wore no makeup. For a woman who wore makeup even when sick, Lindsey thought the absence of it now more than telling. As were her eyes. Normally, they were wide and blue and clear, the fun-filled eyes of someone who had taught her daughter to love life. Now, however, they just looked tired, dull, as though they had cried a seaful of tears.

Lindsey's heart split in two.

Wordlessly, the two women embraced in the middle of the yard. Lindsey could feel her mother clinging to her in something just short of desperation, as though Lindsey had arrived in time to loan her some much-needed strength. But then, as though it were she who had to be strong for her daughter, Bunny Ellison smiled. The smile, however, looked totally incongruous with her weary face.

"Let me look at you," Bunny said, giving Lindsey a quick once-over. Though the women had talked frequently, at least once a week, it was the first time they'd been together since Lindsey had left for London. "You look wonderful," Bunny announced. "Doesn't she look wonderful, Walker?"

A suitcase in each hand, Walker had just come abreast of the women. He glanced over at Lindsey and winked. "Oh, I don't know. I was thinking she'd gone over to England and gotten herself uglied up."

Lindsey grinned. So did her mother. The latter's smile was small, but genuine. Again, the action hurt Lindsey's heart, simply because smiling had once come so naturally to her mother. Lindsey's guess was that smiles had been few and far between of late. They were likely to become even more scarce.

"And what would you know about ugly?" Bunny teased. She and Walker were always teasing. "Except other than what you see in the bathroom mirror every morning?"

Walker laughed. Lindsey wondered just what he *did* look like in the mornings. She knew with a dead cer-

tainty, the kind you'd stake your life on, that it was nowhere near ugly. In fact, she'd put her money on be-still-
my-heart sexy. The kind of sexy that spelled a scratchy
stubble of beard, the kind of sexy that spelled bare chest
covered in dark spirals of hair, the kind of sexy that—

The sound of Walker's voice brought her back to reality, and reality was that they were standing in the quiet,
cool den of her parents' home.

"Where do you want these?" he asked. The question
was directed toward Bunny and referred to the luggage he
still carried.

"You can put them in our ro—" Bunny stopped. Pain
streaked across her face. "You can put them in my
room." At the surprised look that Lindsey gave her
mother, Bunny added, raking her fingers through her
hair, "I, uh, I've been sleeping on the sofa in the den."
What she didn't say, but what was implied, was that there
were too many memories in the bedroom she'd shared
with her husband.

Lindsey had known that her father had asked for a divorce; she even understood, at least theoretically, what
that entailed. She shouldn't have been surprised to discover that he'd moved out of the house. And truly, a part
of her wasn't. Another part of her, however, had obviously, for defensive purposes, denied that possibility.
Or, at least, had conveniently overlooked it. The fact
could no longer be overlooked. The fact also hurt.
Deeply.

Lindsey glanced up to find Walker's gaze on her. It
seemed to silently ask, "Are you all right?"

The very fact that he was there, and that he cared,
made the hurt bearable.

"I could sleep in my old room," Lindsey said to her
mother.

Bunny forced a smile. "With two thousand bears? Or rather," she said, stroking the head of the teddy bear that Lindsey still held, "two thousand and one?" Looking up at Walker, Bunny settled the issue with, "The back room."

Walker didn't argue.

"C'mon," Bunny said to her daughter as she slipped her arm about her waist and squeezed, "I've made us some coffee."

Coffee turned out to be not only a freshly perked brew made from home-ground beans, but also an apple spice cake—Lindsey's favorite. Under the circumstances, considering the stress that her mother was under, Lindsey felt like crying when she saw the cake.

"Ah, Mom, why did you go to this trouble?" she asked, knowing the answer even as she asked it. There was a breed of woman who considered cooking a religion and the kitchen as a place of worship. For them, cooking was an expression of love. Her mother was one such woman. Her father had often teased that he'd married her mother only because of her ability to cook. Lindsey wondered what excuse he'd offer as to why he was divorcing her.

"It gave me something to do," Bunny said, automatically filling a mug with coffee.

Lindsey noticed that her mother's hand trembled. She longed to take the hand in hers and still the shaking. Instead, she set the teddy bear on the countertop and reached for the pitcher of cream her mother had just removed from the refrigerator. As though it had been innately programmed in her genes, as though it wouldn't do to do otherwise, Bunny had placed the cream pitcher on a paper doily.

"Coffee?" Bunny asked when Walker appeared in the doorway.

"No, thanks. I need to run. I'm doubling as a secretary these days."

"Is Gerri still out?" Bunny asked.

Lindsey recognized the name of the woman who'd been the company secretary/bookkeeper for several years. She knew that Gerri was divorced and had a teenage son. She also knew that, at least at one time, Gerri had had eyes for Walker. If Walker had known it, he'd ignored it. But then, maybe he'd changed his mind. Eighteen months was a long time. And, if he was still ignoring Gerri, was there someone else he wasn't ignoring? Maybe even several someone elses?

"Yeah," Lindsey heard Walker say, "and she's gonna be out a lot longer. The doctor says she has mono."

"Oh, no," Bunny said. "I knew she wasn't feeling well. Dean said . . . I knew she wasn't feeling well."

"What are you going to do?" Lindsey asked.

"Call one of those agencies specializing in temporary help, I guess." Walker grinned, slashing deep groves into his cheeks. His whisker-shadowed cheeks, Lindsey couldn't help but notice. "When, and if, I can find the time."

The telephone rang. Bunny reached for the phone hanging on the kitchen wall.

Walker waved a goodbye to her and looked over at Lindsey, who called out, "Thanks for meeting me."

"No problem."

"Hello?" Bunny said into the receiver. She said nothing for a moment, then stammered, "Y-yes, she got in. No, no . . . she's right here."

The ashen shade of pale which she turned, plus the fact that her hand gripped the receiver with white-knuckle force, drew both Lindsey's and Walker's attention. Walker, concern etching his face, halted in the act of leaving.

"It's, uh, it's your father," Bunny said as she passed the phone to her daughter. The woman immediately picked up a rag and began to wipe at the already clean countertop.

"Hello?" Lindsey said, her gaze on her mother.

"Hi, sweetheart," came the voice of Dean Ellison.

Memories swirled about Lindsey—memories of piggyback rides, memories of stories about wolves and trolls and monsters read in a deep, exaggerated basso, memories of dancing on the tops of her daddy's feet. Lindsey felt her throat tighten with emotion. She also felt a twinge of the anger she'd felt before. Why did her father, this man she loved above all others, have to go and change everything?

"Hi, Daddy," she said, unable to hold on to the anger.

"How was the flight?"

"It was good."

"Did Walker meet you?"

At the mention of Walker's name, Lindsey glanced up. Walker was standing in the doorway, looking at Lindsey. She smiled. "Yeah, he met me."

"Good," Dean replied, but Lindsey could hear her father's mind changing gears. She could hear the conversation shifting to the reason for the call. "Listen, sweetheart, I'd planned on seeing you tonight, but I'm stuck out on one of the platforms. Looks like I'm not going to be able to get away."

Disappointment raced through Lindsey. She wanted to talk to her father. The sooner, the better. She wanted to work this nonsense out, so that everything could go back to being the way it was.

"I'm sorry," Dean said, sensing Lindsey's mood.

"If you can't get away, you can't get away."

Walker stepped back into the room. "What's wrong?" he mouthed.

"He's out on a platform and can't get away," she answered Walker, then said into the receiver, "No, I was talking to Walker. He asked what was wrong."

Lindsey could have sworn that her father sounded a little flustered when he added, "Is Walker there?"

"Yeah, we just got home."

"Well, look, I won't keep you, sweetheart," Dean said. "And I promise to see you tomorrow. Okay?"

"Sure," Lindsey answered. Her mother hadn't looked up. She was still wiping the countertop and arranging the cream pitcher just so on the paper doily. "I'll see you tomorrow."

"Tell Walker that I'll—" Dean began, but never got to finish.

"Let me talk to him," Walker said, covering the distance to the phone and reaching for it.

"Walker wants to talk to you," Lindsey said, and handed over the receiver.

"Hey, what's going on?" Walker asked, one hand splayed at his waist.

"Oh, hey there," Dean said, hastily tacking on, "Look, I'm still out at Rig Three."

"Is there a problem?"

"No. I mean, yes and no."

"What's wrong? I thought all you had to do was fly in a replacement for the defective part."

"Yeah, well . . . I thought I'd just hang around to see if the part works. You know how much trouble we've had with this drill. I just want to make certain everything's okay before I fly back in. With our luck, I'd just have to turn around and fly right back out.''

The silence that followed suggested that Walker was having trouble making sense out of his partner and friend's reasoning. For one thing, they weren't accustomed to baby-sitting a part. For another, if the part didn't work, if it, too, had to be replaced, Dean would have to fly in for another replacement.

Dean was obviously hearing the same lack of logic, for he rushed ahead with, ''I'll, uh, I'll see you guys tomorrow.''

''Right,'' Walker said. ''Tomorrow.'' Stretching, he replaced the receiver on the wall phone.

''Problem, huh?'' Lindsey said.

''Yeah. Rig Three.''

Lindsey looked at Walker; Walker looked at Lindsey.

''I didn't know what to do about dinner,'' Bunny said, overbrightly and with the words tumbling over themselves, ''so I thawed a chicken. I mean, I didn't know whether you'd be going out with your father or what, so I thawed a chicken just in case. We could have fried chicken or chicken and dumplings or I could make that chicken casserole you like.''

''Anything's fine, Mom, but don't go to any trouble—''

''It's no trouble. We've got to eat,'' Bunny said, opening the refrigerator and seizing the chicken as though it were a lifeline to her sanity. Her back to Walker, she said, ''And why don't you join us, Walker?''

Lindsey's eyes found Walker's. ''Why don't you? That is, if you don't already have plans.'' Lindsey held her breath, wondering if Walker did, indeed, have plans for a Saturday night. If the women of Galveston had any sense, he was booked through the weekend, through the rest of his life.

"Why don't I take you two out?" Walker asked, unaware of Lindsey's relief.

"Nonsense," Bunny said. "You're tired, Lindsey's tired. We'll eat in." As she said this, she pulled open a drawer and extracted a knife. She began to cut up the chicken with what could only be called exuberance. "Hand me a bowl, would you, Lindsey?"

Lindsey did as bade.

"Is seven o'clock okay with you, Walker?" Bunny asked.

"That's fine. See ya'll then."

"You two have to decide how you want this chicken cooked," Bunny called out, her fingers still going a mile a minute. "We could have chicken spaghetti or lemon chicken or—"

"What if you just fry it, Mom?" Lindsey asked, knowing that was how Walker preferred his fowl.

A lazy grin spread across Walker's mouth as his gaze meshed with Lindsey's. "Now you're talking chicken."

Lindsey's gaze lowered to his lips, lips that had haunted her night and day for the past year and a half. She thought on a suppressed sigh, Now you're talking a first-class reason to cross the Atlantic.

"You need another piece of chicken," Bunny proclaimed that evening over dinner as she reached with trembling fingers for the platter in the middle of the table.

Walker, who had arrived precisely at seven, newly showered and shaved and wearing crisply creased khaki pants, held up his hand. "Un-uh. I've already had three pieces."

"Then what about another roll?" Bunny asked, turning back the daintily embroidered folds of the bread cover.

"No. Thanks. I'm fine."

"Tea. You need more tea," Bunny said as she pushed back her chair and started to rise.

"Stay seated, Mom. I'll get it." Lindsey rose, walked to the cabinet and returned to the table with a pitcher containing an amber-colored liquid. She smiled at Walker as she refilled his glass.

"Thanks," he said, noticing that for all she'd been through, both emotionally and travelwise, she looked good.

In fact, she looked better than good. She looked downright pretty. As he took in the billowy cloud of blond hair, the curvy hips encased in jeans, the high heels that made her long legs seem even longer, he was once more struck by the new maturity that she wore so becomingly. He was also aware of a subtle fragrance that alluringly arrived seconds before she did. The fragrance reminded him of sweetness, freshness, youth. Youth. For all of her newfound maturity, Lindsey was still young, which was probably the reason she looked good after the taxing week she'd had. On the other hand, he was tired, his knee hurt, and he was in less than the greatest mood of his life knowing that he had to work the following afternoon even if it was Sunday. Without a secretary, he'd gotten behind.

"We'll have cake and coffee in the other room," Bunny said now that the meal was in its final stages. All evening she'd chattered like a magpie and flitted around like a hyperactive bee. She started to push back her chair again. "I think I'll put on the coffee, so it'll be ready when we are."

"Don't make coffee for me," Walker said. "I'll be up half the night if I drink caffeine this late. And I don't need any cake." He patted his stomach, which was plain flat and mean lean. "I'll have to do forty laps in the pool as it is to take off these three pieces of chicken."

"I don't want coffee, either, Mom," Lindsey said, placing the pitcher on the table and sitting back down. She glanced over at Walker. "You still swim regularly?"

"Yeah. At least I try to." He grinned. "The older I get, though, the more laps I have to do and the less results I see."

"Oh, I don't know," Lindsey said, "it looks like you're holding your own."

It was foolish, Walker knew, but her compliment—it was a compliment, wasn't it?—pleased him. It was nice to know that, at forty-seven, he hadn't fallen completely apart at the seams. Okay, so a few seams were unraveling, but that wasn't the same thing as falling apart.

"Are you sure about the coffee?' Bunny asked, obviously itching to do something. Anything.

Both Walker and Lindsey assured her that they were. They then talked about the oil business, the weather, Galveston tourism—everything but what was really on their minds. Once the meal was finished, Bunny had the perfect excuse to spring back into action.

"I'll load the dishwasher," she said, shoving back her chair and starting to scrape and stack the plates.

"Let me," Lindsey said. "You and Walker—"

"No, I can," Bunny protested, adding one plate to another as fast as her unsteady hands would allow.

She then reached for one of the tall crystal glasses beaded with cool condensation. No sooner had she picked it up than it slipped from her fingers and fell to the floor. In one deafening crash, it shattered into two dozen pieces. The noise reverberated about the room like a gunshot. Bunny just stared, as though she couldn't believe what she was hearing, as though she couldn't believe what she was seeing. Slowly, with a frightening detachment, she squatted and began to silently gather up the pieces. One by one. With the greatest of care.

"Let me," Lindsey said, dropping to her mother's side.

The older woman disregarded her daughter—in truth, she didn't even seem to have heard her—and continued to pick up the shards of glass. "We bought these when we married," she said tonelessly. "They cost fifteen dollars apiece. That was a lot of money then. I bought one a month for eight months...."

"Mother, please move."

"All these years, I've never even chipped one...."

"Mother, please."

"I've been so careful...."

"It's only a glass," Lindsey said.

"It just slipped out of my hand...."

"Mother, watch it! You're going to... Ah, Mother, you cut yourself!"

As though it were beyond her capability to understand, Bunny stared at the drop of blood that had appeared on the pad of her thumb.

"I cut myself," she mumbled.

Lindsey looked up at Walker, silently asking for his help.

He squatted beside the woman who'd been like a sister to him. "C'mon, Bunny, let's go into the den." When she didn't acknowledge him in any way, but rather continued to watch the drop of blood grow larger and larger until it resembled a sad scarlet tear, Walker tipped her hand, forcing the glass to tumble downward again. "Put the glass on the floor, babe, and let's go get a Band-Aid. Okay?''

With Walker's assistance, Bunny rose and tonelessly announced, "I broke the glass."

"It doesn't matter," Walker assured her. "It's only a glass."

"We bought them when we married."

"I know."

From the doorway, he glanced back at Lindsey, who stood with the fragments scattered about her feet. She looked as if a sculptor had chiseled her face into a pose of concern.

"She's all right," Walker said quietly.

Ten minutes later, the glass cleared from the floor, the dishwasher loaded, Lindsey found her mother, a Band-Aid wrapped about her thumb, stretched out on the den sofa. She was sound asleep. Walker sat in the lounge chair, one leg negligently squared over the other. He held an empty shot glass.

"How did you get her to go to sleep?" Lindsey whispered.

Walker raised the glass and said in the same hushed tones, "Exhaustion and booze are a lethal combination."

"She doesn't look like she's slept all week," Lindsey remarked.

"I'm sure she hasn't."

"She *is* all right, isn't she?" Lindsey asked, suddenly, and desperately, needing some reassurance.

"She just needs to rest," Walker said, adding with half of a grin, "I think you could use a little rest yourself." Earlier he'd thought how unscathed she looked, how resilient youth was, but now he could clearly see that the stressful week had likewise taken its toll on her. She looked tired. Dog tired. Setting the glass down on the coffee table, he said as he rose, "I'm gonna get out of here and let you go to bed."

"What time is it?"

Walker checked the leather watch at his wrist. It was an old watch, one his wife had given him as a Christmas present, but old had a way of feeling familiar and comfortable. "Nine thirty-three."

Lindsey screwed up her face, as though trying to reason out a puzzle. "That makes it..." She sighed, as though the puzzle were too much for her to mentally negotiate in her fatigued state. "That makes it sometime tomorrow in London."

"Well, you need some sleep tonight," he said, starting for the door.

"I'll walk you out."

Bunny whimpered, a sound made in the throes of sleep, restless sleep.

Stepping forward, Lindsey grabbed an afghan from the back of a nearby chair and draped it across her mother. The gesture, Walker thought, was one of pure nurturing. It said warm and caring as only a woman could. Over the years, he had missed such tenderness—the sweetness, the gentleness, the lace and frills of the feminine gender. Of late, he seemed to miss it even more. Watching Lindsey now, he was acutely reminded of how empty he sometimes felt, of how long the after-work hours could be, of how blunt were the rough edges of his masculine life-style and how he sometimes ached for a woman's softness. Damn, he thought suddenly, he *was* getting old. Old and maudlin.

As he and Lindsey stepped outside, the summer heat swarmed about them, reminding them that August was a hostile month in the South. As if in compensation, however, gigantic stars glittered in bounteous plenty, while a slice of crescent moon, a shiny scythe of platinum, rode high in the black sky.

Silently, they headed for the car parked in the driveway. Despite the heat, Lindsey folded her arms about her, as though chilled from some unseen cold. Either that or she was merely holding herself together, Walker thought. Whichever, he longed to comfort her.

"She'll be okay," he said. "She's strong, stronger than even she realizes. Trust me, she'll rise to the occasion."

Lindsey glanced over at Walker. In heels, she stood almost eye-to-eye with him. Funny, he'd never realized just how tall she was. But then, without heels, she'd be considerably shorter, probably coming only to his chin.

"I never really thought much about women's lib," Lindsey said. "I grew up in the middle of it. I grew up reading and hearing about a woman's value. I guess I just took it for granted. You know, all that bit about a woman having her own identity, about a woman fulfilling her own needs, about a woman not being dependent on a man for her happiness. For the first time, I understand just how radical the movement was…at least for women of Mom's generation."

Walker knew exactly what Lindsey meant. "Your mom was from that generation—maybe the last generation here in America—where women aspired only to grow up to be wives and mothers. If a woman worked, it was usually just to put her husband through school. Then she'd quit work and start the family."

"There's nothing wrong with wanting to devote your life to being a wife and mother," Lindsey said. "Each, both, are full-time, honorable jobs, but it can be a deadly trap to fall into. If you don't develop your own identity somewhere along the way. And I'm afraid Mother didn't. She was content to be an extension of Dad.''

They had reached the car. Both now leaned back against it. Walker crossed one ankle over the other. He grinned.

''I'll tell you a secret,'' he said, ''if you promise not to tell your Sisters in Womanhood.''

Lindsey grinned, and her eyes sparkled brilliantly. ''I just love secrets.''

''Well, this one could label me a traitor to my sex.''

''And get you shot at sunrise?''

Walker thought the smile at her lips decidedly impish—irresistibly impish. He thought, too, that if he were to be shot at sunrise, her smile might be the last thing he requested to see. Somehow her enthusiasm for life had always had a way, a pleasant way, of drawing him in. ''Yeah, it could get me shot at sunrise.''

''Oh, great, then it is a good secret. Give.''

''Men are odd creatures,'' he began.

''Ah, you've noticed,'' she interjected. The grin was back...if, indeed, it had ever left. She ran a hand beneath her hair and raised it from her neck. It lent to her impish illusion in a way Walker had no idea how to explain, except that it looked like a ponytail on a teenager. Where had the mature woman disappeared to?

''Do you want to hear this or not?'' he asked, faking impatience.

''Yes. Men are odd creatures.''

''Men are odd creatures,'' he repeated. ''A part of them wants a woman's complete devotion. I guess that's the caveman part. While another part of them is fascinated by a woman with her own strong personality—her own wants and likes and interests. In fact, it's smothering, intimidating to have to give her your life in order for her to have one. Marriage should be a blending of two full, complete lives."

Lindsey was no longer smiling, but had grown serious. "I'll tell you a secret if you promise not to spread it around."

Walker grinned. "If this gets out, are you likely to be shot at sunrise?"

"No, but I'll be strung from the nearest tree."

"I can hardly wait."

"Women are strange creatures," she began. "While it's very important for a woman to fulfill her own needs, the truth of the matter is that nothing is quite as fulfilling as the right man in her life."

The kid had disappeared and the woman had reappeared. Walker wondered, as he had a hundred times before, what had led to the breakup of her marriage plans. Even so, even considering his closeness to Lindsey, a part of him could hardly believe he was asking what he was.

"I take it, then, that Ken wasn't the right man?"

He could tell that the question had caught Lindsey off balance. She didn't shy away, however. In fact, he felt her gaze intensify, until it seemed like a warm light penetrating him.

"No," she answered. Her steel-blue gaze continued to hold his for a fraction of a second before she quickly changed the subject. "Dad didn't have to stay on the rig, did he?"

Walker let the topic of her canceled marriage go, though, oddly, he hadn't particularly wanted to. While she had certainly answered his question, the simplicity of her response invited other questions, questions like: What had made her change her mind? Why had it taken her so long to realize that Ken was wrong for her? Why did he,

Walker, have the feeling that something—some important something—was being left unsaid?

He focused his attention on the subject she'd raised. He considered sparing Lindsey's feelings and decided that he owed her the truth. "No, your dad didn't have to stay on the rig."

"He was just looking for an excuse to avoid seeing me, wasn't he?"

"Yes. That would be my guess." Before she could say anything, Walker said, "But try to understand his point of view. It's going to be difficult for him to face you. He's got to explain why he's hurting your mother and why he's hurting you." Walker sighed deeply. "Heaven only knows what I'd tell Adam if I were in your father's shoes."

"The truth is, though, that you wouldn't be in his shoes."

The comment was an interesting one, made as it was with the force of such certainty. "How can you be so sure?"

Lindsey shrugged. "I just know." She added suddenly, "No, I do know why I know. Loyalty is very important to you. You would never have betrayed your wedding vows by wanting to break them."

Walker thought of his wife and of the happy years they'd shared. The truth was that he couldn't imagine ever wanting to divorce Phyllis. Nor could he imagine why Lindsey's implicit faith in him should move him so. But it did. It made him feel... *special* was the only word that came to mind.

"Do you still miss her?"

The question came softly stealing through the still night. There was no need to clarify whom the question concerned. Walker cut his eyes to Lindsey. In the moonlit darkness, it appeared that her eyes had been waiting for his. If he didn't know better, he might have believed that his answer was of monumental importance.

"I still miss her," he said at last, "but it's as if she were a dream I once had—a nice dream, but a dream. She no longer seems real." He thought of how he felt as though he was just going through the motions of life, as though something vibrant, something vital, was missing. That in mind, he added, though he was unsure why he was sharing something so intimate, "Only the emptiness she once filled seems real."

Walker would have sworn that Lindsey's eyes darkened. Was it possible that she, too, had an emptiness within her that needed filling?

"Phyllis was a very lucky lady," Lindsey said.

The world grew quiet, so quiet that one could almost hear the stars whispering in the heavens. Walker heard the silence, and in it the echo of Lindsey's remark. The kid had disappeared entirely, giving way to a full-grown woman. To a beautiful woman silhouetted in silver moonlight. Her transformation from woman to girl, from girl to woman, was intriguing.

And sexy.

He realized the inappropriateness of this last thought, but could not bring himself to deny the truth of it. He told himself that it was nothing personal, that is, nothing specifically aimed at Lindsey. It simply had to do with the vacillation from youth to adulthood and back again. The child-woman, the woman-child, had had its sensual appeal from time immemorial.

"I, uh, I should go in," Lindsey said.

"Yeah. You need some sleep."

"Yeah," she agreed. "Well, good night—" she pushed away from the car "—and thanks for everything. I mean it. I don't know what I would have done without you to-day.''

As she spoke, Lindsey brought her hand to Walker's elbow. She touched it lightly, allowing her fingers to trail the length of his arm. For just a second, she took his hand in hers—palm to palm, skin to skin. She squeezed, meshing their fingers.

Walker could remember dozens of times over the years when he'd taken her hand in his, when she'd taken his hand in hers. What he couldn't remember was any one of those dozens of times feeling like this time. He could never remember such warmth. But then, she withdrew her hand. He was left only with the memory of their fingers clinging together. And like all memories, it paled by comparison to the real thing. Which was comforting, because it allowed him the luxury of negating what he'd felt. She'd simply taken his hand in hers. It was no big deal.

''Good night,'' Lindsey repeated.

''Good night,'' Walker said. He watched as she took one backward step, then another before starting for the house. At the door, she turned and waved. He waved back...with a hand that curiously still felt warm... despite the fact that all she'd done was to take his hand in hers.

Chapter Three

Bunny Ellison was still asleep. In fact, Lindsey thought she looked dead to the world. Only an occasional twitch told of the dream demons with whom she jousted. Needlessly rearranging the afghan about her mother, Lindsey sighed. She didn't know which was worse— dream demons or those that brazenly roamed the daylight hours. Whichever, she was tired of demons. She wanted to smile and feel it in her heart.

However, no smile danced across Lindsey's lips. Instead, she shut off the lamp and headed for the kitchen. There, she glanced around. The floor was devoid of broken glass, all of which had been discarded in the trash. She wished it were as easy to get rid of the memories of her mother gathering up the shards as though putting them back together would mend her marriage. The scene had frightened her. She'd never seen her mother out of control. She didn't want to see her that way again. Grabbing the wide-eyed teddy bear that Walker had given her, Lindsey turned off the light switch and walked down the hallway toward the back bedroom—her parents' bedroom—where the soft light from a single lamp glowed.

Placing the bear on the bedside table, she bent down before her suitcase, opened it, and rummaged through the contents until she found a cotton nightshirt with a smiling bear emblazoned beneath the question: Have You Given Someone A Bear Hug Today?

Walker rushed to mind.

Only minutes before, desperate to touch him, she'd briefly placed her hand in his. What she'd really wanted, though, was to be in his arms. But then, what was new? It was something that she'd wanted for so long now that she couldn't remember when she hadn't wanted it. Maybe the truth was that the wanting had started long before eighteen months ago, but that she had prudently kept it from herself. She was no longer hiding her feelings, however. At least not from herself. No longer would she treat her feelings for Walker as though they were some-thing to be ashamed of. They weren't. She was in love with him, and love was never a shameful emotion. Nei-ther did love count the years. Her heart couldn't care less that Walker was twenty-four years older than she. All her heart cared about was loving him.

It had taken courage for her to ask if he still missed his wife, but his answer had been her reward. She had feared that his never having remarried meant that he was cling-ing to memories of his dead wife. Obviously, that wasn't the case. Obviously, he just hadn't fallen in love again. Could he with her? She had absolutely no idea, not even a hint of a clue, but surely she owed it to herself to find out. Especially since he'd admitted to being as lonely—wasn't that what feeling empty was all about?—as she.

Slipping out of her clothes, Lindsey drew the night-shirt over her head and let it settle about her. It felt soft and cool against her bare skin—her back, her breasts, her buttocks. Unable to stop herself, she closed her eyes and imagined that it was Walker's hands caressing her. Like her love for him, she no longer censured the feelings that coursed through her. She no longer chastised herself for such sweet musings. How could you chastise yourself for something that felt more natural than breathing? Even so, she knew that such sweet musings could be torture. Because of that, she bridled her imagination and forced herself to the mundane task of brushing her teeth.

Afterward, she pulled back the spread and eased onto the side of the bed. She did not lie down. Instead, she splayed her hand against the smoothness of the sheet. This was her parents' bed. This was where she'd come when bad dreams had awakened her; this was where she'd come, bubbling with excitement, on Christmas morning to awaken her parents; this was where she'd come to tell her parents she was home from a date. There was something tragically wrong about this bed now being empty.

Standing, Lindsey picked up the teddy bear and walked from the room. She left the light on in the bedroom, as though her parents had just stepped out and would return any moment. Following the hallway, Lindsey turned on the light switch of her old bedroom. Hundreds of pairs of teddy-bear eyes, some of glass, others of antique buttons, met hers. Lindsey smiled amid the silent greetings she heard. Lovingly rearranging the stuffed animals on the bed—there were several expensive Steiff bears made of mohair—she turned off the light and lay down among them. She still cradled the latest furry acquisition. It was warm. It was cuddly. It was also a poor substitute for the man she wished were in her arms.

A couple of miles away, Walker pulled the car into his driveway. As expected, the house was dark. Now that his son had flown from the nest, he could never quite grow used to returning to a dark house. He kept threatening to leave a light on, but if he did, he knew he would be admitting that the unwelcoming darkness bothered him. Which it did, but it was just another unspoken game that human beings were so adept at playing. Maybe he ought to get a dog. Naw, he wasn't home enough to do a pet justice. Of course the reason he wasn't home much was because he preferred to stay at the office or out on a rig or anywhere else for that matter. Anywhere that would keep him from returning to an empty, dark house.

The house was the same one he'd lived in with Phyllis. He'd seen no need to move after her death. In truth, moving had been the last thing he'd wanted to do. If the memories were painful, the memories had also been familiar. Something about the sameness had preserved what little sanity he'd had left. He had redecorated about two years ago, or rather had had someone do it for him, since he knew next to nothing about decorating. The decorator had worked her magic with colors she'd called sand, cream and cinnamon.

He'd also had a swimming pool built at the same time he'd remodeled. Sidetracking the house, it was to the swimming pool that he now headed via the outside gate. Not bothering with lights—in fact, they were the last thing he wanted for what he had in mind—he pocketed his car keys and started stripping his clothes at poolside. Yanking the knit shirt over his head, he wadded it up and tossed it at the nearby glass-topped table. His khaki pants, which he unzipped and shucked from his legs in seemingly one motion, he let fall where and as they chose. He kicked out of his shoes, peeled off his socks, and, hooking his thumb into the elastic waistband of his jockey shorts, pared the clingy fabric from his body.

His hot body.

His tired body.

His restless body.

Why did he feel so restless, so damned restless?

Not even attempting to find an answer, he dove into the pool. Hands above his head, he cut through the cool water, feeling his body's heat and weariness begin to dissipate. The restlessness remained, however. In an attempt to counteract it, he began to swim laps. He began to *vigorously* swim laps. Splashing his feet, grabbing fistfuls of water, he traveled from one end of the pool back to the other, then back again. Over and over until he lost count...until his muscles burned...until his lungs threatened to explode.

Bursting from the water, he levered himself onto the side of the pool. He shook his head, slinging water in a wide arc. A drop of moisture rolled from an eyelash and plopped onto his moist cheek. He swiped at it and took a deep breath. At the same time, he took stock of his body. His body heat had cooled, the weariness had eased into his muscles in a way that beckoned sleep. The restlessness, however, remained, making sleep frustratingly elusive. He should have gone ahead and had the caffeine, he thought in irritation, because it looked as if he was going to be awake anyway. Thinking. Worrying.

With Gerri gone, he was behind at work. The business had its fair share of jobs right now, which demanded a lot of time and attention. Then, too, he couldn't negate what was happening to his friends. Because he cared for them, the breakup of their marriage was a stress that spilled over into his life.

Lindsey.

An image of her flashed before him. An image of silky-soft blond hair. An image of sultry gray eyes. An image of a young woman upset by the crisis unfolding in her parents' lives. He would do anything to spare her, but he couldn't.

"Do you still miss her?"

He hadn't been expecting Lindsey's question about Phyllis. Any more than he'd been expecting his answer, but it had come easily enough, truthfully enough. He *did* still miss Phyllis, but it wasn't the kind of missing that tied his heart into knots. It just felt as if some part of him had been removed . . . and that nothing, no one, had ever replaced that missing part. It just felt as if he were empty inside, waiting, wanting, to be touched by some warmth.

Warmth.

The memory of Lindsey's hand in his came sweetly sweeping through his mind, his senses. Against all logic, he could feel his palm heating, as though it had been kissed by the noonday sun. He didn't understand the return of the memory; he didn't understand the power it held over him, though he clearly understood that the memory disturbed him. Greatly. So much so that he erased it from his mind and pushed to his feet. Bare, leaving his clothes where he'd discarded them, he walked toward house.

The dark, empty, lonely house.

* * *

The following Monday morning, the office telephone rang four times in as many minutes. Walker, who'd arrived promptly at seven o'clock—it was now four minutes after seven—reached once more for the receiver. The ringing stopped in midpeal.

"Gal-Tex," he said, thankful now that he'd come in the afternoon before.

Though he hadn't gotten near as much paperwork done as he'd hoped, he at least hadn't had to contend with telephone interruptions. Even so, he'd spent far too much of the Sunday afternoon wondering if Dean and Lindsey had gotten together—surely they had—and what had been said at the meeting. Telling himself that what went on between father and daughter was none of his business had done little to alleviate the wondering.

"Yeah," Walker now said into the phone, "I've got that information right here." As he spoke, he riffled through the thousand and one sheets of paper on his desk. Dammit! he thought, he had had the information right here yesterday. Or maybe it was the day before. Or maybe it was on Gerri's desk. "Give me a sec, will ya?" he said, pushing the button that would temporarily disconnect him with the caller.

He had just started for the secretary's desk when another line of the phone rang. For ten cents—no make that five!—he'd waltz right out the door and forget that the phone was ringing and that one of his foremen was waiting for some important figures.

Instead, he depressed the second lighted button, the one screaming for attention, and said, "Gal-Tex. Could you hold a moment, please?" Walker didn't wait for a response, but rather automatically put the second caller on hold.

In seconds, owing to what Walker considered a lot of luck, he found the list of figures he was searching for on the secretary's desk. He read them to his foreman, then terminated the call.

"Thank you for holding," he said after he'd reconnected the second caller.

There was a pause, then a soft, feminine voice said, "You sound like a zookeeper trying to round up all the animals that got loose during the night."

Walker realized, if only peripherally, that Lindsey's voice was the nicest thing that had happened to him all morning. In fact, it might be the nicest thing that had happened to him since he'd last heard her voice. He grinned.

"Your metaphor is apropos. It *is* a zoo around here. The phone's ringing off the wall, and I haven't even uncapped my coffee." As he spoke, he took the lid off the cup of coffee he'd bought en route to the office. Normally Gerri had coffee waiting for him, but with no Gerri awaiting him, there'd certainly be no coffee.

"Ah, poor baby," Lindsey said in a tone that Walker thought steamier than the vapor rising from the cup.

He grinned again, thinking that the vampy sound was even better than nice, which he hastened to tell himself was all right to think even though Lindsey was his goddaughter. He was, after all, only making an idle observation.

"And here I was thinking that you were going to be sympathetic," he said as he brought the cup to his lips and sipped.

"I am. And to prove the point I'm going to give you time to uncap the coffee."

"I already have, smart aleck," he said around a grin that obviously would not die. "I've already had a swallow, thank you very much."

"And can you feel that caffeine racing through your body, waking up every sleepy little cell?"

What he could feel was something he hadn't felt in a long while. It was so simple, so subtle, that he almost wasn't aware of feeling it at all. And he wasn't at all sure how to define it, except to say it was a sort of hey-isn't-it-great-to-be-alive? feeling. Even with the phone ringing off the wall, even with work stacked up to his chin, even with life less than perfect, it was great to be alive with the day, and its endless opportunities, stretching before him. Lindsey's joie de vivre must be rubbing off on him.

"Has anyone ever told you that you can sometimes be a little too big for your britches?" Walker didn't dare entertain the silk and lace images that flitted just at the corner of his mind. Such images would be so inappropriate that there would be absolutely no way to excuse them.

Lindsey laughed, lilting notes of a cheery song, but then the notes faded and her voice was serious when she asked, "Has Dad come in?"

"No, not yet, but he should be here any minute." Before Lindsey could make any further comment, Walker asked, referring to her meeting with her father, "How did it go yesterday?"

"It didn't," Lindsey answered bluntly.

Walker halted the cup in midjourney to his lips. "What do you mean?"

"Just what I said. I didn't see Dad."

"But I thought—"

"So did I. He called at noon with a list of excuses a mile long. He was still tied up on the job, he was tired, he needed to run by the office, he needed to darn his socks." This last was said with sarcastic flippancy.

Walker but barely heard the sarcasm. He had keyed in to Dean needing to run by the office. Walker knew that he hadn't, however. Not unless he'd come by after seven o'clock, which he doubted seriously. Even though he knew that his friend couldn't be looking forward to the confrontation with his daughter, still it wasn't like Dean to lie. Another thought occurred to him, causing Walker to frown. Surely Dean wasn't seeing someone. Was he?

". . . please."

Walker realized that he hadn't heard a word that Lindsey had said.

"I'm sorry. What did you say?"

"Would you hang on to him when he gets there? Rope him, chain him, hit him over the head, but don't let him get away. Okay?"

"You coming down?"

"I'm leaving in about ten minutes."

"How's your mom?"

There was a pause, then, "I think she's better. It's sorta like falling apart allowed her the opportunity to pick up the pieces and start all over again. In fact, over pancakes, she informed me that she'd never really liked those glasses, anyway, that she'd liked another pattern, but that Daddy had liked these."

Walker smiled . . . and prayed that Dean wasn't having an affair. What in heaven's name would make a man walk away from a woman like Bunny? How in hell could he expect to find a woman who would stand so devotedly by him? He couldn't, and so that put an answer once and for all to the question of whether Dean was having an affair. He wasn't. Something else was motivating him in his request for a divorce.

"So will you hang on to Dad?" Walker heard Lindsey ask.

"I'll do my best, but he's bigger than I am."

"Yeah, but you're quicker."

Walker had heard the comment, which had begun in their high school football days, countless times over the years—brawny Dean and agile Walker. Grinning, Walker said, "Tell that to my middle-aged body."

"Ah, poor baby," Lindsey said once more in that hot-as-a-summer-day voice.

Walker found himself grinning yet again. "Smart aleck."

No sooner had Walker hung up than three more calls came in back to back. Some valve had blown on Rig Four, a foreman needed some time off because of a death in his family and someone was questioning the amount of his pay check. All in all, a pretty routine Monday morning—if he'd had a secretary to help him run interference. But he didn't. All he had were two hands and another ringing telephone. No, make that two lines ringing. As he picked up the receiver, the front door opened and Dean Ellison walked in.

"Grab the other line, will ya?" Walker said, motioning to the phone on the secretary's desk.

Tall—he was exactly three-quarters of an inch taller than Walker, with beefy arms, mammoth shoulders and a solid stomach— Dean did as requested. For minutes, both men spoke to their respective callers, then, within seconds of each other, they hung up.

"Whatever we're paying Gerri," Walker said, leaning back in his desk chair, "it isn't enough."

"Busy, huh?" Dean asked, edging his leg over the corner of the secretary's desk and sitting down.

"That's an understatement."

"You need to hire some temporary help."

"Yeah, I will."

Walker was aware that the conversation was strained. It had been ever since Dean had announced his intention to seek a divorce. Walker supposed that Dean felt defensive, as though he thought he, Walker, was going to judge him. Which Walker was trying hard not to do. Damned hard! He just wished that Dean would open up and talk to him. Walker had thought there wasn't anything they couldn't talk about, but he'd obviously been wrong.

Maybe, though, if he were honest, he would admit that Dean had pulled away from him months before he'd demanded the divorce. Looking back, Walker realized that Dean had pulled into himself. Also, he had become obsessed with health and nutrition and working out. He'd bought a membership at a local spa and spent every free minute there, pumping iron, doing sit-ups, anything that broke a sweat and threatened an inch of fat. It was about that time, too, that he changed his style of dress. Always conservative in his clothes, he began to wear neon-printed pants, jewelry, and sunglasses with iridescent mirrored lenses. It was also during this period that the gray in his hair miraculously disappeared, though there was no way he could eliminate the receding hairline. Maybe Bunny was right. Maybe Dean was simply going through a midlife crisis. Maybe everything would settle back down in time. Then again...

Walker thought of the classic affair that was usually associated with a mid-life crisis. He had a devil of a time thinking of Dean with a woman other than his wife. He just couldn't believe that Dean would stoop to that. No, whatever else might be going on in Dean's life, Walker couldn't believe that he was having an affair.

"How was your weekend?" Walker asked, taking a swallow of coffee.

Dean whipped off his sunglasses and shoved them into his shirt pocket. His eyes didn't quite meet Walker's. "Fine. Rig Three is operational. The part held."

"Good. Did, uh, did you come by the office yesterday?"

Dean's gaze slid into his friend's. He shook his head once. "No, why?"

"Just wondered," Walker said, taking another casual sip of coffee. "By the way, a valve blew on Four."

Something akin to relief sped across Dean's face. He obviously preferred the safe topic of work. "I've got to go out there anyway." He checked his watch. "I guess I could go on and—"

"Lindsey just called. She's on her way here."

Walker thought that the expression on Dean's face would have been funny if it hadn't been so tragic.

"Why's she coming here?" Dean asked.

"To see you. She says ya'll are having a hard time getting together."

"Yeah, well, I've been busy...Rig Three and that hassle.... I can't just drop everything. I've got responsibilities. The valve now on Four..." All this he stammered, one word tripping over the other.

"She thinks you're avoiding her," Walker said, pulling no punches.

"Avoiding her?" Dean asked, his voice pitched a tad too shrilly. "That's ridiculous."

"Is it?"

"Of course, it is!" he said, raking his hand through his tinted hair. "Why would I want to avoid her? Why would I . . ." He stopped, sighed, then swore.

Silently, Walker watched as his friend slipped from the edge of the desk and went to stand before the window. Outside the sun shone, but it did so through a smattering of clouds. The weather forecaster predicted showers. So did Walker's knee.

Dean turned suddenly, saying, "What am I going to tell her?"

It was the old Dean asking the heartfelt question, the Dean who'd been his friend all through high school and college, the Dean he called his best friend, the Dean he'd die for if need be.

"How about the truth?" Walker said softly.

Dean laughed harshly and speared his fingers back through his hair. "And just what the hell is that? How can I explain something to her that even I don't understand?"

Walker stood and, rounding his desk, perched on the edge in a pose similar to the one Dean had only moments before abandoned. "Then tell her that."

"I owe her more than that, man." His voice displayed his self-anger. "A helluva lot more."

"She'll settle for what you can give her. If it's all you can honestly give."

"Yeah, sure, just the way Bunny did."

The sarcasm clearly revealed that his confrontation with his wife hadn't gone well. But then, Walker hadn't supposed it had.

Dean sighed, as though he bore the weight of the world on his shoulders and that, even though those shoulders were massive, they weren't up to the burden.

"I don't know, Walker," he said, obviously mystified himself by what he was feeling. "Have you ever felt like life was choking you to death? Have you ever woken up in the middle of the night wondering if this is all there is to life? Have you ever broken out in a cold sweat because you thought maybe that it was, that you were never going to have anything more than you already did?" Before Walker could respond, his friend added, "Hell, we're getting old, or hadn't you noticed?"

Walker angled his knee into a more comfortable position. "Yeah, I noticed."

"Don't you want anything more than you've got?"

Walker didn't even have to ponder the question. "Yeah," he answered, "I want what you're throwing away. I want someone in my life who loves me—warts and all. I want someone to smile at me first thing in the morning. I want someone to give a damn whether I come home in the evening."

"See, I can't make even you understand," Dean said.

"Okay, so I don't understand, but I'm not condemning you, either."

"Yeah, well, you're not Lindsey. I'm not divorcing *your* mother."

It was a fact that Walker couldn't deny. Lindsey would be prejudiced in a way he wasn't.

"What is it you want?" Walker asked after a few seconds of silence.

Dean shrugged. "To be young again, to have my hair again, to feel the same excitement about life that I did twenty years ago, to have the chance to play pro football like you.... You didn't know that I'd wanted to play pro ball, did you?''

Walker shook his head. "Why didn't you?"

"I didn't think I was good enough."

"If I was good enough, you were good enough."

"Yeah, well..." Dean answered, leaving the sentence as unfinished as the issue was unresolved.

"Believe me," Walker said, "it wasn't what it was cracked up to be."

"The point is that you got to find that out for yourself."

Walker couldn't argue the logic. Logic. There was still something about all this that didn't make any sense, and so he said, "Up to a point I understand what you're saying, but I still don't understand how divorcing Bunny is going to make you young again, keep your hairline from receding, and make up for not playing pro ball."

Pain streaked across Dean's face, making him look even older than he was complaining of being. "Look, I just can't..." He was obviously searching for the right words, but ultimately had to settle for the paltry, "I just can't be tied down anymore. I don't expect you to understand. Just believe me when I say I can't. It's nothing personal. I mean, I don't hate Bunny or anything—I could never hate Bunny—but I can't be tied down."

Walker refrained from saying that Bunny had probably taken his decision personally. Very personally.

"Talk to Lindsey for me," Dean implored.

"I can't do that."

"Yes, you can. She'll listen to you."

"It's not my place."

"Maybe not, but—"

"No," Walker said firmly, then added, "There's not much I wouldn't do for you—you know that—but this I can't do. Lindsey has a right to hear this from you."

Hiking his hands at his hips, Dean gave a weary sigh. "You're right. I know you're right. Besides, I can hardly avoid her forever."

Dressed in casual denim, Lindsey entered the office. Her gaze immediately went to her father, who sat at the smallest of the three desks in the room. Since he was in the office less than anyone, the smallest desk had seemed the logical choice for him. Now, two things crossed Lindsey's mind in tandem: One, as always, his stature dwarfed the desk, making it appear even smaller than it was, and two, if her mother had changed since last she'd seen her, so had her father.

Lindsey took in his pants—bright yellow, blue, and sherbet pink. A drawcord cinched the waist, while the ankles were pegged. Over his chest fit a shocking-pink cotton jersey. There was nothing wrong with the clothes—far from it. It was just that for a man who'd once balked at any color other than drab gray or basic black or brown, the carousel colors looked wildly out of place. Sadly out of place. The bracelet at his wrist and the iridescent sunglasses in his pocket wouldn't compute, at all!

"Hi, Daddy," Lindsey said in a voice that was hardly more than a whisper. Somewhere in the back of her mind, she noted that Walker, who was on the telephone, had looked up when she'd opened the door. His presence was comforting. Particularly since the other man in the room, her father, seemed a little bit like a stranger.

At his daughter's entrance, Dean had glanced up, too. The eyes of father and daughter met, held, probed. Slowly, Dean pushed back his chair and stood.

"Hey, sweetie," he said in a voice that Lindsey thought sounded a little uncertain, though maybe she was mistaken. Maybe she was the one suddenly feeling uncertain, as though afraid that not only did he want to cast her mother aside, but maybe her, as well.

Lindsey crossed to him; Dean crossed to her. And then, she was in his arms. Though his appearance might be different, his arms were wonderfully familiar. These arms, hugging her so tightly that it hurt, were the loving arms of her dad, the man who could slay dragons, the man who could heal young and tender hurts, the man who'd always had implicit faith in her.

"You look great," Dean said at last. "Doesn't she look great, Walker?"

When Bunny had asked Walker the same question, he'd teased that Lindsey had gone and gotten herself ugly. Now, taking in the soft taffy-blond curls that tumbled about her shoulders and the snug jeans that cupped the curves of her shapely rear, even to tease so seemed outrageously ridiculous. And so he simply spoke the truth, "Yeah, she looks great."

For a moment, Lindsey's gaze connected with Walker's. The honest tone of his voice warmed her.

The intensity of Lindsey's steel-blue eyes, a look that said what he thought was important, equally warmed him. Though, to be honest, he wasn't quite sure why. He just knew that it did.

The phone rang again, and Walker swore something decidedly unflattering about Monday mornings and sick secretaries.

Lindsey turned her attention back to her father. "Could, uh, could you take a break? I'll buy you a cup of coffee."

Before Dean could answer, another line rang. Dean punched in the call. It was about the valve on Rig Four.

"Yeah . . . okay . . . no, I'll be on out."

Disappointment, frustration, even a bit of anger flowed through Lindsey. "Dad, I really want to talk to you."

Dean looked up at his daughter and covered the mouthpiece with his palm. "And I promise we will."

Lindsey looked skeptical. Highly skeptical.

"Within a couple of hours," Dean said into the mouthpiece. "Do ya'll need anything else?"

Lindsey looked ready to do battle. Just as her father hung up, she said, "Couldn't you spare—"

"Let me get this done, sweetheart, then we'll talk. In fact, I'll tell you what. Why don't I pick you up at seven and we'll have dinner?"

Lindsey's skepticism looked on the verge of returning.

"I know I've been avoiding you, I know we have to talk, and we will tonight. I promise. Okay?"

"Do you mean it?"

Dean made the appropriate sign over his heart. "Cross my heart and hope to choke." As a little girl, her father pledging to cross his heart and hoping to die had frightened Lindsey, so he'd modified the saying.

Lindsey smiled. "Okay. Seven."

The smile faded, however, as she watched her father, after a peck to her cheek, walk from the office. She turned to Walker.

"Do you think he'll show up?"

"Yeah. He'll show."

"How can you be so sure? His track record isn't exactly sterling."

"I just know," he answered, grinning as he added, "Besides, I'll kick his butt if he doesn't."

"That'll be the day—when you and Dad fight."

Walker's grin faded as he thought of his best friend. "Yeah."

Lightening the mood, Lindsey said, "I don't suppose I can buy you a cup of coffee?"

"I'd love to, but there's no way I can get away. Not with Gerri out and all the zoo animals loose and on the prowl."

As if to prove his point, the phone rang. He sighed.

"Let me get out of here and let you go to work," Lindsey said, heading for the door. Before Walker could answer the phone, she turned and said, "I thought you said I'd gone and gotten ugly."

The truth was that Walker could never remember thinking anyone more beautiful—beautiful and something more. Alive. Lindsey was alive. Appealingly alive.

The grin recaptured one corner of his mouth. "It's remarkable what a little rest will do."

Lindsey's heart gave a bumpy thump-thump at the sight of his all-male smile . . . and at his words. She said nothing. She simply smiled, waved, and walked out the door.

Walker watched her go. Curiously, her absence left him feeling . . . flat. Deflated. As though life had shifted from technicolor to black and white. He had no idea how long he stood staring at the spot where she'd been only seconds before. When the ringing of the telephone finally penetrated his consciousness, he felt like a first-class fool. What was wrong with him?

Brushing thoughts of Lindsey aside, he reached for the phone. "Gal-Tex," he said. "May I help you?"

Chapter Four

When the telephone rang, Walker ignored it. He'd had his fill of telephones for one day. Besides, the cool water felt too good to abandon as he lazily glided the length of the swimming pool. It had rained earlier in the afternoon, which meant that his knee had ached all day and he really needed this exercise. Badly. Plus the heat had set in with a vengeance once the rain had stopped, making the night air thick and sticky like a blob of bubble gum. No, he thought, as the water purled across his body, the last thing he needed was another phone call.

And yet...

What if it were Adam calling about the baby? Or what if it were Bunny needing something? Or what if it were Lindsey calling to say that her father hadn't shown up, after all? This last had been on Walker's mind all evening. Surely Dean had kept his promise. Surely Dean wouldn't disappoint Lindsey again. Would he?

Before he knew quite what he was doing, Walker converted his gliding strokes into something faster and in seconds hefted himself onto the side of the pool. He'd again swum in the nude, the way he most often did, owing to the sheltered privacy the redwood fence and privet hedge provided. Then, too, the houses in this secluded neighborhood were set discreetly apart. He reached for the portable phone that lay on the glass-topped table even as his bare backside registered the heat still contained within the concrete.

Adjusting the phone's On button, Walker said, "Hello?"

There was a pause, then, "Am I interrupting anything important?"

The voice belonged to Lindsey. The memory of her standing in the office doorway that afternoon came to mind. The memory was clothed in denim—clinging denim. As always, he was uncomfortable with these errant thoughts. Denying them, he grabbed his watch and checked the time. Ten minutes after ten o'clock. Surely she'd have called earlier if Dean failed to show.

"No," Walker said, "I was just getting in a few laps." Before she could answer, he added, "How did the evening go with your father?"

At the mention that Walker had been swimming, a bold—even a brazen—image flashed through Lindsey's mind. The image consisted of sun-tanned skin, silver-tipped ebony hair foresting a wide chest, the same ebony-tinted hair scoring stomach and legs and...

She focused on the question Walker had asked. "Who knows?" she said in answer.

Walker halted the towel he was passing through his hair. A renegade drop of water ran down the ridge of his straight nose. "He did show up, didn't he?"

"Oh, yeah, he showed up."

"Well, did you talk to him?"

"Not really. I mostly talked *at* him."

"I see," Walker said, seeing only too clearly. Dean wasn't into communication these days.

"In short," Lindsey said, "he told me to mind my own business. Oh, he wasn't quite that blunt. No, as a matter of fact, he was that blunt. He told me that what was going on between him and Mother was their business only, that no third person, not even a daughter, could sit in judgment on a couple's marriage, that no one could judge what two other people were feeling in their hearts." Lindsey gave a weary sigh. "And if you tell me that you told me so, I'll scream."

Or cry, Walker thought, hearing the strain in her voice. She was trying hard to control her emotions. As always, he wanted to protect her, shield her. In fact, the thought of her crying did strangely painful things to him.

"Hey," he said, "get that chin up off the curb before it gets run over."

"And how do you know my chin's on the curb?"

"Having been there a time or two myself, I recognized the sound of one's voice bleating against concrete."

Lindsey giggled, then sobered. "What really upset me was his categorical rejection of counseling. He doesn't need counseling, he said. He wasn't nuts, he told me." She sighed again. "Oh, Walker, he's so different. I mean, he is and he isn't. He's still my dad, but he seems like someone else, too. And when did he start dressing like...like...I don't know, like he was twenty instead of forty? Not that forty is old or anything," she hastened to add.

Oh, but it was, Walker thought, drawing the towel through the hair on his chest, which was now as silver as it was black. It was at least old enough for a man to know that he couldn't recapture his youth, which was what Dean was trying to do.

"Don't be too hard on him, Lindsey. He's being hard enough on himself right now."

"I know that. I could hear his suffering. He practically admitted that he still cares for Mother, but that he just can't be tied down right now. What does that mean, Walker? I thought that loving someone was wanting to be tied down to them—for forever."

The image of that kind of loving bondage was not an unpleasant one for Walker. It was what he wanted, too. It was what he'd missed so sorely since his wife's death. "Not everyone defines love the same way. Plus people change. Their needs change. What you need or want today, you don't need or want tomorrow."

"In other words, people fall out of love?" Lindsey asked, then didn't even give Walker a chance to answer. "I don't believe that. If people fall out of love, they were never in love."

Walker heard the idealism of youth, an idealism that reality had not yet tarnished. The hard, cold truth was that people did fall in love, then grow apart . . . and the reasons were many and myriad. Life was never static. People were never static. And yet, Walker had always believed that in an ever-changing, dynamic world, love was the only thing that stood a chance of surviving. The commitment that some couples were able to make did outlast everything, perhaps even the people themselves. Hundreds of times over the years, he had imagined that he could feel the love Phyllis had left behind. So, perhaps the truth was that Lindsey was right. Maybe he was faulting her for her naïveté when he should be applauding her maturity. Maybe some people did fall in love for forever, while others just fell into something less than love.

"Are you there?" he heard her ask. The tone of her voice suggested bewilderment at the silence.

"Yeah, I was just wondering when you grew up on me."

This time the silence came from Lindsey. Her heart skidded to a stop before galloping forward. "Is that what I've done?"

"Yeah, I think so," he answered, images of her playing through his mind once more. He saw her standing in the airport, all prettiness and bright eyes. He saw her standing in the office doorway, all curves and long, silky hair. He heard her talking of love, all wisdom and maturity.

"Well, I hear that it happens to everyone sooner or later," she answered.

"Yeah. Sooner or later."

Lindsey made no reply.

Neither did Walker.

Each let the silence, like a soft, fluffy cloud, drift about them. A subliminal tension, however, floated along with the silence. Even had he been aware of the tension, Walker would have denied it, for it felt a lot like the tension, the sexual tension, that crackled between a man and a woman. The right man and the right woman. Unaware of his movements, Walker drew the towel into his lap in order to hide his nakedness.

"So," he asked, "what do you do from here? I mean, about your parents?"

Lindsey wondered what he'd thought about during the silence. She wondered, too, what he would have thought if he knew what she'd thought about during the silence;

namely, did he swim in the buff? The thought that he might left her in definite need of a full breath of air.

"Well," she said, pushing this thought aside, "I'm not my father's daughter for nothing. I've inherited every ounce of his stubbornness. I'm going to hang around, at least for a little longer, to see if he comes to his senses. It's obvious I'm going to have to lead him in the right direction."

"Lindsey—"

"Don't!" she said. "Don't caution me about interfering. Don't tell me that it's none of my business. Don't tell me that I shouldn't involve myself in someone else's marriage, even if the marriage is that of my parents. Don't tell me that I should pack my bags and go back to London."

"I thought you were going to Timbuktu."

Lindsey could hear the grin that nipped at Walker's lips. "I'm going there only if you'll go with me."

"After today, I'm tempted. Believe me, I'm tempted." Even as he spoke, the endless phone calls rang in his head.

"Well, actually, that's what I'm calling about," Lindsey said, adding, "And I'll bet you thought I called just to whine."

"That never crossed my mind."

"Well, maybe it should have, because that's what I did. And I'm sorry."

"Don't ever apologize for sharing with me how you feel. You're my—" He started to say godchild but, for reasons he didn't acknowledge, he chose another word. "You're my friend."

Lindsey had no problem with that description of their relationship. She wanted to be his friend. The only problem was she wanted to be something else, as well. Something like his lover. In due time, she thought, she'd test the waters. She no longer wanted to live in a state of limbo. Even if it meant losing Walker completely, she had to know if they had a future.

For now, she'd settle for "friends." "You're right. We're friends. Listen," she added, "did you find anyone to fill in for Gerri?"

"I called the temporary-help agency, but the woman I needed to talk to was at lunch. She didn't return my call—not that she could have gotten through."

"Why don't you let me help you out? I'm going to be here and I do know my way 'round an office."

"Are you serious?"

"Absolutely. I'll even work for free."

"Oh, I think we can do a little better than that."

"Does that mean, yes, I'm hired?"

Walker chuckled. "I'd be crazy to refuse that kind of offer."

"Then it's settled. I'll see you at eight in the morning."

"Thanks," Walker said, his mood sober.

"You're welcome." There was a slight pause before she added, "I'll see you in the morning."

"Lindsey?" Walker said, sensing that she was about to hang up.

"Yes?"

"I wasn't going to caution you about interfering. I was just going to tell you not to expect a miracle."

"Oh, but I do," she said. "They happen only if you expect them."

And that, Walker thought minutes later as he once more lazily swam the length of the pool, might very well define the difference between youth and middle age.

Youth still expected miracles, while middle age dared them to happen.

In the days that followed, Lindsey and Walker each made a heretofore unknown revelation. Lindsey learned that her father's list of excuses for spending any extended time with her was endless, while Walker learned that the office of Gal-Tex was smaller than he'd ever imagined.

As for Lindsey and her father's excuses, she tried to be patient and understanding. She knew that he was uncomfortable around her. This fact saddened her, primarily because they'd always been so close, but she understood that that very closeness was now working against them. He knew that Lindsey wanted answers, but answers were something that he couldn't, or wouldn't, give. This pressure to explain was always there when they were together. As was a certain guilt. At the core of everything, Lindsey sensed that her father felt guilty about hurting her as he most assuredly was.

On the other hand, Walker was beginning to envy Dean his list of excuses for staying out of the office, although he never truly formalized the thought. That would have been too telling, too troubling. That would have forced him to ask some questions that he knew he was avoiding. Questions like: Why was he suddenly aware of Lindsey's least little movement? Why was he going out of his way to avoid any physical contact with her? When had the office shrunk to dimensions more appropriately represented not by feet squared against feet, but rather by the fragrance of her perfume squared against her lilting voice?

''Mr. Dowell won't be able to return your call until tomorrow, these are the figures you asked for, and here is a cup of coffee, which you didn't ask for, but which you look as if you can use."

Walker glanced up at Lindsey's approach. It was Thursday afternoon, her third day of work, and there was no denying that office efficiency had improved a hundred times since that chaotic Monday. There was also no denying that, despite the unrest he felt in her presence, an unrest he couldn't define or explain, he was nonetheless glad she hadn't returned to London. Her energy, her spirit was definitely habit-forming.

"Thanks," he said, reaching for the cup she was offering him, but taking great pains not to touch her. A part of him realized the strangeness of that. Why shouldn't he touch her? He'd touched her a hundred times over the years. Another part of him, however, just accepted the restraint as prudent.

"Oh, by the way, this is the last of the coffee," Lindsey said, thinking that Walker looked decidedly appealing with his end-of-the-day appearance. His hair had been mussed by busy fingers, while his cheeks and chin had darkened with stubble. He'd loosened his tie, pink and black and a perfect match to his pleated black slacks, giving him a roguish look. The look played havoc with her senses, but then her senses had been taunted and teased by his proximity all week.

"Have you checked in the cabinet above the sink?" Walker asked. "Gerri usually keeps a spare can."

In way of an answer, Lindsey crossed the room and opened the cabinet door. She stood on tiptoe, bringing her weight to the balls of her feet, which were encased in simple, but stylish white heels. The white skirt she wore, which normally struck her at midcalf, rose upward, allowing the hem of her slip to show.

Walker instantly spotted the delicate lace edging the undergarment. Like a siren, it beckoned to him and, once it seized his attention, it wouldn't let go. He stared at it, wondering how something as simple as silk and lace could be so out-and-out powerful. But it was. In fact, it was so powerful that it conjured up other images—images of lace-trimmed bras, images of skimpy, lace panties, images that were startling and more than a little unsettling.

"Yeah, there's a...can." Lindsey faltered at the stark, starved look in Walker's eyes, but before she could do more than wonder as to the why of it, it disappeared, leaving her to think that she had imagined it, after all.

Diverting his gaze back to the papers on his desk, Walker said, in a tone crisper than usual, "I need to talk to your dad. He's out on Platform Four. Will you see if you can get him, please?"

Telling herself that wishful thinking did strange things to a person, Lindsey, via ship-to-shore connection, contacted the rig and asked to speak to her father.

"I see," she said. "How long ago did he leave? Fine. No, no message. We'll see him back here in the office. Yeah. Thanks." She hung up the phone. "He's been gone about three hours."

Walker checked his watch. It was four o'clock—give or take a tired Thursday minute. Even considering dropping the helicopter off at the airport, he should have been back in the office by now.

"Shouldn't he be back by now?" Lindsey asked, echoing Walker's thoughts.

Walker shrugged. "He may have had an errand to run. He'll be here."

He wasn't there by five o'clock. Concerned, Lindsey called the airport. The Gal-Tex helicopter had been logged in a little after three o'clock.

"I don't understand," she said. "Doesn't he usually come to the office when he isn't out on the platforms?"

"Yes and no," Walker said, trying to downplay the incident. He was doing it not only for Lindsey's sake, but for his own, as well. The truth was that Dean usually was at the office when he wasn't on site. "Like I said, he probably had an errand to run. He sometimes has to chase down parts." At the worry that still shadowed Lindsey's eyes, Walker smiled and pointed her in the direction of the door. "Go home. The day's over. Your dad's okay."

"If you hear from him—" Lindsey began.

But Walker cut her off with, "I'll tell him to call you."

Lindsey smiled. "Have you noticed that I'm sounding like the parent here?"

Walker grinned, primarily because he couldn't stop himself when subjected to the grandeur of Lindsey's smile. "Trust me, parents worry needlessly about ninety-nine per cent of the time. Your father's fine. I promise."

Twenty minutes later, concerned despite the positive rhetoric he'd spouted for Lindsey's sake, Walker drove by the apartment Dean had rented after moving out of his house. Walker was on the verge of pulling into the driveway when the front door of the apartment opened. A redhead, a smiling, hair-tousled redhead, stepped—bounded—onto the small porch. Dean stepped onto the porch, as well. As though reluctant to part with her, he pulled her back into his arms. The only thing that Walker's brain would register was that he wished he hadn't promised Lindsey that her father was fine. Not that, in a technical sense, Dean wasn't fine. In fact, he was a little too fine.

Even as Walker discreetly watched, Dean lowered his head and planted a kiss, a thorough kiss, to the woman's lips. The woman leaned into Dean, unabashedly pressing her svelte body to his. Dean slipped an arm about her waist and hauled her even closer. Walker felt sick—sick at heart. He, likewise, understood, and never more fully, the reputed blissfulness of ignorance. God, how he wished he hadn't seen what he just did! That acknowledged, he admitted that he couldn't say he was surprised. He'd had a nagging suspicion that he just couldn't shake. However much he longed to believe that his friend wasn't capable of such duplicity, the truth remained that an affair was an important component of a mid-life crisis.

And there was no doubt about it, Dean Ellison was square in the middle of a mid-life crisis! He'd also unwittingly put his friend square in the middle of a moral dilemma. Walker owed allegiance to all three parties involved—Bunny, Dean and Lindsey. Lindsey. God, she'd be crushed if she knew that her father was seeing another woman!

Pulling around the corner, Walker watched and waited, hating what he was seeing, yet captivated by it. In minutes, the woman walked to her car, got in and pulled from the drive. She turned at the corner, and Walker leaned forward as though retrieving something from the glove compartment. He looked up just as she was passing by... and got the shock of his life. Up close, the woman became nothing more than a child. She couldn't even be as old as Lindsey. Dean was having an affair with a woman, a child, younger than his daughter!

Walker drove home with his thoughts alternately clouded by gray confusion and a red blaze of anger. What should he do? Should he tell Bunny, tell Lindsey? Should he confront Dean? The truth was that he felt like punching Dean out for putting him in this hotter-than-hot spot. Which, in and of itself, was upsetting. He could never remember wanting to punch out his best friend.

Once home, Walker showered, went through the motions of eating, then called Lindsey. He had no idea what he was going to say until he heard himself saying it. Her father was fine, he told her. He'd had an errand to run just as he'd suspected. Hanging up the phone, Walker cursed at the out-and-out lie. He felt betrayed by Dean. Furthermore, even though he'd decided that there was no way he could tell Lindsey about her father's affair, he felt as though he were betraying her. He wasn't certain which was worse: being betrayed or being the betrayer.

That night he slept restlessly and, when he did manage to drop off to sleep, he had wild and disturbing dreams. He dreamed that he and Dean were fighting it out, crude fisticuffs that bloodied noses and bruised knuckles. Interestingly, Dean's punches to him didn't elicit pain. It was only those he landed to Dean that caused him to writhe in physical agony. The blood was crimson and reminded Walker of flame-red hair... the flame-red hair of the woman coiled sensuously, serpentinely about Dean. Dean was kissing her and telling her that he'd wanted to play professional football.

Another time—or perhaps this dream simply flowed into the other—Walker was comforting Lindsey. In the background, her father embraced the red-haired woman, while Lindsey cried. The tears, flowing from her silver-blue eyes, looked like diamonds—pale blue-tinted diamonds. Walker tried to capture them as they bled onto her cheek, but the softness of her cheek distracted him. It was softer than anything he'd ever felt, softer than fleece, softer than clouds, softer than silk and lace. Silk and lace. Like the hem of her slip. Like the hem of her sexy slip.

And then he was embracing her, pulling her into him...comforting her...reassuring her...sighing at the softness of her...threading his fingers through the satin fullness of her hair...tilting her head back...brushing her lips with his....

The next morning he awakened tired and restless. He had dreamed something—something about Dean, something about Lindsey. The something about Lindsey he couldn't remember. What couldn't he remember? He didn't pursue the question. Intuitively, he knew that he'd be happier without an answer.

"I don't believe it," Lindsey said later that morning. If her words had not betrayed her disbelief, her voice most assuredly would have.

Walker glanced up. Lindsey stood staring out the window and into the parking lot. She wore a candy-pink skirt and a pink, blue and yellow summer sweater. Pink flats encased her feet, while her hair was pulled back into a ponytail with a pink ribbon. She looked like a girl; she looked like a woman. The combination, coupled with a restless night and troublesome dreams, had unnerved Walker all morning. So much so that he'd hidden behind a facade of professionalism.

Lindsey had wondered at Walker's mood, which had bordered on, if not cool, then at least withdrawn, but now everything fled from her mind except the sports car strutting to a stop in the space reserved for her father.

"What is it?" Walker asked.

"I don't believe it," Lindsey repeated, watching her father spill from the car. "When did Daddy buy a sports car?"

"Sports car?" Walker asked, rising and walking to stand just behind Lindsey. He'd been right. The top of her head came midway of his chin when she wore low-heeled shoes, which provided a good location for her perfume, a bedeviling scent of summer flowers, to subtly swirl about him. Glancing up and outward, Walker saw a sports car, a convertible whose color was red, as in flame red, as in redhead, sitting in the parking lot.

"Don't tell me you didn't know about it," she said.

"I didn't know about it."

"Hi!" Dean called, bursting through the office door as though it were the most glorious morn that had ever dawned. He still wore his iridescent sunglasses, which entirely hid his eyes behind a deep purple tint. "Isn't she a beauty?" Before anyone could answer, he rushed on with, "I went by just to look. Next thing I knew, I'd bought it! I said, what the heck? You only live once." Again, before a comment could be forthcoming, he asked, "What do you think?"

What Walker thought was that, if his friend were flying any higher, he'd bump into a cloud. He also sensed a tension in Lindsey. It was a tension that had not been there minutes before.

Lindsey, on the other hand, thought her father had already run into something...and knocked what little sense he had clean out of his head. She felt her disbelief boil over into irritation. No, maybe it wasn't irritation at all. Maybe it was a clear-cut case of anger. Here she was worried sick about her mother, here she was trying to salvage their marriage and here her father was out buying a new flashy, splashy sports car, as though the only thing of importance was him zooming about like a playboy!

"C'mon, let me show her to you," Dean said. "I'll even take you for a spin." As he spoke, he slid an arm about Lindsey's shoulder.

Lindsey discreetly slid away. "You two go on. I'll stay and man the office."

"Ah, c'mon," her father said. "The office'll be fine for five minutes."

"No, really, ya'll go on," Lindsey insisted, stepping back behind the desk and starting to shuffle the papers. "I've got a couple of calls to make." Lindsey's gaze shifted to Walker, as though she was begging him to understand her feelings and run interference for her.

"Call and see if you can get Ed Dowell," Walker said. "If not, just leave the message that I'd like to cancel the meeting for next week and reschedule."

Lindsey gave a silent thank-you and reached for the phone.

"I'll take you for a ride another time, sweetheart," Dean said, seemingly oblivious to his daughter's dark mood. "C'mon," Dean said enthusiastically to Walker. "Wait till you hear this engine, wait till you feel this power."

All the way to the parking lot, Walker listened to technical chatter: the car had a five-speed manual transmission and a 32-valve V8 engine, which allowed it to soar from zero to 60 mph in 6.2 seconds. Then there was the antilock brakes, air bags, the ten-way electrically adjustable seats and a fully automatic soft top, which could be raised or lowered at the touch of a button. Walker heard, but didn't hear, saw, but didn't see, felt, but didn't feel. In truth, all he heard was the drone of Dean's voice, all he saw was the redhead buried in Dean's arms, all he felt was the tension that had instantly coiled in Lindsey at the sight of the automobile.

"Look at her," Dean said, drawing his hand across the side of the car, as though in a caress.

The gesture reminded Walker of Dean's hand sliding around the waist of the young woman. He told himself that he had no right to judge Dean, but the truth was that he guessed he was. Dean was hurting two people whom he cared deeply about.

"Wait till you see how she handles," Dean said, tossing the keys to Walker.

With lightning speed, Walker caught them, then sailed them back to Dean. "You drive. I'm not used to anything that goes from zero to sixty in 6.2 seconds."

Dean laughed. "Believe me, you can get use to this baby's performance. Not that I've opened her up on the streets, but the power's there. You can feel it."

Walker thought his friend sounded orgasmic.

Opening the car door, Dean bustled inside. Walker, less enthusiastic, followed suit, feeling the warmth of the sun-heated leather penetrate the fabric of his slacks. In seconds, the car hummed. Dean's hand on the gearshift, the convertible, its nose pointed in the direction of the street, roared from the parking lot. In a gusty surge, the wind tunneled through Walker's hair, teasing it like sensuous fingers. Dean's hair flew wild, too, ironically playing up the receding hairline that Dean fought so valiantly to disguise.

Dean looked over at his friend, grinned, then shifted into another gear that sent the car barreling down the street. Not dangerously so, but enough to challenge the speed limit. Several turns here, several there, and Dean maneuvered the vehicle onto an asphalt road that ran just at the edge of town. The road was deserted, except for an occasional car. Without warning, Dean floored the gas pedal. The car, like a bullet, shot forward, causing the wind to whip violently at hair and clothes and senses.

"Great, huh?" Dean shouted above the howl.

Walker said nothing. He simply rested his arm across the back of the seat in a negligible pose that said he was out for nothing more than a snail-paced Sunday drive.

Slowing the car, which had indeed lived up to its fast claim, Dean pulled the vehicle to the shoulder of the road, made an illegal U-turn and started back into town at a more reasonable pace.

Looking over at Walker, he asked, "Well, what do you think?"

What he thought was that he was about to do something he'd probably regret. "Who is she?"

On the surface, Dean's expression went absolutely blank. Below the surface, however, Walker thought he saw a streak of panic flash behind the purple-lensed sunglasses. The flash was so quick that it made the sports car's speed seem drop-dead slow.

"Who's who?" Dean asked calmly—too calmly.

"The young girl I saw you with?"

"What girl—"

"For God's sake, Dean, don't insult my intelligence or our friendship!"

Dean said nothing. Neither did he look in Walker's direction. It was as though the road had become the sole focus of his attention.

Obviously realizing he'd have to make a comment at some point, he said finally, "How'd you find out?"

"I saw you."

"Where?"

"On the porch of your apartment," Walker said, adding angrily, "Didn't discretion ever cross your mind?"

"I was discreet!" Dean bellowed back.

"On the porch of your apartment? For God's sake, Lindsey could have been the one to find you!"

Dean jerked his head in Walker's direction. "She doesn't know, does she? She and…Bunny don't know?"

"Not that I'm aware of."

"You're, uh…you're not going to tell them, are you?"

Walker had been looking at his friend. He now turned his eyes back to the road. "No," he said, flatly, but emphatically. Just as he'd known in a split second that he couldn't tell Lindsey, so, too, in just such a split second did he discover he couldn't betray his friend. Being caught in the middle was an unbearable position, one he hoped to never be caught in again. Assuming he ever got out of the viselike jaws of this unbearable middle.

At his answer, Walker could feel Dean's relief. He could hear the soft sigh that whispered at his lips. It crossed Walker's mind that maybe Dean was offering up a prayer of thanks.

Neither spoke for a while, then, blocks from the office, Dean said, "I, uh, I met her at a diner. She's a nice kid."

Kid. Walker thought the word more than appropriate. He was relieved, though, that at least Dean wasn't denying the woman's youthfulness.

"I mean, she's not underage or anything—she's nineteen—but that's…" He sighed. "That's still a kid, huh?" He laughed mirthlessly. "I've got a daughter older than my girlfriend."

Walker said nothing. He wondered what Dean would think if someone his age was seeing Lindsey. He didn't pursue the thought, because, quite frankly, he himself didn't much like the idea of an older man with Lindsey. Something in him said maybe he wouldn't like seeing

Lindsey with any man, regardless of his age. He told the something to get lost, that the subject was something he didn't want to consider too closely.

"I didn't leave Bunny for her," Dean said. "Our relationship isn't that serious. I mean, I did start seeing her before I left Bunny. God knows, I hadn't intended to, it just happened. I stopped at the diner one day for lunch, and she got to kidding around and then...well, one thing led to another, but we're not serious. She's going off to college this fall. She's sweet and everything, but our relationship's just not that serious."

"Then why are you seeing her?" The question was blunt. Determinedly so. At its core was Walker's need to understand. His desperate need.

Dean looked over at his friend. His unvarnished answer rang with painful honesty. "Because she makes me feel young. I said that I didn't leave Bunny for Michele, and I didn't. I left her for the way Michele makes me feel. She makes me feel young. She makes me feel alive."

Somewhere during the discussion, Dean had driven the car back into the parking lot of Gal-Tex. He hadn't killed the motor, though, and Walker was aware of the engine's powerful thrumming vibration. Understanding equally rumbled through him. He could identify with wanting to feel alive. Growing older didn't necessarily bother him, but the emptiness he felt did. He was tired of feeling that he was standing on the sidelines watching everyone else live life.

"I know it's not an excuse, and I'm not trying to pretend it is," Dean said, "but Bunny's the only woman I'd ever been with. Hell, I used to talk big about scoring with the girls—we all did!—but the truth was I never did. I met Bunny the summer I graduated from high school, and we went together until we got married. She's the only woman I'd ever been with.''

Walker grinned despite the seriousness of the discussion. ''Yeah, I guess we all exaggerated a little.''

Dean grinned, too. ''What about Sissie Pennywell? We all thought that you and she . . . I mean, you never said anything, but then again you didn't deny anything, either.''

Walker's grin grew. ''Let's just put it this way, I wouldn't have ruined her chances of getting into a nunnery.''

For a moment, both men sat smiling at high school memories. For a moment, both were bound in the close camaraderie they'd shared for most of their lives.

Dean's smile slowly disappeared. ''Like I said before, I don't expect you to approve or to understand.'' His voice had deepened when he added, ''I just don't want you to hate me.''

There was no doubt in Walker's mind that Dean Ellison had just bared his soul. Nor was there any doubt in Walker's heart that it had taken courage to do so. But then, his friend had never lacked for courage. Not on the football field. Not flying helicopters through the war-torn skies of Vietnam. Not hustling back and forth across a sometimes stormy gulf. No, Dean may have his faults, but lacking courage wasn't one of them. Any more than it had ever been, or ever would be, in doubt how Walker felt about this man, this man who was closer than a brother.

''I could never hate you,'' Walker said. ''I don't always like what you do, but I could never hate you.''

Dean said nothing. The two men simply stared at each other. Finally, his voice noticeably blank, Dean said, ''To tell you the truth, I don't always like what I do, either... and I'm not always as kind as you. Sometimes I despise myself."

The heartfelt words slammed into Walker's heart, bringing with them a new realization, a realization that Walker's narrowed thinking had not taken into account. While it was true that Dean was hurting innocent people—Bunny and Lindsey and even his best friend—it was also true that he was hurting himself. In fact, perhaps it was he who was hurting most of all.

Chapter Five

"I'm sorry."

Walker, who was sitting at his desk, glanced up from the drilling chart he was perusing. It was all Lindsey could do not to reach out and brush back a swath of hair that slanted across his forehead. Ever since he'd returned from the sports car outing several hours before, his hair had been attractively mussed, as though the wind had played a game of tag through the silver-tinted black strands. But Walker had been too pensive to even take heed of his hair's tousled condition. Lindsey couldn't help but notice, however. Just the way she couldn't help but wonder what had transpired between the two men.

"For what?" Walker now asked, removing the reading glasses he'd been forced to put on in order to make out the detail chart figures.

"For the surly mood I've been in," Lindsey said with a sheepish smile. "It isn't your fault Dad bought a sports car. It isn't your fault that he's acting like a jerk."

Walker wanted to tell Lindsey how badly Dean was hurting, but he knew that Lindsey herself was in pain. It was hard to see another's pain through your own. Instead, he laid the glasses on the desk and, pushing back his chair, he stood. "You haven't been in a surly mood."

She made a little sound that could only be interpreted as contradiction. "Yeah, sure," she said, thinking that, despite the fact that it was the end of the day, Walker still looked good. Real good. The jeans that earlier had been crisply starched now hugged his form in a way that was guaranteed to attract a woman's attention. At least, it had attracted hers.

Stepping toward the cooler of bottled water, Walker poured himself a cup, drank and tossed the cup into the trash. He had known that Dean's buying the sports car had upset Lindsey. He just hadn't known what to say to make Lindsey feel better. If she knew the extent of her father's aberrant behavior, if she knew about his affair, Walker doubted seriously that anything anybody said would help Lindsey's feelings. In fact, knowing would destroy her. In a way he couldn't explain, he still felt as though he himself was betraying her simply by being in possession of the knowledge. On the other hand, he couldn't betray a friendship. Dean's tormented face still haunted him.

To tell you the truth, I don't always like what I do, either... and I'm not always as kind as you. Sometimes I despise myself... despise myself... despise myself....

"I know your dad buying the car upset you, and I can understand why. I just don't know what to say."

As he spoke, he brushed back the strand of hair from his forehead. Fascinated, Lindsey watched him, wondering if his hair felt as soft as it looked. And was the hair on his chest—she could see raven-colored sprigs peeking from the vee of his white knit shirt—just as soft? This last thought caused her pulse to accelerate.

"You could say yes," Lindsey said, ignoring the racing of her heart . . . or at least trying to.

As she spoke, she stepped toward Walker. His eyes went to the gentle sway of her ponytail, around which hung a pert pink bow. It was a mesmerizing sway that reinforced the notion he'd conceived earlier. Namely, that Lindsey was a combination of both woman and child. A beguiling combination, if he listened to his heart. Which he tried not to do. Instead, he focused on what she'd said.

"I could say yes to what?"

"To letting me buy you a drink." Before he could respond, she added, "My way of apologizing for my surly mood this afternoon."

Interestingly, the mention of their having a drink together—or maybe it was that damned provocative sway of her ponytail!—caused his heartbeat to flutter. Whichever, he felt it in his best interest to ignore it.

"I told you, you weren't in a surly—"

"I was," Lindsey interjected. "And I insist upon buying you a drink."

Walker's heartbeat fluttered again. Again, he ignored it.

"Hey, I'm not dressed—"

"You're fine," Lindsey said, forcing her eyes not to take a sensual inventory of the length and breadth of his body. "We'll go somewhere casual."

"You're too young to drink," he said, feeling as though he were being backed into a corner. It wasn't an altogether unpleasant corner, which made him feel all the more backed into it.

"You told me just the other day how adult I was."

Walker remembered having done that very thing. And as he stood watching her this moment, he couldn't in good conscience retract what he'd said. Despite the fact that the ponytail emphasized her youth, she looked very much like the woman her years claimed that she was. If nothing else, the way she filled out the pastel-shaded sweater attested to her maturity.

"You want to see my ID?" she asked teasingly.

What he wanted was to get out of the corner. Or maybe he didn't want out of the corner at all. Maybe he wanted to be pressured into having a drink with Lindsey. When you got right down to it, what was the harm in it? Wasn't it acceptable for a goddaughter to buy her godfather a drink? Where was it written that it wasn't?

Suddenly the teasing lights vanished from Lindsey's gray-blue eyes. "I promise you I'm all grown up," she said. Her eyes held Walker's for the fraction of a second necessary to prove her point.

Walker heard the challenge in her voice. He saw it in her eyes. There was no way he could avoid it. Even if he'd wanted to, which he didn't, because he suddenly needed to prove to himself that everything he'd been feeling of late—his superawareness of Lindsey—was nothing more than an emotional mirage. He glanced up at the clock. It read ten minutes after five o'clock.

"Let's go," he said, his voice strong and sure in the conviction that he'd just made the right choice. After all, a drink was simply a drink. Why try to make something more out of it?

In answer, Walker's heart skipped another beat.

Within twenty minutes, each having driven his own car, both Lindsey and Walker sat in the lounge of a hotel located in the city's historic Strand district. The bar's dark walnut paneling, its polished hardwood floors, its Victorian ambiance created not only an air of elegance, but also one of intimacy. Scattered among wicker tables stood tall palms, their fronds cascading downward as though bending to whisper a lover's secret, while delicate romantic bouquets of sweet-scented posies graced each table. To add to the intimacy, soft piano music wafted from the back of the lounge.

"What can I get you?" the waiter asked.

"I'll have a white wine spritzer," Lindsey said. On the drive over she'd repaired her makeup, adding a pale pink lip gloss to her lips and dabbing perfume behind her ears and in the vee of her sweater.

"Bourbon and water on the rocks," Walker said, normally not ordering more than a beer. On the drive over, however, as tight muscles had begun to make themselves known, he'd realized that he'd had a bitch of a day. Confronting a friend about his affair made for a bitch of a day, a real bourbon-and-water kind of day. The sight and smell of Lindsey as she exited the car, her lips gleaming in pink, her skin bathed in perfume, her ponytail contrasting markedly with the long, shapely, white-stockinged legs that slid from the vehicle, did nothing to ease the tension of said bitchy day. In fact, they had once more sent his heart into that crazy uneven rhythm. "Just make that bourbon on the rocks," he said, only several notes away from a growl.

"Tired?" Lindsey asked when the waiter stepped away. She'd heard the dark timbre in Walker's voice. She also noticed the plain aviator sunglasses tucked in his shirt pocket. He'd been wearing them when he'd gotten out of the car. It crossed her mind that her father had wasted a lot of money on fancy colored lenses when the gray-tinted ones Walker was wearing were enough to make a woman salivate.

"Yeah. I guess so." Totally surprising himself, he grinned. "Either that or I'm in a surly mood."

Lindsey smiled. "No more surly moods, no more talking about business, and no more talking about Mom and Dad. Agreed?"

"Agreed. So what do we talk about?"

"'Of kings and queens or simpler things,'" she quoted from a book that Walker had read to her and Adam dozens of times when they were youngsters.

Walker's grin turned to a laugh. "I hadn't thought of that in years. Whatever happened to that book? Was it yours or Adam's?"

"It was mine, and I have it in a chest in the attic. Thanks," Lindsey added as the waiter delivered their drinks.

"Thanks," Walker repeated, though he had to admit that he felt less in need of a drink than he had minutes before. It was strange how laughter could relax coiled muscles. Maybe that was what was wrong with his life. Maybe that was what all the emptiness was about. Maybe he'd just forgotten how to laugh. Although laughter, like most all things in life, was better when shared with someone else.

"Plus, I've got all my Winnie the Pooh books," Lindsey said. "I think those must have been the beginning of my love affair with bears."

Walker took a swallow of his drink, then said, "Ten to one, you missed your teddy bears more than anyone when you were in London."

"Oh, I don't know. They're great to cuddle, but they don't cuddle back."

As once before, for just a heartbeat, Walker had the feeling that there was more to what Lindsey was saying than merely the words she'd spoken. The way she was looking at him, so intensely her gaze burned, only corroborated this. But then, she dropped her gaze to the wineglass, sipped the spritzer, and spoke so normally that Walker thought, again as he had before, that he'd simply imagined the whole thing.

"Have you heard anything about the baby?"

"I talked to Grace yesterday, and there's still no sign of Junior. The doctor says any minute, though."

"That must be exciting—waiting for your first child to be born."

Lindsey's voice held a wistfulness that Walker couldn't help but hear. Neither could he help but wonder what had happened to cause her to call off her wedding. If plans had gone according to schedule, she'd now be a wife and possibly even a mother. Inexplicably, he found the thought disturbing. Especially the part about her being some man's—Ken Larey's—wife.

"Do you remember when Adam was born?" Lindsey asked, thankfully breaking into Walker's unsettling thoughts.

He grinned. "Yeah. He was two and half weeks late. Phyllis was so uncomfortable that she was about to jump out of her skin."

"Night or day?" At Walker's inquiring look, Lindsey clarified. "Was he born at night or during the day?"

Walker grinned again. Was this becoming a habit? he wondered. If so, he could grow accustomed to it. "Babies are never born during the day. They always come at night. Usually after midnight."

"I take it Adam was born after midnight."

"Three-oh-six." Walker took a swallow of his drink, then said, "And I never slept through the night again. At least not for a long while. There were diapers and feedings and colic and nightmares and, then, just when I thought I had him out of my hair, he got his driver's license, and I stayed up half the night listening for the car."

I stayed up half the night. Not *we* stayed up half the night. Only in the last few months, as she'd matured into a full-fledged adult, had Lindsey realized how difficult it must have been for Walker to raise his child alone. The fine job he'd done gave her a deeper appreciation of the man. It was just one more reason for her to love him.

"Do, uh, do you ever wish you could start over?" Lindsey asked as she stroked the cool tulip-shaped wineglass. "I mean, do you ever wish you could have another child?"

"Good heavens, no!" Though he'd been undeniably emphatic, he realized that the days of raising his son, the early days which he'd shared with his wife, were probably the most enriching of his life. In those days, he hadn't felt empty. In those days, he hadn't felt as if he were simply going through the motions of living.

His answer wasn't what Lindsey had wanted to hear, though it was pretty much what she'd expected. Every woman knew, though, that a man could be made to change his mind.

"I'm too old to start over," she heard Walker say.

"You're not too old."

"Besides, all the women my age have already raised all of the babies they want."

Lindsey smiled and said, as casually as though they were discussing the weather, "What you need is a younger woman."

Walker laughed, but the laugh was forced. He kept seeing the image of Dean and a flame-haired young woman—a woman young enough to be his daughter. "Yeah, well, I'm the last thing a young woman wants or needs."

"I don't know. Could be you're selling yourself short."

The sincere look she gave him made his heart skip a beat. It also made him change the subject.

"So, tell me about your job in London."

The topic led quite naturally to her fill-in job at Gal-Tex and, even though they'd vowed not to discuss work, they found themselves doing so.

"Does that prospectus have to be ready Monday?" Lindsey asked. "I could do it this weekend."

"Uh-uh. It won't be needed until the end of next week. Besides, you don't need to spend your weekend working."

"You don't spend yours working?"

"That's different."

"How?"

"I own the company. . . at least half of it." Uncomfortable with the direction of the conversation—he might have to confront the loneliness that forced him to work late and weekend hours—he said, "I thought we agreed not to discuss work."

"Fine. Let's dance."

Her request, so blandly, so bluntly given, caught Walker totally off guard. His startled look said so.

Lindsey laughed and leaned forward, as if speaking of a conspiracy. "I don't know how to tell you this, but women have been liberated. They can now ask men to dance."

"I have heard of women's liberation, smart aleck. And I have no problem with women asking me to dance."

"Then what do you have a problem with?"

He glanced around the room, indicating the occupied tables. The pianist, a blonde chicly dressed in black chiffon, was playing and crooning a ballad about the first time ever she'd seen her lover's face. "No one's dancing," Walker pointed out.

"So? There's a dance floor. See, right there by the piano."

"I see, but—"

"But what?"

"I have two left feet."

"I'll bet you don't."

"Trust me, I do. I also have a bum knee."

"No big deal. We'll slow dance." She pushed back her chair. "C'mon."

"Lindsey!" he whispered, grabbing her hand to keep her seated. Her hand felt warm—just the way it had the night she'd taken his hand in hers. He pulled his hand away, uncertain why he was fighting the warmth, uncertain why he was fighting her offer of a dance. He just felt he should. On the off chance that all of her was as warm as her hand.

"You need to loosen up, Walker. Live a little. How am I ever going to get you to run off with me to Timbuktu if I can't even get you to the dance floor?" Rushing ahead, she said, "Look, I'll make you a deal. If the pianist plays...oh, I don't know, 'Misty,' let's say...yeah, 'Misty'...if the pianist plays 'Misty' next, we dance. If she doesn't, we don't. Fair enough?"

The expression on Lindsey's face, the spark in her slate-gray eyes, was one of utter playfulness. Once more Walker was reminded of how alive Lindsey was. Of how alluringly alive she was. Of how irresistibly alive she was. Leaning back in his chair, he heard himself assume the same playful posture.

"Let me get this straight," he drawled. "If the next song the pianist plays is 'Misty,' we dance. If it's not, we don't."

"Right. Deal?"

Walker considered all the songs—the hundreds, the thousands, the tens of thousands—that the pianist had to choose from. What were the chances of her playing one specific song? Walker gave a half grin, the sign of a man confident of his win because the deck was stacked in his favor. "You've got yourself a deal."

"Good," Lindsey replied, pushing her chair back farther and rising. "Excuse me a moment. I'll be right back." With that, she crossed to the pianist, bent and whispered something, then started back toward the table. The triumphant look she wore said that Walker had been had.

Despite his loss—which curiously he also viewed as a win—he had to admire her style. "You, uh, you wouldn't call that cheating, would you?"

"Not in the least. I'd call it guaranteeing that I get what I want." She held out her hand. "Time to pay off."

The beginning strains of "Misty" spilled from the piano and filled the silence.

In a single gulp, Walker downed what was left of his drink. Something told him that he was going to need what fortification he could get. Standing, he placed his hand in hers—dammit, why was her hand always so warm?—and, following as she led, walked to the dance floor. It was he, however, who stopped, turned her and pulled her into his arms. After all, a deal was a deal, right?

He took Lindsey by surprise. She'd known that he'd have to take her in his arms, but she'd expected to be the one to make the move. She might even have to force the issue. His assertiveness startled her, pleased her and left her wholly breathless. She'd been in his arms before—countless times when she'd been growing up—but she'd never been in his arms after she'd realized her love for him. Except for that moment at the airport, which was marked primarily by its brevity. Now, however, she was in his arms in earnest . . . and for the duration of a song. What was that? Two minutes? Three minutes? Could she force the brief time to make up for all the lonely nights she'd lain awake wondering what it would feel like to be held by him?

"See," she said, hoping that she didn't sound as breathless as she felt, "you don't have two left feet."

Her eyes were on his, and he could never remember seeing anything that looked more beautiful. The blue of a peaceful ocean shone through, a shimmering blue shaded with silver. The look, almost translucent, was one of serenity. The thought crossed Walker's mind that maybe that, serenity, was what was missing from his life. Maybe he was blaming emptiness, and more recently, lack of laughter, when the truth was that he lacked serenity in his soul.

"That may be open to debate," he responded to her comment about his feet.

"How's the knee?" she asked.

"Fine," he said. His knee hurt. Like hell. But suddenly the pain seemed unimportant, even irrelevant.

The pianist sang softly, of not knowing one's right foot from one's left, one's hat from one's glove, because one was too misty and too much in love. Walker realized that he was about as confused as the person in the song, for suddenly, slowly, he seemed to have stepped into a surreal world. A world he could never remember inhabiting before. A world composed of nothing but sensation. He was keenly aware of the small of Lindsey's back, the slight concave where his hand rested; he was painfully aware of her palm merged with his; he was bewilderingly aware of the occasional brush of her thighs against his. He was also aware of wondering if people were watching them and, if so, did they think them father and daughter? Or, worse, did they think him an old fool? On this last score, Walker told himself that he was just ultrasensitive because of Dean's affair.

Lindsey, too, was inundated with feelings. The hair at the nape of Walker's neck felt soft and silky beneath her hand, while the hand that held hers felt solid and strong and big. And then there was the brush of his thighs against hers—intimate, yet not intimate, socially proper, yet bringing to mind things forbidden on a public dance floor.

The song continued, the pianist singing that a thousand violins begin to play when her lover takes her hand.

Hand. Her hand. It still felt incredibly warm. Baby warm. Womanly warm. Father. He didn't feel like her father. Not in the least. In fact, the way she felt in his arms was decidedly alarming. Primarily because it might be worth risking feeling like an old fool just to feel this alive.

Alive. He made her feel alive. Wonderfully alive. So many times she'd wondered if what she was feeling was right. Was there something wrong in what she felt for this man? This she'd pondered, questioned, worried about to the nth degree. She'd decided, though, even before returning home, that what she was feeling had to be right, simply because it felt right. If she'd needed that fact corroborated, the feel of his arms did so. In spades.

Acting on pure instinct, Lindsey sighed and, slipping her hand from his, slid it along the back of his neck to join her other hand. At the same time, her cheek nestled against his, while she eased her body one step, two steps closer. The pose was unquestionably that of a lover's pose.

Lover.

The thought struck Walker. She felt like a lover in his arms—her fingers gently kneading the back of his neck, her cheek flush with his cheek, her body swaying softly, sensuously against, and into, his. It struck him like a bolt out of the blue that he liked the lover's feel of her. God help him, he liked it!

Abruptly, he stopped. So did Lindsey. So did the music. As the last dying notes of the song echoed throughout the room, Lindsey pulled back until her gaze found Walker's. A lazy, hazy sultriness danced in her eyes. For one crazy moment, Walker could almost believe that Lindsey was feeling the same thing he was. In the next instant, however, reality snatched him by the collar. The moment wasn't crazy. He was. He had to be to think that Lindsey would ever entertain anything but daughterly feelings for him. As for himself, he was appalled at his unfatherly feelings. For the love of heaven, he cried silently, what was happening to him?

Lindsey saw Walker's confusion and could only pray that she knew its source. Surely she could not be imagining the longing look in his eyes. Surely she couldn't have imagined the perfect way their bodies had fit. Surely he had felt that perfect union, too. For the first time since coming home, Lindsey allowed herself to be encouraged. That encouragement bubbled like vintage champagne in her veins. God willing, she'd find a way to make him love her. She had to, because her heart would allow no less.

The following week proved interesting. At least as far as Lindsey was concerned. Her father, for unknown reasons, actually chose to spend some time with her. They went to lunch twice and dinner once. He still refused to talk to her about the divorce or, rather, cleverly avoided even letting the topic come up. It was almost—almost—amusing how he headed the subject off at the pass. Perhaps fueled by her father's reticence, Lindsey remained convinced that a good discussion—for that matter, any discussion—between her mother and father would end their ridiculous separation.

If the week saw Lindsey spending more time with her father, it saw her spending less with Walker. In the beginning, she didn't think much about it, but as day after day passed with Walker finding more and more flimsy reasons to be out of the office, Lindsey started to wonder if he wasn't manufacturing them. At first the thought dismayed her. Maybe she'd misinterpreted his reaction. Maybe he hadn't been attracted to her. Furthermore, maybe he'd sensed her feelings, which in no way matched his, and he was trying to spare her as best he could.

On a miserably sleepless Thursday night, however, it occurred to her that maybe the opposite was true. Maybe she had been right about his reaction. Maybe for one unguarded second he had seen her as a woman and not merely his godchild, and maybe that vision had scared the living daylights out of him. Hadn't she been frightened in the beginning? And, if he was frightened, wouldn't his behavior, his refusal to be near her, make sense?

It was that same Thursday night that an idea regarding her parents came to her. She didn't kid herself; she knew that the idea wasn't exactly fair, that is, that it would be based on a lie—a white lie, to be sure, but a lie nonetheless. Did the circumstances warrant such a breach of honesty? She'd always believed that there was such a thing as situational ethics. Did she believe it strongly enough to justify her actions in this case?

Bright and early Friday morning she called Walker, who sounded as sexy as sin being awakened from a dead sleep. Forcing herself to concentrate on her parents, and not on his gravelly voice or the image of him naked to the waist with the sheet pleated about him, she informed him that she wouldn't be able to come in to the office until the afternoon. She took a secret delight in knowing that her absence would force him to spend some time in the office. She wondered, though, what excuse he'd drum up for leaving the minute she got there. After she hung up, she went down to breakfast.

"Hi, Mom," she said, suspecting that her mother hadn't slept well again. Once more it broke Lindsey's heart to see her mother, usually a typically vain woman, with no makeup and her hair in need of some loving attention.

Bunny smiled, or gave a facsimile thereof, as she automatically picked up the coffeepot and poured her daughter a cup. "Good morning, darling. What do you want for breakfast?"

"Just toast."

"No, let me make you pancakes," she said, reaching for a mixing bowl. "A working girl needs a hearty breakfast."

"Toast is fine, Mom. Besides, I'm not a working girl this morning."

Bunny Ellison looked up, her tired eyes connecting with Lindsey's. "Why not?"

"Because I'm taking the morning off. We're—that's you and I—are going to pamper and pet ourselves. We're getting a facial, getting a massage and getting our hair done. Oh, and I think we'll toss in a pedicure and a manicure."

"Lindsey, I'm not in the mood."

"That's all the more the reason to do it, isn't it?"

"Lindsey—"

"My treat, and I won't take no for an answer."

"Lindsey—" Bunny tried again.

"It's not negotiable, Mom. You're going to return to the land of the living whether you like it or not. That's it, final, over and done with."

Bunny seized the mixing bowl, as though it were the only way she knew to cope with this new crisis. "Then we'll need a hearty breakfast," she said, proving that her daughter wasn't the only stubborn member of the family.

Lindsey moaned.

It was nearing two o'clock when Lindsey sashayed into the office of Gal-Tex. She had been pounded and pumiced, powdered and polished—all in the name of beauty. Refreshed, she felt optimistic about both her parents and about Walker. She had only to believe that she could make something happen in both quarters and she could. For her parents, she had a plan for that very evening, a plan she'd set into motion with a call to her father following breakfast.

Though Walker had no idea how Lindsey had spent the morning, he knew that his breath fled the second he saw her. From her rosy skin to her gleaming blond hair, which coiled in riotous curls down her back, to the shell-pink nail polish that covered both her fingernails and her toe-nails—the latter peeking out from strappy high-heeled sandals—she looked gorgeous. Positively, absolutely come-on-give-my-pounding-heart-a-break gorgeous.

"Hi," she said, sounding as perky and sassy as the brassy sun beating down on the island. "Sorry I'm late."

"H-hi," he managed to get out after he'd cleared his froggy throat. He tried to ignore the way her white slacks molded her derriere, but couldn't. Some things, some perfect things, a man couldn't disregard however much he tried. "What have you been up to?" Good, he thought, he sounded normal. Or close enough.

"Mom and I had a make-over. What do you think?" she asked, slowly pirouetting.

At the sight of soft curls and sweet curves, the frog jumped back into Walker's throat. What he thought was that he needed to get away from her. Now. Or possibly sooner. "N-nice," he stammered. "Look, I'm glad you're here. I need to check on something outside the office. I'll be gone—"

"All afternoon?" Lindsey ventured knowingly. She fought a smile.

"I, uh, I don't know about all afternoon. I'll, uh, I'll probably be back. I don't know. It, uh, it depends."

On whether it's five o'clock and I'm gone, Lindsey thought. "Well, before you go, do you know where Dad is?" As she said this, she picked up the phone and started to dial her mother's number.

"He's checking on some part."

"Here in town?"

"Yeah."

"Then I can reach his beeper?"

"You should be able to." For a reason he couldn't explain, Walker hung around to see what Lindsey was up to. There was a suspicious glimmer in her eyes.

"Hi, Mom," she said. "Look, I've just had a marvelous idea. I don't know why I didn't think of it earlier." She hoped the idea sounded spontaneous. She hadn't mentioned the plan earlier because phone-to-phone deception was easier than face-to-face deception. "Since we're all dolled up, why don't we go out to dinner tonight...? No, Mom, we can eat in anytime. Let's eat out." She mentioned the name of a restaurant. "I'll meet you there at seven o'clock, okay? I'm going to work a little late here.... No, I've got a couple of things to catch up on.... No, we'll have the pork chops tomorrow night. Mom, just meet me at the restaurant, okay?"

She hung up before her mother could offer any more resistance. Without hesitation, she dialed her father's beeper and left a message.

"Hi, Dad. Don't forget about dinner tonight." She confirmed the restaurant. "And be there at seven o'clock. Not a minute later."

Frowning, Walker asked as she replaced the receiver, "And just what are you up to?"

"Matchmaking," Lindsey answered without apology. "If they'll just sit down and talk, they can work this out."

"Lindsey—"

She held up her newly manicured hand. "I don't want to hear how this is none of my business. I don't want to hear how underhanded and deceitful this is. Trust me, when they're back together, you'll see that I was right."

"Lindsey—" Walker tried again.

"Please," she whispered so plaintively that Walker would have done anything she asked. What she was doing was not only foolhardy, but also potentially explosive, but he supposed he had to let her find that out for herself.

Raking his hand through his hair, he sighed. Hell, maybe she was right! Maybe all Bunny and Dean did need was to sit down and sort through their differences. He wasn't exactly the one to be giving anyone advice these days, since his own sanity seemed to be sitting on such unstable sand. He was the one who couldn't sleep at night for thinking thoughts so forbidden, so verboten, that their very existence shamed him.

It took Walker and Lindsey a while to realize that they were staring at each other. And even then, neither seemed inclined to look away. Lindsey was remembering being warmly tucked against Walker while they danced. She could remember, vividly, the hard, muscular wall of his chest, the iron strength of his thighs. Walker was remembering how he'd lost his breath at the sight of her only minutes before. The way he was still losing his breath, because, disbelievingly, she seemed to grow more beautiful as the seconds passed.

"I, uh, I need to go check on that, uh...on that..." Exactly what *was* he going to check on?

As though in response to his query, the phone rang. It rang again. And again. Walker never did seem to notice it. At length, however, Lindsey forced her gaze from the man before her and down to the telephone. Walker's expression said that he was surprised to find it ringing.

"Good afternoon. Gal-Tex. May I help you?" she answered, then said, "Oh, hi. Yeah, it's me. Fine, thanks." At the question that the caller posed, she looked back up at Walker. "Yeah, he's right here. Hold on." Passing the phone to Walker, she added, "It's Adam."

Careful not to touch Lindsey's hand, Walker took the receiver. "Adam?" He listened, then grinned. "That's great! Is the baby all right? Good. What about Grace?" Walker laughed. "Tell her that she'd better get some rest while she can." There was silence as Adam spoke, then Walker's answer. "You bet I'm coming to see him." Walker glanced at his watch. It read a little after two o'clock. "I'll leave here about five. Right. See you, then. Oh, Adam...congratulations." He replaced the receiver and glanced back at Lindsey. He'd purposely stared out into the parking lot while talking to his son. Lindsey looked as beautiful as he was trying to persuade himself that she didn't.

"A boy?" she asked with a glowing smile.

God, yes, she was beautiful! How had he ever hoped to convince himself otherwise? "Yeah," he answered, "a boy. Eight pounds, eight ounces. Born at 1:21."

"Baby and mother are fine?"

"Yeah."

Lindsey's smile widened. "One-twenty-one this afternoon?"

Walker couldn't help but grin. "Okay, so he blew my theory about babies being born only at night. But," he hastened to add, "that's what kids do best—blow all your theories."

Once more they were staring, he at her, she at him. This time, though, they were smiling. She thought his smile as sexy as moonlight and satin. He thought her smile wonderfully vibrant. Slowly, however, Walker's smile began to fade as he realized that he was simply staring.

"I, uh, I need to go check...something." He was still obviously uncertain just what he was leaving the office to check. He was certain only that he should be leaving.

"You're going to see the baby after work?" Lindsey asked.

"Yeah," he answered, telling himself that he'd be-fine once he got away from Lindsey. He'd be able to breathe again then...which was what he needed—a decent, mind-clearing breath in his lungs.

"Would you mind if I went with you? I'd love to see Adam, and what better time than now?"

Walker's heart turned over in his chest. He searched for a reason to deny her, but couldn't find one. The truth was that it was natural for Lindsey to suggest accompanying him to Houston. After all, she and Adam were as close as brother and sister. What wasn't natural was what he was feeling. On the one hand, being with Lindsey pleasured him. On the other hand, it pleasured him too much, leaving him to grapple with feelings he didn't understand.

What he did patently understand was that she was waiting for an answer. Which he couldn't avoid much longer. Corner. He felt himself being backed into a corner. A velvet-lined corner. Oh, God, where was that decent breath of air?

"Sure," he heard himself say as the velvet-lined corner closed in around him, smothering him in its folds. He didn't want her to go. He truly didn't. Even so, he couldn't help but feel a burst of excitement. The excitement shocked him and shamed him. Most of all, however, it made him feel alive.

Chapter Six

Walker peered through the nursery window at the baby bundled in the fleecy-soft blanket. Blond hair the color of honey sculpted the infant's head, while eyes as blue as a Texas sky lit the baby's angelic face. The child also had a teeny mouth into which it was trying to wedge a teeny fist. Suckling, slobbering, then suckling again, the baby obviously concluded that there was no nourishment in the clenched hand. This realization produced a whimper, which was closely followed by a cry. Then, as though he decided it wasn't worth the effort, the crying died back down to a whimper. At the same time, eyelids closed so that the sandman could come acalling.

Love, deep and unqualified, filled Walker's chest until he felt he must surely burst from the precious pressure. This was his grandson. Flesh of his flesh. Child of his child. He had loved his son the moment he'd seen him twenty-four years ago, but the love he felt now was different. Not any greater, not any less, just different. Perhaps it was love factored with maturity, hopefully with even a little wisdom. Whatever, it was a love that said you belong to your parents, but you also belong to me—in a very special way because I'm now old enough to know the value of love, old enough never to take it for granted.

"What do you think?" a voice, reverently hushed to befit the occasion, asked.

Walker turned, his eyes meeting those of his son. Tall and lithe, Adam Carr had his father's nut-brown eyes and his mother's blond hair. Blond hair. It crossed Walker's mind that although Adam and Lindsey had blond hair, they were totally dissimilar shades. Adam's was ash blond, while Lindsey's hair reminded Walker of homespun threads of gold. Even so, there was similarity enough that Adam and Lindsey could have been brother and sister.

That fact reminded Walker that he was old enough to be Lindsey's father. He immediately shelved the thought, along with memories of the drive from Galveston to Houston. It had been a long drive, which had had nothing to do with mileage and everything to do with soft laughter, billows of golden-blond hair and glossy pink lips. Thank heaven that Lindsey had chosen to visit Grace before seeing the baby. It had given him a moment to breathe again... and to convince himself that he truly wasn't losing his mind and that he wasn't harboring unnatural, even immoral, feelings. Somehow or other, he'd just stepped into a surreal world for the past few days. It probably had something to do with the stress he'd been under. Yeah, that was it. He'd just been under stress.

"He's perfect," Walker said, slipping his arm around Adam's shoulders and luxuriating in the reality of his son. There were no surreal imaginings here. Adam was real. And so was this newborn child.

"Yeah," Adam agreed in awe as he stared down at the sleeping infant. "He's so little, though."

"Babies are supposed to be little, although eight pounds, eight ounces isn't all that little. In fact, he weighs a pound more than you did."

"He's bigger than I was?"

Walker nodded. Adam looked as though he'd accomplished something of paramount importance—producing a son who weighed a pound more at birth than he had.

"Yeah, I guess he isn't all that small," Adam said, adding, "What do you think? Tackle or linebacker?"

Walker laughed. "He'll be tough enough and rough enough to be either... if we can just keep him from sucking on his fist."

Adam grinned. "He stays hungry."

"So did you. If I remember correctly, you can still pack it away pretty good."

Adam's grin turned to soft laughter. "Yeah, I guess I can." The grin faded slowly, replaced by a dead earnestness as the young man looked over at his father. "The baby's great and all... and I'm excited... but, I don't know, the whole thing's kinda scary, too. I, uh, I wasn't expecting to be scared, but I am... I mean, being responsible for another human being is scary." He shrugged his shoulders. "They don't pass out instruction booklets with babies. At least they didn't with this one. How the heck are you supposed to know what to do?" Adam grinned sheepishly. "I guess I'm asking just how easy babies are to break and am I supposed to feel scared?"

Walker tightened the arm still thrown across Adam's shoulder. "Babies are tougher than they look and hell, yeah, you're supposed to be afraid. You can't make a decent parent unless you're scared spitless about ninety percent of the time. But you'll learn to handle the fear. You'll learn to put it on the back burner. Plus, you'll have Grace to share it with. That'll make it tolerable."

"You didn't have anyone, did you?" Adam asked.

Walker withdrew his hand from Adam's shoulder and shoved it into the pocket of his khaki pants. He had changed into clean clothes as Lindsey had awaited him in the living room of his house. He'd felt odd undressing with her there. It made no sense, but then again neither did much else in his surreal world.

"I did in the beginning," Walker said. "Your mom was there when you were a baby. By the time it was just you and me, you were too old for me to break."

"But still, it couldn't have been easy."

"No," Walker said, once more feeling an emotional weight shackle his ankle as he recalled the solitary years of rearing his son, "it wasn't easy. Raising a teenage boy alone isn't easy. Not when you've got to make a living, too."

"I didn't cut you much slack, either, did I?"

Walker grinned. "You weren't supposed to. You were just a kid."

Adam looked back at the baby. "I, uh, I hope I can do as good a job as you did." The young man looked up at his father. "I mean that. You haven't made too bad a father."

A knot formed in Walker's throat, though he grinned to downplay the moment's emotional intensity. "You haven't made too bad a son. And you'll make a great father."

"I guess we'll see, won't we?" Adam said. He then added, "You, uh, you haven't asked what we named him."

"I thought you were going to name the baby Stephen if it was a boy."

"Yeah, we did. We named him Stephen—Stephen Walker Carr."

There had been few times in Walker's life when he'd been moved to speechlessness. Now was one such time. He honestly didn't know what to say and feared that he wouldn't have been able to say it even if he'd known the right words. The knot that had been in his throat before had doubled in size.

"I, uh, I don't know what to say," Walker finally managed to get out.

"You don't have to say anything."

But he did. Walker knew that he had to say something. Why was it so hard for men to verbally express their feelings? In the end, however, he said nothing. He simply reached for his son and unabashedly hugged him. Adam hugged him back. As comfortable as the men were with the exhibition of affection—hugs had been commonplace in the Carr household—enough sentimentality was enough. Especially in a public place.

"I'm glad you brought Lindsey with you," Adam said, as eager to lighten the mood as was his father. "It's good to see her again."

Walker mumbled some response. He refrained from saying that he'd actually had little choice in the matter, that Lindsey had invited herself along. Neither did he go into the fact that he both loved and hated being near her. More to the point, he felt like a man walking a very high tightrope when he was around her. He felt exhilarated and scared half out of his mind. But mostly, he just felt confused.

"She looks great, doesn't she?"

Walker groaned inwardly. If one other person asked his opinion of how Lindsey looked, he was going to scream. Loudly. The truth was that she looked sensational. Even better than sensational. Which he was trying real hard to ignore. Not that he was doing anywhere near that. In fact, the opposite seemed to be true.

"Yeah, she looks great," Walker mumbled, the memory of Lindsey coiled in the corner of the car swamping him. Her long legs, encased in the white slacks she'd arrived at the office in, had curled under her in a cozy kind of fashion that had emphasized their length and sleekness. The sweater, in pretty pink, had lovingly hugged her breasts, while her pink-tipped toes had teased his masculine senses.

"How's she taking the divorce?"

"About like you'd expect."

"Having your parents separate after all these years must be a real bummer."

"Yeah."

"Lindsey doesn't strike me as the type to sit around and do nothing," Adam said. He smiled. "Remember how she could never stand to see the kids fight? Remember how she always tried to act as mediator?"

Walker thought of the dinner Lindsey had tricked her parents into. He thought, too, of how Lindsey had always been a serious child, a sensitive child. Yes, she was capable of great caring. Maybe too capable. One had to learn when to care and when to save one's own soul, rather than give it away piece by piece.

"Yeah, well," Walker said, "I'm afraid she's setting herself up to be hurt this time." Before he even knew what he was saying, he heard himself ask, "Did she ever tell you why she called off the wedding?"

Adam shook his head. "No. But then she left for London so quickly that we didn't even have a chance to talk. I got a couple of cards from her. On one she just said that she was sorry for the pain she knew she'd caused Ken. That was all."

Disappointment filled Walker. He'd always wondered what had happened, but he seemed to be wondering more of late.

"It had to be something pretty serious," Adam continued. "She wouldn't have hurt Ken otherwise."

Walker agreed. He'd once seen her cry because she'd dropped a teddy bear. Lindsey, who couldn't have been more than five or six at the time, had explained that teddy bears had feelings, too, and that they cried when they were hurt, but that they didn't cry in front of just anyone. They cried only in front of special people. Walker hadn't had to ask if they cried in front of her. He'd known that they did.

Suddenly, with a certainty he in no way questioned, Walker sensed Lindsey's presence. He glanced up to see her walking down the hospital corridor. He felt her bright sun warm the cold lonely night that had become his heart. In that moment, he was glad that she'd come along. As confused as her presence made him, he was glad.

"Let me see the baby of all babies," she said, her face wreathed in a dazzling smile. "Oh, my," she whispered, looking through the glass at the sleeping infant.

For seconds, she said nothing. Her palms pressed against the glass, she just stared. Walker couldn't have taken his eyes off her under penalty of death. She was absolutely glowing as she watched the silent, still baby.

"Oh, Adam, he's beautiful," she said in a voice so soft that it sounded like the patter of snowflakes. "Look at his little hands. And look at his hair. He has your hair. And your nose. He has your nose."

Once more, Walker heard her enthusiasm building to a youthful level. He hoped, though, that she never outgrew that enthusiasm. It was what made her so special. It, and her sensitivity, was what made teddy bears cry in front of her.

"Do you ever wish you could start over? Do you ever wish you could have another child?"

Walker heard the question she'd once before asked him. He'd answered an unequivocal no. Yet as he watched the way she devoured the sight of the baby, he felt a strange tugging at his heart. It was obvious that Lindsey wanted a baby. It was equally obvious that she'd make a wonderful mother.

"Oh, Walker," she said, and the calling of his name sent a strange feeling down his spine, "you have a gorgeous grandson."

Grandson.

Grandfather.

Interestingly, the word *grandfather* ensnared his attention as the word *grandson* had not. Grandfather sounded so old. It conjured up images of stuffy men, crotchety men set in both their chairs and their ways. Hell, there was no denying it! He *was* old. His hair was turning gray, he couldn't read without his glasses and his knee ached with a vengeance unless he pampered it, in which case it ached with only half a vengeance. And that wasn't the worst of it. He thought old.

Except when he was around Lindsey.

She honestly made him want to run off to Timbuktu. She honestly made him feel less than old. Or, maybe she just made him feel that forty-seven wasn't quite as old as he thought it was. The truth was that she even made him think that maybe starting over with a baby wasn't all that ridiculous. He could see it now—diapers, feedings, sleepless nights—none of which would seem too intimidating if there was someone there to share it with. The someone began to take shape in his imagination. She had long blond hair, steel-blue eyes and a smile that melted away the loneliness he'd felt for so many years. The woman by his side was . . .

Lindsey.

The realization startled him. But it did more than that. It appalled him. Principally because it didn't appall him enough.

"Coffee?"

He glanced up, realizing belatedly that his son had spoken to him. Both Adam and Lindsey wore expectant looks.

"What?"

"You want to go down to the cafeteria for coffee?"

"Uh . . . no . . . I mean, ya'll go ahead. I'll visit with Grace."

"You want us to bring you back a cup?" Lindsey asked.

"No," Walker managed to say, thinking that what he needed was Scotch. Straight up and long. Real long. Like the length of a whole damned bottle!

"The baby's beautiful," Lindsey said minutes later. Cups of coffee sat before her and Adam, sending up slender spirals of steam. Around them rose the muted chatter of cafeteria conversation.

"Yeah, he is, isn't he?" the proud new father said without a trace of apology.

Lindsey smiled, causing slight dimples to form. "You bet he is. And Grace looks wonderful. She looks more as though she's been on vacation than in the delivery room. She's radiant, she's gorgeous, she's...beautiful."

"Yeah, she is, but then so are you. You look wonderful. Even Dad said so."

Lindsey's heart went pitter-pat. "Did he?" she asked, nonchalantly uncapping her dispenser of cream and dribbling a few drops into her coffee.

"He did. And you are. It would take a blind man not to see it. You've...I don't know...you've grown up. Not that you weren't grown-up before—you were—but now...wow!"

Lindsey laughed. "You're good for my ego, Adam Carr."

"And it's good to see you," Adam said. "God, it's good to see you," he said, suddenly turning serious. He reached for Lindsey's hand and squeezed.

She squeezed back. "It's good to see you, too. I've missed you."

"I've missed you. Dammit, Lin, you left without even a word to me."

Lindsey could hear the hurt in Adam's voice. Under the same circumstances, should their roles have been reversed, she would have been hurt if he'd left without giving her some clue as to why he was going. They were—had always been—best friends. Best friends shared. But how could she have shared what was in her heart a year and a half ago? How could she have told Adam that she was calling off her wedding because she'd discovered that she was feeling something for his father? Even now, what would Adam's reaction be? Approval? Disapproval? Disgust?

Lindsey pulled her hand from Adam's and encircled her cup. The heat felt comforting, reassuring. "I know I left without a word," she said. "I just had to get away. I had some feelings that I had to sort through."

"You couldn't have told me about them? I couldn't have helped you sort through them?"

Lindsey smiled faintly. "I didn't know what I was feeling. How could I have made you understand what I didn't understand myself?"

"I could have listened."

"Not this time, Adam. This time I had to go it alone. This time I had to find my own answers."

"And did you?"

"Yes," Lindsey said emphatically.

She'd come home knowing that she was in love with Walker. Every act, every word since had only confirmed that fact. And unless she were really losing her mind, she'd seen a spark of interest in Walker. Something had happened on the dance floor. He'd been aware of her as a woman. Not as a child, not as his godchild, but as a woman.

"I, uh, I realized that I wasn't in love with Ken," Lindsey said, feeling that she owed some explanation to Adam. Moreover, she now wanted to share with him. At least up to a point. "Let me rephrase that. I loved him, but not the way I should have. Not the way a woman should love the man she's about to marry." She glanced down at the coffee, then up at her friend. "The truth is that I was, am, in love with someone else."

Lindsey could tell that the news took Adam completely by surprise, though, to his credit, he recovered quickly. "I had no idea that there was even anyone else in contention. You'd gone with Ken for so long. I just assumed that there'd been no opportunity for anyone else.'' He shrugged. ''I know you weren't dating anyone else. At least, I assumed you weren't. I mean, I *know* you weren't. You wouldn't have dated someone else while you were going with Ken. I mean... Ah, hell, you know what I'm trying to say!''

Lindsey took Adam's hand. ''I know. The truth is that I didn't know there was anyone else in contention, either. I've known this man for a long time. My feelings for him just sort of slipped up on me.''

''And?''

''And what?''

''That was eighteen months ago. What's happened since?''

''Nothing.''

''Nothing? Doesn't this guy have any sense? Why aren't you two married?''

Lindsey's heart skipped at the very thought of being married to Walker. ''There's, uh, there's a complication.''

Adam's face fell. ''He's married?''

Lindsey couldn't help but laugh. ''No, silly, he isn't married.''

''Then what?''

Lindsey hesitated. Was she saying too much? Maybe, and yet she did need to talk to someone. ''He's older than I am.''

''So?''

''Considerably older. As in twenty-some years older.''

''So?'' Adam repeated. ''Is he in love with you?''

Lindsey's heart went pitter-pat again. ''Who knows what he's feeling? I'm not even sure he knows.''

Adam gave a suspicious frown. ''Does he know you're in love with him?''

"No," Lindsey said, "I haven't had the courage to tell him."

Adam's answer was soft and sage. "You've never been a coward, Lin. Why start now?"

Adam's words whispered in Lindsey's ear as she and Walker began the drive back to Galveston. Adam was right, she concluded. She wasn't a coward. Now was the time to play her hand. Now was the time to find out if she was holding aces or jokers. But what if she ruined everything? What if she destroyed the beautiful relationship that she and Walker had? What if she had only imagined his reaction to her?

Fear swept through her—a cold, gnawing beast eating at her hurting heart.

What would she do with the rest of her life if he rebuffed her? One thing she was certain of. There would be no going back to what they'd had. Once she revealed her feelings, she was taking a step that could never be retraced. But then, there was one other thing of which she was certain. Things couldn't go on as they were, either. Not if she were to remain sane. Besides, wasn't it true that if one were to succeed, one had to be willing to fail?

She willed the cold, gnawing beast back into chains.

Twisting her head, she peered through the darkness. Walker, his wrist nonchalantly maneuvering the steering wheel, sat silently staring ahead. He'd said little since leaving the hospital, and then only when she'd spoken to him.

"If you'll stop, I'll buy us dinner."

At the sound of Lindsey's soft-spoken voice, Walker angled his head toward her. She sat in the corner of the car, her long legs stretched before her, her blond hair, a mass of defiant curls, fluffed about her. It was all he could do to look at her after the thoughts he'd had back at the hospital. He didn't deserve to look at her. That taken into consideration, it was all he could do to keep from pulling to the side of the road and ... And what? The answer was simple. Touching her.

Dammit, he wanted to touch her!

In some way.

In any way.

Instead, he answered in a tone that surprised even him in its normalcy, "You hungry?"

Lindsey smiled. "Famished. And I know you must be."

Yeah, he thought, he was hungry. For all the wrong things.

"Is Mexican food okay?" he asked, more gruffly than the question demanded.

"Fine," she answered. She'd heard the roughness in his voice and wondered at its motivation. She'd give anything to know what was going on in his head. More important, she'd give anything to know what was going on in his heart.

"I'm buying, though," Walker said, adding, "and I don't want any argument about it."

She didn't argue.

Within minutes, just on the outskirts of Houston, Walker spotted the restaurant he was looking for. Gravel crunched beneath the tires as he pulled the car into the parking lot and brought it to a stop in a slot in the second row. Silently, he opened his door, got out and crossed around to the passenger side of the car. He opened the door. He did not reach out his hand to her. Did he usually do so? Yes. No. She couldn't remember, and she was heartily annoyed with herself for looking for telling signs in every breath, in every word, in every movement he made.

Twisting around, she levered her feet onto the gravel. It crossed her mind that gravel and sandals didn't mix. In particular, gravel, sandals and a fresh pedicure didn't mix, because one didn't chip the polish one had just paid good money for. That in mind, she cautiously picked her way toward the restaurant.

One step here.

Another there.

And then an unsteady step on a large rock.

Her ankle gave up the struggle to remain upright.

Crying out, Lindsey reached for anything to balance herself. The something she found was Walker. Or rather, he found her. Though he wasn't touching her—he wouldn't allow himself to—he was attuned to her every step. When he sensed her falling, he reacted instinctively. With one hand, he grabbed her upper arm. With the other, he reached for her waist, encircling it with his arm. Both her hands splayed wide against his chest.

It all happened in seconds. She was looking up at him. He was looking down at her. She was aware of one of her legs alongside one of his. He was aware of the slenderness of her waist. She felt the buckle of his belt pressing into her stomach. He felt the roundness of one breast nestled against his arm. He also felt the beating of her heart. Just as she felt the beating of his—the battered beating of his.

Time slowed to a slumbering pace.

A heartbeat. His and hers. His gaze, languid and as hot as a sleepy summer sun, lowered to her mouth. The action had been as instinctive as reaching for her when she was falling. In an equally instinctive way, her gaze raised to his.

Time stopped.

Is he going to kiss me?

Am I going to kiss her?

Both—each—pondered the question for what seemed like the passage of eternity. Lindsey prayed that he *would* kiss her. Walker prayed that he wouldn't. He prayed, too, that his soul wouldn't burn in hell because of what he was feeling. He could no longer hide from the naked truth. He desired Lindsey. In every corner, crook and cranny of his body, he desired his goddaughter! The realization shamed him, excited him . . . angered him.

Abruptly releasing Lindsey, he growled, "Let's eat!"

The meal was long. As was the rest of the drive home. Lindsey wondered what Walker was thinking. In turn, he wondered what she was thinking and if she'd known what had gone through his mind back in the parking lot—and what pond scum she must think him if she had.

And yet . . .

As once before, he could have sworn she was feeling the same thing. Even now, as they neared Galveston, a thick tension lay between them. The tension huddled like a lightning-driven rain cloud.

"I wonder how the evening went for Mom and Dad," Lindsey said, breaking through the stifling silence. Despite the fact she'd been preoccupied with Walker, her parents had never been far from her mind. Nor would they be until she'd talked some sense into their stubborn heads.

Walker glanced over at Lindsey. Despite the confusion he was mired in, he could think clearly enough to know that he didn't want Lindsey hurt. In fact, it was the last thing he wanted. "Listen, h—" He'd started to call her hon, but that which had always been so natural suddenly seemed fraught with danger. "Listen, don't expect a—"

"I know. I know. Don't expect a miracle."

A miracle, however, was exactly what Lindsey allowed herself to believe in a few minutes later. She had left her car at the office since taking it home would have alerted her mother to the fallacy of the dinner plans. On the drive back, Lindsey had decided to leave her car at the office overnight. That in mind, she'd directed Walker to drop her off at her parents' house.

As they pulled into the driveway, Lindsey noted that her mother's car wasn't there. Nor was there a light on inside the house. Though almost ten-thirty, it was clear that Bunny hadn't returned yet. Surely that was a good indication that the evening had gone well. Wasn't it? Lindsey chose to believe it was. She even chose to believe that maybe, just maybe, her mother and father were settling their differences. Maybe even making up in true lover's fashion. Maybe they were necking on the beach. Maybe they were snuggled up in a hotel room. Maybe—

"Don't expect a miracle," Walker repeated.

Through the darkness, Lindsey's eyes found his. She saw concern in his, concern that she'd expect too much and, in the end, wind up hurt. His protectiveness was endearing.

She smiled faintly. "I told you once before that, if you don't expect a miracle, it won't happen."

"I don't want to see you disappointed."

"I know you don't," she said softly. "And that's really very sweet."

Sweet. Walker wasn't certain that anything he was feeling for Lindsey would fall under the heading of sweet. What he wanted, and he'd wanted it all evening, was to touch her—and it wasn't for any sweet reason. Then again, maybe it was for the sweetest reason of all. Damn! he thought. Just walk her to the door, see her safely inside and get the hell out of here. The irony of the situation did not escape him. He was keenly aware that he was protecting her from himself.

Cutting off the headlights and the engine in seemingly one motion, he reached for the door handle. He had just unlatched it when he felt and heard Lindsey.

"Wait!" she called quietly, her fingers banding about his forearm.

Walker hesitated—lost in the velvet of her voice, the satin of her hand. His gaze merged with hers. She was leaning forward, her hair tumbling about her shoulders, the curves of her breasts just barely visible as the scooped neck of the sweater fell gently forward.

"It's late," he said, the words sounding as if they'd been polished with sandpaper.

"It's not that late. It's only ten-thirty."

"But I have to go to work in the morning."

"You shouldn't work on weekends," she said, loosening her fingers and beginning to seductively trail them up his arm.

He lowered his gaze to her hand, studying it as though he'd just arrived from another planet and had never seen such an appendage—long slender fingers, a pearl ring where she'd once worn an engagement ring, prettily manicured nails. Walker dragged his gaze away and back to hers.

"Lindsey?" he whispered. He hadn't intended to whisper. The word had just come out thus.

"Yes?" she said, her voice sounding like lace and silk. By now her fingers had made their way to the inside of his elbow. The sensitive inside of his elbow. They stopped there. She felt him tremble beneath her touch.

"What—" he swallowed "—are you doing?"

"What do you think I'm doing?"

Driving him mad, he thought, but he answered, "I don't know."

Lindsey brushed her knuckles against his cheek, whose stubble felt wickedly sexy to her, and whispered, "You really are working too many weekends if you don't know what I'm doing."

Walker reached for her hand, ostensibly to stop whatever feel-wonderful something she was doing to his face, but he managed only to take her hand in his. Once he'd done so, he seemed unable to turn loose. Warm. God, her hand was so warm!

"Lindsey..."

Her fingers entwined with his.

"... this is not ..."

She leaned forward.

"... a good idea."

Her breath fanned against his mouth milliseconds before her lips brushed his.

Walker moaned, then told himself to stop this...while he could.

"Lindsey—"

"You talk too much, Walker," she whispered, grazing his lips yet again. Then once more, before sensuously settling her mouth on his.

A part of Walker tried to resist, but the part of him that had resisted kissing her earlier in the evening could resist no longer. He wanted this kiss. He needed it. And if it meant paying the devil with his soul, he'd have it. On a deep, shattered groan, he tugged her to him and buried his hot mouth in hers.

Chapter Seven

Heaven.

He might well be on his way to hell, Walker thought dimly in some far recess of his mind, but he'd made a pit stop in heaven. Nothing in all of his life had prepared him for the sweetness, for the sensualness of Lindsey's kiss, nor for the effect it had on him. He felt as though he'd shattered into a million crystal shards of sensation, each possessed of a rainbow of lights. He felt as though he were racing in a star-studded sky, flying high, flying low, flying without any net to catch him, which made the experience more exhilarating simply by dent of the danger. In a word, he felt alive.

In spite of the beauty of what he was feeling, however, his conscience was troubled. What was happening shouldn't be happening. He knew that. He just didn't seem able to stop it. But he had to. He had to....

Lindsey moaned at the way Walker's mouth slanted over hers, at the way it melded with hers. In response, she parted her lips, bringing their mouths into even more intimate contact. Somehow she'd become wedged between Walker and the steering wheel. Somehow she'd ended up partially draped across his lap. She could feel his hard thighs. She could feel his taut stomach. She could feel his masculinity growing strong. He wanted her. His kiss told her so. His body told her so. And yet, she could feel him holding back. She didn't want him to hold back. She'd waited too long for this moment. Guided by instinct, emboldened by feelings that had been too long denied, Lindsey sent her tongue forward. The tip, nimble and eager, touched Walker's.

He tumbled from his high-flying flight, falling downward into a sea of sensuality. He groaned, grinding his mouth more desperately against hers, shoving his fingers deep into her hair. In proportion to his desperation, in proportion to his growing need for this woman, so, too, did his conscience flare. The intimacy of the kiss, the feel of her in his arms, the way his body was boldly responding to her—each and all appealed to his sense of right and wrong. Along with one brazen question: How in hell could he explain this to Dean and Bunny?

"No!" Walker cried, wrenching his mouth from Lindsey's at the same time he pushed her from him.

Startled, Lindsey simply stared. To have gone from the fullness of his arms to the emptiness of nothing left her bereft of all feeling. She felt nothing but loss—a grievous, soul-gouging loss. She thought it the worst she'd ever felt. She was wrong, however, for into the void slowly crept a cheek-reddening embarrassment.

He had rebuffed her. She'd obviously misinterpreted his actions, read the wrong meaning into them. Yet how could she have mistaken the way, the man-woman way, his mouth had moved over hers? How could she have mistaken the masculine response of his body? Dummy, she answered herself, throw yourself all over a man and he responds . . . whether he wants to or not.

Feeling like a fool, wishing the earth would split wide and swallow her, Lindsey threw open the car door and, without once looking back, slammed the door behind her and ran toward the house. She didn't give her pedicure the first thought.

"Lindsey, wait!" Walker called, pushing wide his door, too.

She ignored him, digging instead into her purse for the house key. She found it—though heaven alone knew how with her trembling fingers—jammed the key into the lock, and, flicking on the lights, fled inside the house. She sent the door sailing shut. Walker caught it in midswing.

"Lindsey?"

Again she made no response. She just headed for her bedroom. This time the door closed with a deafening bang. Right in Walker's face. Dragging his hand to his waist, he closed his eyes, lowered his head, and let out a long, frustrated sigh.

Dammit! he thought, how could he have let things get to this point?

Turning the knob, he opened the door slowly and entered Lindsey's bedroom. She stood staring out a window with her back to the door. In the dim glow of a single lamp, Walker could see that she clutched something to her. He suspected that something was a teddy bear. As though the thought made him ultra-aware of his surroundings, he made a quick scan of all the stuffed bears in the room. Each pair of eyes stared back accusingly. He deserved their censure.

Walker looked back at Lindsey. Remembering her womanly kiss, he thought she looked incongruous in the youthful setting. He also thought that she was crying because, even as he watched, she swiped at her eyes. Fancifully, he wondered if the teddy bears knew that she was crying, just the way she knew when they were. Not at all fancifully, he wanted to take her in his arms. God, how he wanted to take her in his arms! To comfort her, to hold her, to kiss her lips once more. He forced himself to settle for calling her name. Softly. As softly as her lips had felt against his.

"Lindsey?"

It was hard to tell whether she'd known that he was in the room before he spoke. Walker suspected she had. At the sound of her name, she turned. As though it were her only friend, she clung to a teddy bear—the one he'd given her at the airport. She was also crying. At least, she'd been crying, for her eyes still glistened with tears. Her pain crushed him, and he fought, as he'd never fought anything before, to keep from going to her.

"I'm sorry," he whispered. It was a paltry, worthless thing to say, but it was all he had to offer her.

She smiled sadly, mirthlessly, with lips still swollen from the bruising pressure of his. "What are you apologizing for? I'm the one who made a fool of myself. I'm the one who threw myself at you." Before he could respond, she added, so softly that it was more silence than sound, "I'm sorry."

Her lips, which had been sweeter than anything he'd ever tasted, trembled, and Walker groaned inwardly. He rammed his hands deep inside his pockets, because if he didn't he was going to cross to her and yank her into his arms.

"Don't, Lindsey," he said. "Please." He wasn't certain what he was pleading for her to do. Not to cry? Not to apologize? Not to make him want her even now, because—God, help him!—that was exactly what he wanted!

"No," she said, emboldened by what she'd already said. "I have to say this. I am sorry. I misunderstood. I thought... I thought... I just assumed..." She clasped the teddy bear closer, garnering the courage she needed to say, "I thought you were feeling what I was." She smiled again sadly, but this time so prettily that Walker thought he was going to die from her sheer beauty. "Wishful thinking plays strange tricks, huh?"

Her frank admission humbled him. How, though, could she not know that he'd wanted her, too? Hadn't his body signaled that loud and clear? The thought that he had wanted her still mystified him, still mortified him, yet he could not deny it. Not even to her. Especially in the face of her honesty. "You know I wanted you," he said.

He could have sworn that her cheeks pinkened. Minutes before, like a siren *extraordinaire*, she'd initiated a kiss, the likes of which he'd never known before and now here she was blushing. But it was that very dichotomy, the child-woman, the woman-child, that charmed him so.

"I know you reacted like any man would have under the circumstances. Reacting in a biologically prescribed way isn't the same as wanting someone. I mean, it is and it isn't. I thought... I thought you wanted to want me. I mean, I thought there was something—" she shrugged "—some chemistry going on between us. I thought you were feeling what I was. I thought..." She suddenly looked lost, confused, as mortified as he. Raking one hand through the blond tumble of her hair, the hair he'd minutes before devoured with his hands, she moaned, "I don't know anymore what I thought."

Walker took a step toward her. Only one. It was all he dared. "I felt what you felt. I wanted what you wanted." He took a deep breath. "I wanted you," he said hoarsely. His voice was torn and ragged when he added, "Heaven help me, I still want you!"

Lindsey, her heart hammering a discordant song, stood perfectly still. She was barely able to believe what she'd heard. She wanted to shout this wonderful news from the highest hill, yet, if he had indeed wanted her, she was more perplexed than ever.

"Then why—" she began, only to be cut off by Walker, by an emotional Walker who savagely thrust his fingers through his hair.

"My God, Lindsey, you're young enough to be my daughter! Which you are in a sense. You're my god-daughter! Which quite possibly makes what just happened incestuous!"

"That's a bunch of bunk!" Lindsey shouted, matching the pitch of her voice to his. "There's nothing inces-tuous—"

"Yeah, well, explain that to your parents!" As though weary to the bone, Walker plopped down on the side of the bed, gave a deep sigh and buried his head in his hands. He muttered something about explaining it to him while she was at it.

Lindsey could see Walker's pain. It was a tangible thing, jagged and serrated and ripping at his guts. He was just now facing what she'd faced months before. She remembered the emotional agony she'd endured. She remembered wondering if she was losing her mind. She remembered thinking that somehow there was something inappropriate, even downright wrong, about what she was feeling.

"I know," she said softly as she stepped across the room and eased down beside him. She was careful not to let her body touch his. "It takes some getting used to."

He pulled his head from his hands and glanced over at Lindsey. His look said that he'd heard the subtlety of her remark, namely, that she'd obviously had some time to consider the matter.

Lindsey admitted nothing more, however. She wasn't certain that Walker was ready to learn the depth of her feelings, nor how long she'd been nurturing them. She didn't want him to have to deal with anything more than he was already having to deal with. Frankly, he looked overwhelmed enough. "I'm not your daughter," she did say with defiance. "No matter what our relationship has been in the past, I'm not your daughter. Nor are you my father."

"Not in a biologic sense, of course, but—"

"I'm not your daughter, period. You're not my father, period. It's that simple."

Her nearness making him feel things of a decidedly unfatherly nature, Walker rose from the bed and stepped to the window, where he stared out into the black night. A car, its headlights bright, eased down the quiet street. It crawled past the house. Its presence reminded him, however, that it could have been Bunny returning home. How could he explain this scene to her should she find him in Lindsey's bedroom? The fact that he couldn't—at least not easily—underscored the complexity of the situation.

"It's not that simple," Walker said.

"It is just that simple," Lindsey repeated.

He turned around. "Lindsey, I'm twice your age."

She laid down the teddy bear and stood. "Which is it? Are you worried about the age difference or about my being your goddaughter?"

"Both, dammit!"

"What's the big deal about age?"

"Lindsey, I'm old enough to be—"

She groaned. "I know! I know! You're old enough to be my father!"

"Well, I am!"

"So what?"

"So what? So doesn't that bother you?"

"No. Not particularly. When you kissed me, your age was the last thing on my mind. I was hoping that it was the last thing on yours."

Her honesty disarmed him again, especially since the truth was that age, neither his nor hers, had been the last thing on his mind minutes before. All that had been on his mind had been the satin-softness of her lips, the honey-eyed sweetness of her mouth. Walker closed his eyes and sighed.

Lindsey saw her chance and pressed her advantage. Slowly, she walked toward him. Without actually touching him, she stopped so near that she could feel the heat of his body. Her voice was only a whisper when she said, "Tell me that you were thinking about age when we kissed."

When he felt her moving toward him, he opened his eyes. And watched as she closed the distance to him. She stopped only a heartbeat away. A tantalizing heartbeat away. Her perfume wafted about him, causing him to feel giddy. Or maybe it was just her nearness... or maybe it was her eyes that had turned a smoky, hazy blue.

"Was that what you were thinking about?" Lindsey repeated, prepared to give him no quarter.

No, he thought, the word thundering through him.

"Lindsey—"

"You owe me an answer."

He did. He knew he did. But to answer her truthfully meant another slight alteration, an irrevocable alteration, of their relationship. He wasn't certain he could stand many more.

"Lindsey—"

"Answer me," she demanded.

"No!" he spat. "I wasn't thinking of our age, but that isn't the point."

"What we feel isn't the point?"

"No. Just because you feel something doesn't make it right." He groaned suddenly. "My God, I can't believe this is happening. I can't believe we're having this discussion. I can't believe we..." He couldn't bring himself to even verbalize what had just happened in the car. Instead, he repeated, "I can't believe this is happening. Look," he added quickly, as though he were desperate to wind up this discussion and go back to the safe security of believing that all he'd been feeling ever since Lindsey returned home had been nothing more than his overwrought imagination, "forget this happened. We were both tired. We've both been under a lot of stress. Just forget it happened. Find yourself someone your own age and...and...and..." None of the and's that came to mind pleased him. In fact, each displeased him. Mightily.

With each word, Walker had backed farther and farther away from Lindsey and closer and closer to the safety of the door. He now stood directly in front of it.

"I don't want anyone else," Lindsey said. "I want you."

Walker heaved another sigh, this one caught between frustration and exhilaration. "Lindsey, you don't know what you're saying."

"Oh, but I do. I know exactly what I'm saying. I'm saying that I want you. I'm attracted to you and I want everything that attraction entails. And, furthermore, Walker Carr," she added, a sweetly wicked gleam in her otherwise innocent eyes as she walked toward him, "I intend to have you."

The child had disappeared again, replaced by a sultry, sexy vamp. Walker groaned, as though the vamp had clipped him at the back of the knees. He was falling, falling, falling, but what a heavenly descent! The quick hands of sanity snatched him back just in the nick of time. He mumbled something that vaguely resembled "Good night," and fled.

On the drive home, Lindsey's silken threat taunted and teased, teased and taunted Walker, until he arrived home uncertain of which he feared more—that she would pursue him exactly as she'd promised or that she'd take his advice and find someone else. He groaned.

How in hell was it possible for a grown man, a supposedly mature man, to make such a mess of everything?

"I swear I'd divorce your father if he wasn't already divorcing me!" Bunny said the next morning in answer to Lindsey's question of how the evening had gone.

Because her mother still hadn't come in by midnight, the hour at which Lindsey had gone to bed and, unbelievably, immediately fallen asleep, Lindsey had allowed her hope to soar. Her mother's words now dashed that hope.

"And, furthermore, young lady," Bunny said, beating the pancake batter as though it was what she had the grievance against, "I'm angry with you. You set the whole evening up." Here Bunny slopped several tablespoons of batter onto the griddle, puddling an irregularly shaped pancake that the woman ordinarily wouldn't have even come close to settling for. "You set *me* up," Bunny added, creating a companion pancake vaguely in the shape of Texas. "How could you do that to me, Lindsey?"

With the death of hope had come the anger that Lindsey had experienced once before. Her parents were obviously not inclined to cooperate. On a frustrated sigh, Lindsey poured herself a cup of coffee and sat down at the table. "I was hoping that you and Dad could work out your differences like two rational human beings—"

"Rational?" Bunny asked, tacking on a disgusted "humph" as she flipped the first pancake. It landed in the squishy middle of the second, bonding the two cakes like Siamese twins. "That's a word your father hasn't the vaguest concept about these days." As though just thinking about it, she asked, "Did you know he has a red sports car?" She didn't give her daughter time to answer. "Which he drives like a sixteen-year-old showing off! My God, a man of his age driving around like some sixteen-year-old, pimply-faced kid!"

She slapped the pancakes—one of which was still doughy because it hadn't been turned—onto a plate and slapped the plate down in front of Lindsey.

"I don't know who in heck he thinks he is, but if he thinks I'm going to sit around pining for him while he's out making a fool of himself, then he's mistaken. *Sadly* mistaken. Don's right. I have a life of my own, and it's too short to waste it worrying about your father."

Lindsey frowned. "Don? Who's Don?"

"The man on the beach," Bunny answered, pushing the syrup, which was still in the plastic container it came in, toward Lindsey.

Lindsey's frown deepened. "What man on the beach?"

"The man on the beach last night. When your father stormed out of the restaurant, I drove down to the beach and walked. I ran into Don."

The frown of perplexity turned to a frown of disbelief. "You spent the evening with a beach bum?"

"He was not a beach bum. He was a perfectly decent man on vacation here on the island. He was just taking a walk...the way I was. Anyway, he's divorced himself and said that no spouse is worth trying to hang on to if they don't want to be held on to. I think his wife must have hurt him. Anyway, he said I ought to get on with my life."

Lindsey was speechless. Utterly speechless. "L-let me get this straight," she said finally. "You won't seek professional counseling, but you'll take the advice of a strange man on the beach?"

"It wasn't me who nixed the idea of counseling. It was your father. But now that I really think about it, I'm not interested in counseling. It's your father who has the problem. Not me. Your father is scared to death of growing old. All I want is to salvage my life—and grow old gracefully and peacefully."

"But—"

"Lindsey, the best thing for you, for everyone, is to just stay out of this. I know it's difficult, but there it is. There's nothing you can do."

"If you and Dad would only talk—"

"I tried. He won't. And that's that. Don says that if pride is all your father left me, then it's pride that'll have to sustain me."

"That sounds great, but— Hey, where are you going?" Lindsey asked when her mother started from the kitchen.

Bunny turned in the doorway. "To the paint store. I'm going to paint that lawn furniture your father never had time for. And I want to get an early start."

Lindsey silently watched her mother go. A part of her—the mature woman part—applauded her mother's quest for an independent life, while another part—the child of her parents part—feared that independence, for it might drive yet a wider wedge between her parents.

She also felt an escalation of her anger. How dare her parents resist her efforts to get them back together! Mostly, though, she just felt as flat and deflated as the untouched pancakes—and all on a beautiful Saturday morning when she should have been basking in the warm glow of the evening before.

She and Walker had kissed. Really kissed. Like a man and a woman. And nothing would, could, ever again be quite the same.

On Monday, after seeing an article in the newspaper, Bunny decided to enroll in college for the fall term, which was only a couple of weeks away. Going back to school was something she'd always wanted to do and now, she'd told Lindsey, was the perfect time to do so.

Lindsey hadn't been able to argue the point, though once more she wished her mother were at least still trying to talk to her father. She wasn't, however. She had apparently taken the tack that enough was enough. If Dean wanted to talk to her, he knew where to find her.

Curiously, Lindsey began to suspect that her mother, with the actualization of a new attitude, was getting her father's attention in a way she'd been unable to heretofore. When Dean found out about the newly painted lawn furniture, he was downright angry. Hadn't he told her that he'd take care of that? He was still capable of taking care of his responsibilities, thank you very much! Bunny's response to her husband had been a quiet so-was-she.

And then, on Tuesday morning, Dean learned that his wife had enrolled in college. College? He hadn't even known that it was something she wanted to do. Bunny politely told him that there were obviously a lot of things that he didn't know about her. Amused, Lindsey had watched the interplay. Though not amicably, they were at least talking.

And then came Wednesday morning, when Dean realized that Bunny had accepted a date with somebody named Don.

"Don? Who the hell is Don?"

When Lindsey had casually announced moments before that her mother was going out, she had gotten both Walker's and Dean's attention. Dean, who wore red slacks, sunglasses and a multicolored braided bracelet, looked as though he'd been poleaxed.

"Some man she met on the beach," Lindsey said, rising from her desk and slowly making her way to the filing cabinet.

She sensed not only her father's gaze, but Walker's, as well. In fact, she'd sensed Walker's subtle glances all week. Though he hadn't touched her in any way—he'd comically gone out of his way not to—his look said that he'd like to. Lindsey had done everything she could to drive him wild. She appreciated the struggle he was engaged in. It was a struggle she intended for him to lose.

"What man on the beach?" her father asked.

"Just some man," Lindsey said. She was uncertain how she felt about this man, but she was prepared to use him to her own advantage. "After you left the restaurant Friday night, Mother went to the beach."

"She met him there?" Dean asked incredulously.

"That's what she tells me," Lindsey said, closing the file cabinet and starting back toward her desk. Her eyes met Walker's. Their gazes held for a fraction of a hot second.

"She's going out with some guy she met on the beach?" Dean asked.

"Mmm," Lindsey confirmed, looking over at Walker and asking, "Do you want this priced by the end of the day?"

What he wanted was for her to look less enticing, Walker thought as he took in the snug fit of her summer-white sweater and jaunty sway of her ponytail. What he wanted was a decent night's sleep. What he wanted was to forget the way her lips had felt on his. What he wanted was to get the hell out of the office! he thought, jumping to his feet and heading for the water dispenser. He grabbed a paper cup and filled it.

"Yeah," he muttered in response to her question.

"You don't seem too upset over this date," Dean accused his daughter. "You don't even know this guy and you're willing to throw your mother at him."

"I'm not throwing her at anybody. And I'm not even sure she's calling this a date. They're just going to have lunch at Christie's. Besides, both you and she have made it clear that this is none of my business."

"But a date—"

"You *are* getting a divorce, Dad. I'm sure that you'll want to start dating soon, too."

Walker turned from the water dispenser just as Lindsey made this last remark. This time his eyes collided with Dean's. Embarrassed, Dean looked away first. Instinctively, as though it were his job to protect Lindsey, Walker sought her out. He was relieved to note that she hadn't noticed the exchange. He was not relieved to note that several strands of hair had slipped onto her cheek and curled about her lips. As she absently brushed them aside, she glanced up. At the sight of Walker watching her, she hesitated, the crook of her finger at the corner of her mouth.

I don't want to remember the taste of your mouth, his look seemed to say.

I don't want you to forget, hers returned.

He crushed the paper cup in his hand and threw it at the trash can. At the same time, he asked Dean, with more roughness than the question required, "Are you going out to the platform?"

"Yeah," Dean grunted, still smarting from his wife's date.

"I think I'll go with you."

Dean looked surprised. "Why?"

Because your daughter is driving me crazy, Walker thought, but said, "Just thought I would. Okay?"

"Sure," Dean said, heading for the door. "Let's go."

"I'll, uh, I'll see you tomorrow," Walker said to Lindsey. There was an unspoken implication that tomorrow would somehow be better than today. Tomorrow he wouldn't remember the candy-sweet taste of her lips. Tomorrow he wouldn't wonder what his tongue would taste if it dipped into the corners of her mouth or the dimples that sometimes appeared. Tomorrow his sanity would be returned.

"Ya'll be careful," Lindsey said softly, her glossy pink lips challenging his logic.

Walker groaned silently. Tomorrow *had* to be better. It just had to be.

Tomorrow wasn't any better. In fact, it was worse. Walker slept poorly—again—leaving him nothing better to do than toss and turn and swim restless laps in the pool. At a quarter till five, he stopped trying to sleep and put on a pot of coffee. By six-thirty, he was at the office and up to his eyebrows in work. The strong coffee, the bright September sun and the pleasing distraction of his job buoyed his spirits and left him feeling emotionally stronger than he had in some time. Everything was going to be fine. Whatever had happened between him and Lindsey was over—nothing more than a fleeting aberration.

His optimistic mood lasted until Lindsey walked through the door.

Dressed entirely in white—white slacks and a white blouse with an enormous square, lacy collar—she was gorgeous. Both virginally wholesome and awesomely sexy. She literally took his breath away, reduced him to the restless creature he'd been the night before. He was lost, and she didn't try to save him. In fact, she did everything in her power to drive him over the edge. She caressed him with her eyes, she moistened her lips with the tip of her tongue, she touched him every chance she got and made chances at every opportunity. She pursued him just as she said she would. Walker didn't know whether to throttle her or throw her down on a desk and make love to her.

At four-thirty she placed a mug of steaming coffee before him. He glanced up, wondering why the long day hadn't taken some toll on her. Instead, she looked as fresh as when she'd arrived that morning. And as gorgeous. Up close, he could see the straps of some lacy undergarment beneath her blouse. A brassiere? A camisole? Or maybe a... What did they call those things? A teddy? Whatever it was, it ought to be illegal.

"You look as though you could use this," Lindsey said.

"Yeah," he grumbled, wrapping his hand about the hot mug and drawing it to his lips. After a swallow, he asked, "Are you having fun?"

She gave a coy look. "I don't know what you mean."

"The hell you don't."

A tiny smile at her lips, she said, "Oh, you mean my flirting with you."

Despite the circumstances, despite the miserable havoc she was playing with him, he couldn't help but smile. He forced himself to limit it to a half smile. "Yeah, I think that's what they call it."

"Well, is it working?" she asked, easing to sit on the edge of his desk.

At the tantalizing fragrance of her perfume, Walker, the mug in his hand, leaned back in his chair. "You were the one who said I looked as though I needed this."

Her smile turned to a vixenish grin. "Now, exactly when are you going to stop fighting me?"

This time Walker didn't smile. He knew that it wasn't so much a matter of fighting her as fighting himself. His answer was appropriate in either case. "I'm not."

Lindsey didn't look in the least perturbed. "We'll see." Scooting from the desk, she said, "Oh, by the way, you want to buy me a drink after work?"

"Yes," he answered, "but I'm not."

For a moment her smile disappeared entirely and she looked like a consummate adult. A concerned adult. "Poor Walker. I'm not making it easy for you, am I?"

He didn't answer. What was the point of stating what was blatantly obvious?

If Thursday had been worse than the days preceding it, Friday was the worst of all. Dean had been uncommonly surly—Friday noon had been Bunny's luncheon date with the elusive Don. That, on top of another sleepless night, had left Walker about as surly as his friend. To add insult to injury, Lindsey had flirted outrageous, if subtly. He was, quite frankly, about ready to scream, get drunk or throw a royal fit. Maybe all three.

"Who in hell wrote this?" Walker grumbled. "I can't read a damned word of it."

Lindsey crossed to his desk and looked down at the notation. "You did."

That only angered Walker more, that and the fact that all he'd wanted all day was to be near Lindsey. God, he'd sell his soul to reach out, pull her down onto his lap and smother her mouth with his! Which really showed what a sick son of a bitch he was! Dropping his head, he tunneled his fingers through his hair. He was vaguely aware that his knee hurt like hell. Was it going to rain? Was he ever going to be at peace again? Was—

He felt her hands at the nape of his neck, her fingers gently kneading and massaging.

"It says call Ramsey," she said. "Isn't he the foreman on Four?"

"Hmm," Walker mumbled, unable to stop her from what she was doing. Her caressing fingers felt too wonderful on a neck whose muscles were strung tight.

"You need to relax, Walker," she said, her voice having dropped to a few notes short of a whisper. "You're tight."

Tight. God, she didn't know the half of it! Every inch of his male body was stretched to the point of popping. He couldn't take much more. Intuitively, he knew that.

"Stop fighting," she whispered. "I want you. You want me. There's nothing wrong with that."

"Lindsey..." He felt the brush of her lips against the back of his neck and moaned.

"Why don't we buy some wine and cheese and bread and go to the beach," she said. He could feel her lips smiling against his neck. "I can't attack you there. I can flirt a little maybe, but your virtue's safe."

"Lindsey..." This time he felt her nibble at his ear. He also felt her lean forward. Her breasts nestled into his back. She'd worn another see-through blouse, the ivory fabric of which was so soft as to be almost nonexistent.

He moaned.

"Or," she growled softly, "we could take the wine and cheese and bread and have a picnic in your backyard. Your virtue, however, is definitely not safe there."

"Lindsey—"

"Come to think of it..." she said, biting the back of his neck.

"Stop it."

"...It might not be safe on the beach, either."

"Lindsey—"

Her tongue rasped across his neck.

His control gone, Walker grabbed her hand and pulled her from him. "Dammit, don't!" At her sudden wide-eyed, very startled look, he added hoarsely, "Please." When she still said nothing, he said, the words tattered and torn, "I'm begging you."

For long, long, eternally long seconds, neither said anything. There didn't seem to be anything to say. Walker could see her hurt. She could see his frustration. She could also see that he'd just arrived at the end of his rope.

Slowly, Walker realized that he was still holding her wrist. He released his hold, feeling oddly bereft by the loss of her touch. It was strange, he thought, but all it took to make him happy these days was her touch. He could never remember when so little seemed like so much.

"I, uh, I think I'll leave early today," he said.

She said nothing.

"Why don't you, too? There's nothing here that won't keep over the weekend."

Still, she said nothing.

He rose. "I, uh, I'll see you Monday." When she still said nothing, but rather stood looking as though he'd struck her, he added, "Lindsey—"

"It's all right," she said quietly.

They both knew that it wasn't, however. In fact, everything was a damned sight short of all right, and there was the real possibility that nothing would ever be right again.

Chapter Eight

Lindsey sat in her car, staring at the unturned key. Minutes before, she'd paid for the piña colada that she'd nursed for the past hour and left the hotel bar where, weeks before, she and Walker had shared a drink. She wished now that she hadn't chosen that particular bar. It had too many memories. But then, memories plagued her no matter where she went.

"Dammit, don't... please... I'm begging you."

Walker was nearing the breaking point. It was what she wanted—for him to lose the struggle with his emotions and, thereby, for her to win. She hadn't realized, though, that his losing would be so painful for him, so soul-wrenchingly painful. She had heard the pure agony in his voice. He wanted her, and that fact was eating him alive, for it was making him go against every fiber of his integrity. He had not yet—and maybe never would—come to terms with what was happening between them. He saw his feelings for her as a betrayal of her parents and a breaching of his godfather responsibilities. How stupid of her not to know how hurtful this betrayal of his principles would be. How stupid! How insensitive! How naive? Yes, how incredibly naive.

So, where did she go from here? She didn't want to keep hurting Walker. She couldn't keep hurting him. When you loved someone, you didn't hurt that someone. At least not if you could help it. All of which meant, she guessed, that she'd have to rethink her battle plan.

She sighed, feeling the September heat ooze through the sheer lawn fabric of her blouse. Though almost seven-thirty, it was still as hot as Hades, and the humidity was as dense as a chunk of wood. The radio had earlier reported rumblings of a storm in the Gulf, which could, ultimately, mean wind and rain for the island. At the present she would welcome such a cleansing, although it might be days down the road... if at all. Right now, she had to decide where to go, because she couldn't very well sit in this parking lot all night.

Home.

She thought of home, but didn't want to go there. She knew that her mother was out again with this Don person. According to her mother, lunch had been nice, and she'd volunteered to show Don some of the off-the-beaten-path sights before he left the island the next day. Lindsey didn't know how she felt about her mother being out with a man other than her father. Well, actually, she did. She didn't like it any more than her father did. When he'd heard that Bunny was going out again that evening, he'd become sullen, quiet, withdrawn. For the first time, Lindsey had felt encouraged. Maybe her father was having second thoughts.

Her father.

Maybe he could use a little tender loving care tonight. Maybe she herself could use a little of the TLC that he was so good at dispensing. Over the years, no one could ease her pain the way her father could. No pair of arms had ever been able to so completely hug away life's hurts. Suddenly, more than anything in the world, Lindsey wanted to feel her father's arms about her. Even though she couldn't tell her father about Walker, wouldn't it be wonderful just to have her father's silent assurance that whatever was bothering her would be all right?

Turning the key, Lindsey started the car and headed it in the direction of her father's apartment. Though she'd never been there, she knew the address. At least, she knew the small apartment complex. All she'd have to do was look for a red sports car, which, as luck would have it, she caught sight of several blocks from the apartment. The car, its top up for a change, had just halted at a stop sign, then lurched forward with the power of a team of wild horses. Lindsey knew it was her father because of the temporary license plate.

At closer inspection, Lindsey realized that there was someone else in the car with him. For the duration of one unsteady breath, she toyed with the idea that it might be Walker, but the idea fled when the car turned the corner. The passenger was clearly a woman with long flowing red hair, the ends of which fluttered out the open window. Lindsey's unsteady breath vanished entirely at the sight. Her first reaction was to deny what she was seeing. Her second, to minimize it. There could be lots of reasons that her father had a woman in the car with him. Yeah, she heard a voice saying deep inside her, name a couple. The truth was that she could come up with only one. One very hurtful reason.

Lindsey's pain grew by leaps and bounds as she watched her father pull into the driveway. From a position of a block away, she saw him get out of the car, round the hood and open the passenger door. A woman, all red hair, long legs and a giggly smile, tumbled out . . . and into her father's arms.

Lindsey couldn't believe what she was seeing. Her father with another woman! Woman? Maybe, but Lindsey would guess that she barely had reached that chronological point, and there was no doubt whatsoever that the flame-haired sprite was younger than she. It was equally obvious that this wasn't the first time her father had dated the young woman. They were too chummy, too personal, too downright intimate. This Lindsey thought as she watched the redhead brush her mouth across her father's.

At the sight of her father returning the kiss, Lindsey grew numb. As though she could not help herself, as though compelled to watch, Lindsey's gaze followed the couple as they walked, arm in arm, up the sidewalk and toward the apartment. At the door, they paused as her father searched through his pocket for the key. All the while, the two of them laughed and kissed. As Dean fitted the key into the lock, the woman's hand roamed onto his rear end and splayed wide, as though staking a claim. Lindsey noted that her father in no way objected. In fact, he dragged her into the apartment and closed the door, leaving the impression that he couldn't get her alone fast enough. Lindsey had no doubt what was about to occur behind the closed door.

Suddenly, she felt sick to her stomach, sick at heart. In all of her life she could never remember feeling this way. She felt hurt, in such an abundance that she wasn't certain she could bear it. It was like a mighty weight pressing down on her chest. In equal proportions, she felt anger—a hot, scalding, how-the-hell-could-he-do-this anger. She felt...alone. So bitterly alone. She also felt like crying, but this she stubbornly refused to let herself do.

Lindsey had no idea how long she sat a block away watching the apartment. She saw the downstairs lights go out and the upstairs lights go on. She then saw them go out, too. Still, she continued her dark vigil until she finally became aware that the night had closed in around her. Outside, stars had begun to twinkle. Inside the car, she had grown uncomfortable sitting in one limited position. With a start, she realized that the motor was still running. She eased the gear into drive, turned on her lights and let the car take the lead. She hadn't the foggiest idea where she was headed.

Wearing only a pair of worn stone-washed jeans, Walker reclined in a chaise lounge at the side of the pool. Except for the sparse illumination of the pool lights, he sat in darkness. A beer can rested on his flat belly, its cool drops of condensation mingling with the sweat that had formed on his body. Beside him, the radio played a string of love songs—songs of passion, songs of devotion, songs of love gone painfully wrong.

"...And now an update on the weather," came the male voice on the radio. "In case you hadn't noticed, it's hot here on the island. At present it's eighty-eight degrees, with another sizzling day predicted for tomorrow. For those of you following the progress of the tropical depression in the Caribbean, it's still harmless enough, but seems to be gaining momentum. We'll keep you informed of its movements. And now, here's a song for all of you out there who are in love. It's called—"

Walker abruptly shut off the radio and brought the beer can to his lips. He was sick of love songs, as in fed up to the gills. He also wondered about the storm. When you lived on the coast, when you operated oil rigs in the Gulf, each manned by a crew, you never took storms cavalierly. They were always worth watching. Sometimes a storm was nothing more than a naughty lady. Then again, it could be bold and brazen.

Lady.

Bold and brazen.

An image of Lindsey shadow-danced through Walker's mind. She was all he'd thought about since leaving work. Hell, she was all he'd thought about for days, weeks! He'd give anything if he could just stop thinking about her, if he could just stop wanting to be near her, wanting to touch her, if he could just stop remembering every nuance of how she looked, how she smelled, how she sounded.

"Oh, you mean my flirting with you."

"Poor Walker. I'm not making it easy for you, am I?"

"Stop fighting. I want you. You want me. There's nothing wrong with that."

Walker groaned. To indicate just how far he'd fallen, there were actually times when he thought wanting Lindsey wasn't wrong. How could something that felt so right—and the feel of her in his arms *did* feel right—be so wrong? How could feelings so strong be false?

The flash of headlights cutting across the privet hedge brought his miserable thoughts to a halt. Who in hell? he wondered, momentarily hearing the slam of a car door. Maybe, if he pretended not to be at home, whoever it was would go away. He didn't want company. Not anybody's. At the sound of the doorbell, Walker didn't stir. The bell rang again. Walker held his breath. Once more the doorbell rang—three times in rapid succession. Walker uttered a profanity and pushed himself from the chaise lounge. Whoever it was wasn't going away. That much was clear.

En route to the front door, Walker turned on a couple of house lights and deposited the beer can, with a spewing thud, onto the kitchen cabinet. He hit the porch light at the same time he yanked open the front door. His mood was only three growls short of a grizzly bear's.

"Yeah?" he barked, the word clipped in the middle of its delivery.

Lindsey stood on the doorstep, the harsh porch light bleaching her skin to a sickly pallor. At least that was Walker's first interpretation of her paleness. He revised it when he saw the blank look in her eyes, the vacantness in her expression. It wasn't the orange glare of the light washing the color from her face. She had managed to be pale all on her own.

"Lindsey, are you all right?" Walker asked, his concern apparent.

"I, uh, I didn't know where else to go," she said. Seconds, heartbeats, regrets by the score passed. "I don't want to hurt you . . . I promise I won't flirt . . . I promise I won't tease. . .I promise. . ." Her voice trailed off as if she couldn't remember exactly what she was promising. She then repeated, "I didn't know where else to go."

As instinctively as breathing, Walker stepped aside. Lindsey accepted his unspoken invitation, noting, even in her muddled state, that he wore neither shirt nor shoes. An ebony matting of hair, some shaded in silver and moistened in sweat, covered his chest. Though the woman in her clearly recognized his blatant sensuality, the child in her just wanted to be held, and comforted, against that chest. Abruptly, she realized that she was just staring at the object of her interest. She raised her gaze from Walker's chest to his eyes.

She had promised not to flirt, but the very look of longing on her face was more powerful than any blatant teasing she might have engaged in. Walker's body suffused with heat, with longing, with a need so profound it was frightening. Only the fact that something was wrong—very wrong—kept him from pulling her into his arms.

"What is it?" he asked. "What's happened?"

Lindsey smiled in self-deprecation. "I must be incredibly stupid. Or naive." She laughed as she drew back the long blond hair from her face. "Or maybe I'm both. Yeah, I guess that's it. I guess I'm both."

"You're going to have to tell me what you're talking about," Walker said.

"What I'm talking about is being as blind as a bat. All the signs were there. I just refused to put two and two together."

"Lindsey..."

"I mean, he was exhibiting all the classic signs of a mid-life crisis. Why did I think he wouldn't have gone all the way?"

"...You're going to have to tell me..."

She laughed mirthlessly, and her voice had risen in anger when she said, "Well, I guess it's pretty obvious why I didn't want to add two and two together. Four hurts. In fact, it's downright unfair!"

"Lindsey—"

"Dammit, he's having an affair! My father's having an affair!"

In that moment, Walker could have throttled Dean. The pain he was inflicting on those who loved him was inexcusable, unforgivable. Walker could also have throttled himself for not anticipating that Lindsey would find out. Affairs never remained a secret for long. Why hadn't he told her himself? Because he hadn't had the guts, that was why. Now, angry with both himself and Dean, Walker gave a long, weary sigh.

Something in the sound of the sigh caught Lindsey's attention. That and the fact that Walker looked less than shocked. Disgusted, yes. Frustrated, yes. Shocked, no.

"You knew, didn't you?" she asked with a certainty that didn't need confirmation. "You lied to me," she said disbelievingly. The hurt she'd experienced earlier that evening, the revelation of her father's affair, now compounded and magnified until she felt that she would surely smother beneath her suffocating pain.

Her accusation cut through Walker like a sharp saber. "I didn't lie to you! When I told you I didn't know of any affair, I didn't. I found out later."

"And you didn't tell me?" She now refused to be placated. Frankly, it felt good to be taking her anger out on someone. Anyone.

"And I suppose you rushed right home and told your mother," Walker said, his own emotions peaking to the same hot high.

"Of course, I didn't! How could I tell her that Dad is screwing around? How could I be the one to hurt her?"

"My point precisely. I didn't want to be the one to hurt her, either." His voice had lowered to a rich huskiness when he added, "I didn't want to be the one to hurt you."

The words lapped about her like heated honey, their tone telling her of the strength of his feelings, feelings he was fighting, but feelings he had nonetheless.

"Maybe I should have told you," he said suddenly. "Maybe it would have been better coming from me."

"No," she answered softly, wisely, "it wouldn't have been any better. And, if it's any consolation, I probably wouldn't have told you, either. I wouldn't have wanted to be the one to hurt you. I couldn't hurt you. At least not intentionally."

Walker knew that she was apologizing for all the times she'd taunted him, teased him. That apology, coupled with her remarks when he'd first opened the door, remarks about her no longer going to flirt with him, had an unexpected and strange effect upon him. He'd begged her to stop, but now that she was, disappointment seized him. My God, was he going totally crazy?

"You want a drink?" he said, starting for the liquor cabinet. The fact that it was so meagerly stocked said that he wasn't normally a drinking man. All that might change if his life didn't get back to normal. Normal? All he could remember of normal now was that he'd been drowning in dullness, sameness, with one day plodding slowly into another. And then Lindsey had returned home.

"You told me once that I wasn't old enough to drink," Lindsey said, watching Walker pour a dash of brandy into a snifter.

"Believe me, we're both getting older by the minute," he said, downing the drink in one gulp.

It was hot and mixed poorly with the cold beer sloshing around in his stomach. He splashed more brandy into the glass and handed it to Lindsey. She took it. He noted that her hands were inordinately cold for the hot weather flooding the city. It crossed his mind that he could think of a lot of ways to warm them—sexy ways, sweetly sinful ways—then realized that it was just such thoughts that he was trying to curb.

After swallowing the brandy, Lindsey made a face. "Brandy and piña coladas don't mix."

"Tell me about it," Walker grumbled as the beer and brandy battled.

Suddenly, as though just remembering what had driven her to this man, Lindsey spoke. "Oh, Walker, my father's having an affair. And the worst of it is, she's just a kid. My God, she's just a kid! She makes me look ready for Social Security."

"She's nineteen," Walker supplied, adding what he knew she wanted to ask, "He met her at a diner."

Disbelief streaked across Lindsey's face. "He left Mother for a nineteen-year-old he met at a diner?"

"No, he didn't leave your mother for her. Their affair isn't serious. Even your father says so. The truth of the matter is that he's running scared. He would have had an affair with the first skirted thing that crossed his path. Let me rephrase that, with the first *young* skirted thing. He needs to feel young right now."

"Why? What happens to make a man go crazy at an age when he should be moving toward wisdom?"

Walker shrugged, sending his bare wide shoulders up and down. "The reasons are as varied as the men, but basically it's fear. Fear of aging, fear of dying—" Walker recalled his friend's comment concerning the professional football he'd never played... and never would "—fear of never realizing a dream."

"But you're Dad's age and you're not afraid."

Walker took inventory of the woman before him and of the fury of feelings she unleashed in him, feelings he wasn't certain he could contain much longer. They might be wrong, but they were strong and, with each breath he drew, they were growing stronger. Just how much longer could he resist them? Not long, he was afraid. His gaze unswervingly on her, he said, "We're all afraid. Of one thing or another."

Afraid.

Yes, she, too, was afraid, Lindsey thought. She was afraid that she'd dreamed a dream that just wasn't going to come true. She loved Walker so much, wanted him so much, that she'd thought she could conjure up a miracle. He did care for her, that much she knew. But caring wasn't enough. He had to be willing to commit. Naively, she'd believed that would happen in time. Now she wasn't sure. Any more than she was sure that her parents' marriage could be salvaged.

Lindsey smiled. Sadly. "You're right," she said. At Walker's quizzical look, she explained, "I am immature."

"I never said—"

"You implied it." She laughed, bobbing her head so that her hair swirled about her. "And you were right. I foolishly thought I could save my parents' marriage. Well, the truth is that some things just can't be mended. And even if their marriage can be mended, I'm not the one who has to mend it. It was never in my power."

"It takes maturity to reach that conclusion...and guts to admit it."

"Maybe. Maybe not. The point is, though, that no matter how you cut it, I've acted immaturely, naively. You hurt me this afternoon, and so I ran to Daddy for him to hold me and tell me everything was all right. When he upset me, I ran to you for you to hold me."

Walker was uncertain which fact moved him more— the fact that he'd upset her or the fact that she wanted him to hold her and tell her everything would be all right. This latter was precisely what he wanted to do.

His voice was husky when he spoke. "Everyone needs comforting, Lindsey. No one ever becomes that self-reliant."

"Yes, but adults stand on their own feet. Which," she added, setting down the snifter she'd just then realized she was still holding, "is something I'd better learn to do."

Second bled into second as their gazes became one. Lindsey fought the urge to lower her eyes to the chest that she wanted so desperately to be held against. She lost the battle. When she once more raised her gaze to his, he saw her naked need. What she saw was that she was once more hurting him. With hesitant steps at first, then practically running, she started for the door. She already had it open when she felt him behind her.

Walker's hand shot out of nowhere, closing the door in her face, hemming her between him and it. Neither spoke. Neither moved. It was as though the moment were frozen in time. Lindsey could feel the heat of his body. She could feel his chest—so near, yet so far away. Closing her eyes, she let the nearness of him burn through her.

Similarly, Walker was aware of every nuance of Lindsey's being. He smelled the sweetness of her perfume, saw the blond curtain of her hair as it flowed across her shoulders, felt her back against his chest. He closed his eyes, praying that she would ease back into him, praying that just once more she'd be a sweet siren. But she didn't move. And Walker could never remember regretting anything more profoundly. Suddenly, he had struggled all he could. Suddenly, he knew he'd lost the battle. And frankly, he didn't care. He simply wanted her in his arms.

On a deep groan, he whirled her around and hauled her to him. Instinctively, his arms went around her...just as hers went around him. He crushed her to him, her breasts plumping against the bare, hair-dusted wall of his chest through the thin fabric of her blouse. But even that wasn't close enough. Even that didn't satisfy all the lonely nights he'd lain awake wanting her. Only one thing would do that. Only one intimate act.

"Everything'll be all right," he whispered, his lips near her ear. "I promise. Everything'll be all right." He was aware that his comment was as much for his benefit as it was for hers. Maybe more so. Because he knew what was coming. He knew what he was about to do. Simply because he could no longer stop himself.

God, please don't let me do this! Please don't let me...

The decision was jerked out of his hands by Lindsey's angling of her head. What she was doing was not deliberate. That Walker would have staked his life on. She had said that she would no longer tease him and she wasn't. At least not knowingly. But what she was doing with such consummate instinct was allowing him access to her neck.

At the sight, at the feel of her hair falling away like silken honey, Walker was lost. Totally. Completely. And if he were to die on the spot, he could not have kept his lips from the ivory column laying so sweetly before him. In truth, he was already dying, dying with yearning. He brushed his mouth across her skin, then brushed her flesh again and again—cheek to chin, the hollow of her throat—until a fine fury trembled through him. Moaning, he buried his fingers in her hair, anchored her face, and crushed her mouth beneath his.

The savage beauty of his kiss tore at Lindsey's senses. Beyond thinking, beyond caring, she just wanted what Walker was giving her—himself. She didn't care what lay beyond this moment. For now, time and place forgotten, she just wanted to taste him, to touch him, to feel him. She wanted him to chase away the loneliness that dwelled within her heart. She wanted to share her over-flowing love.

At the parting of her mouth, Walker drove his tongue deep. Then deeper. Tremors sluiced across Lindsey, making her weak, making her strong, making her want. Caught up in Walker's fury, as though she had to touch all of him at once, she wrenched her mouth from his and began delivering kisses across his face, down his neck, onto the flat furry planes of his chest.

He moaned as her fingers tunneled through the thick hair; he groaned as her fingers grazed the sensitive nipple of his breast. When her lips, her tongue, found the same knotted bud, he died. Died of the most exquisite pleasure he'd ever known. Backing her against the door, his rock-hard body pinning hers, he dragged her face up to his. They stared, he at smoky-blue eyes and wet lips, she at eyes that had gone from brown to passion black. His nostrils flared with his heavy, moist breath.

"I'm sorry," she whispered. "I didn't mean—"

Walker silenced her by slipping the pad of his thumb across her lips.

"I want you," he said. "I don't know whether it's right. I don't know whether it's wrong. I really don't give a damn anymore. I just know that if this isn't what you want, you better say so now."

Her answer was simple and silent. She kissed the pad of his thumb, then drew his hand away. Angling her head, stretching, she placed her mouth on his—slowly, gently, a provocative counterbalance to the wild storm that had only seconds before raged through them. When Walker could no longer stand this sweet slaughter, he whispered something that could equally have been a prayer or a curse and scooped her into his arms.

The bedroom was dark except for the faint light of a cloud-streaked moon. Even in the misty shadows, however, shapes could be seen—Lindsey's arched neck as Walker traced it with his mouth, the wide spread of his shoulders as Lindsey clung to them, dug into them, for support, their bodies, though clothed, straining to merge, each with the other.

Accompanying the shadowy sights were muted sounds—the whispered "Oh" that trickled from Lindsey's parted lips, the soft calling of Walker's name, the urgent gasp she gave when Walker kissed her still-clothed breast. Walker, too, sang notes that filled the silence. He breathed her name, he moaned at her touch, he hissed as her hands slipped inside the waistband of his jeans.

More important than either sight or sound, however, was feeling. Hot mouth merged with hot mouth. Hand caressed hand and fevered skin. Body melded with body. Lindsey felt Walker's unsteady fingers unfastening the buttons of her blouse. Walker felt Lindsey's fingers tighten on his shoulders. Painfully tighten. Gloriously tighten. Pulling the blouse from the waist of her slacks, Walker slowly slid it from her shoulders. Moonlight dappled her skin and air, cooled from the air conditioning, flitted across her shoulders. Even so, she could feel Walker's heated gaze. It blistered her senses. It scorched her soul.

In the dusky darkness, Walker could see the lacy straps of the undergarment that had driven him crazy on more than one occasion. Running a finger beneath the thin teddy strap, he played with the fabric, feeling its softness slither over his skin. Then, with all the laziness of a new day dawning, he drew it from her shoulder. Similarly, he tugged the other strap onto the other shoulder.

The garment clung to the swells of her breasts. Walker's gaze clung to hers.

Child.

Woman.

She looked so youthful standing before him, her hair a wild, beautiful mass of gold. She looked unspoiled, virtually untouched by the harsh realities of life, and yet there was a maturity about her that couldn't be denied. Maybe it had to do with all she'd been through of late. It most definitely had something to do with the blatant way she was returning his gaze—fully, completely, like a woman who knew exactly what she wanted. And that something was him. No aphrodisiac could have been as powerful as her desire.

"Ah, Lindsey," he whispered, not trusting himself to say more.

Her eyes never leaving his, she slowly—oh, so slowly—untied first one bow, then another of the teddy. With each unfastening, the garment slipped lower and lower, revealing more and more of her breasts—the rounded swells, the gentle curves, the darkly crowned centers.

Walker's breath faded away, leaving him light-headed, dizzy. Reaching out, he drew the back of his hand across one breast. The dark center beaded, causing what little reason he had left to scatter. Lowering his head, he kissed first one breast, then the other. The taste was sweeter than honey. The taste was headier than wine. The taste practically buckled his knees. Yanking her to him, he buried the softness of her breasts into the hard planes of his chest. His mouth sought hers, saying scalding-hot things that words alone never could have. In the fervor of that kiss, in the intimate contact of their bodies, the desperate yearning, the biting desire, returned.

On a growl, his lips still on hers, Walker found the waistband of her slacks. With but one goal—removal— he wrestled the button, fought the zipper. Likewise, Lindsey unsnapped his jeans. Denim and doubt, cotton and caution, fell to the floor in a forgotten heap.

The bed sagged beneath Lindsey. She registered this only marginally, for something far greater overrode all else. Walker was beside her, his flesh touching hers, his hands seeking and finding all the feminine places that begged for his attention. Was this really happening? she thought. Or had all those nights in London, those lonely, endless nights when all she'd thought about was Walker, finally pushed her over the precarious edge? Was this only a dream?

"Walker?" she whispered, wanting, needing confirmation that this moment was real.

He spoke only with his mouth, his hands, his body. He, too, wondered if he'd once more stepped into a surreal world. But then, it didn't matter if he had. Lindsey's sweetly bold, boldly sweet kisses joined with his. She matched his passion, his desire, devouring him with her mouth. Everywhere her lips touched, he burned. Everywhere her hands roamed—his back, his hips, the heat of him—begged for more. He had no idea whether what was happening was right or wrong, but he knew without a doubt that he couldn't live another second without her.

He took her, the way a man takes a woman, the way a man takes *his* woman. He buried himself deep. She was hot and soft and, ironically, filled his emotional hollowness even as he filled her physical being. On a deep moan, he gave himself up to feeling, setting a rhythm that she lovingly, sexily followed.

The end came, but he had no idea whether it was soon or late. He knew, though, that it was like racing through time, through space. It was the powerful acceleration of a sports car. Like the wind, ecstasy whipped about him. Exhilaration raced through his veins. Speed... power... pleasure... a blissful, soul-shattering pleasure.

He cried her name.

She cried his as she, too, reached the pinnacle of pleasure.

And then peace. A peace like neither had ever felt before. A numbing, please-let-this-last-forever peace.

Lying on their sides, they peered at each other. Their bodies were yet entwined simply because neither could bear the thought of separating. Though slowing, their breathing filled the silence with a grated rasp. Lindsey could feel her mouth tingling from the bruising pressure of Walker's kisses.

Walker could feel his heart pounding. Its message was loud and clear. Nothing in his life had ever felt so right.

Lazily, he drew his knuckle across Lindsey's cheek. She laid her hand on his and, like lovers, their hands joined, palm to palm. Walker remembered the night weeks before when she'd first taken his hand in hers. The warmth of that hand had teased and taunted him, making him want to touch her again... and again... and again....

"Why did you call off the wedding?" Walker heard himself ask. The question had come out of nowhere. No, not nowhere. It had been in his mind for months, in his heart for weeks. He had to have an answer.

"Don't you know why?" Lindsey whispered.

Did he? Did he know the reason? Had it revealed itself slowly to him these past few weeks, and had he simply chosen to hide from its truth?

"Tell me," he said, needing to hear the words.

"I realized that I was in love with someone else." Lindsey smiled softly, sweetly. "That's a devil of a thing to realize on the eve of your wedding."

Walker's heart, the one that hadn't yet slowed from their lovemaking, sprinted into a new and wilder rhythm.

Lindsey's smile faded. "Actually, it wasn't as emotionally simple as it sounds. I didn't realize I was in love with someone other than my fiancé. I just knew that something went very wrong at the rehearsal. A bride-to-be shouldn't be feeling more for the man walking her down the aisle than for the man waiting for her." Lindsey's voice lowered to the sound of lace being drawn across satin. "I shouldn't have been wondering what your lips would feel like on mine."

Her confession wrapped itself around Walker, warming him as her presence did.

"I love you," she whispered. "I don't know when it happened or why it happened or how it could have happened." She smiled. "I just know that it happened."

Strangely, what she had said didn't surprise Walker. Even more strangely, he clung to her words as though they were the most precious gift he'd ever been given. He just didn't know what to answer back. He didn't know what he was feeling. His emotions were still too new to put a name to. But he had to say something. He *wanted* to say something.

"Lindsey..."

As he had earlier that evening, she now placed the pad of her thumb across his lips. "You're not required to say anything," she said, adding, her voice now husky with feeling, "just make love to me. If only for tonight."

On a dark, desperate growl, Walker hauled her to him.

Chapter Nine

At ten minutes to two o'clock, both as naked as the day they were born, Walker scooped Lindsey into his arms and started from the bedroom. He was aware, but only vaguely, that his knee hurt. The truth was that there was little room for any awareness other than that of the woman cradled against him.

Laughing even as she tightened her arms about his neck, Lindsey asked, "Where are you taking me?"

"Timbuktu," Walker said, uncertain whether he liked her best when she was laughing or when she was serious. He guessed that he liked her both ways—any way. Mostly, though, he just liked the way he felt around her. As if he were a seed that had lain dormant and was only now sprouting to life. Only Lindsey's sunshine had provided the stimulus for growth.

He tried not to think about what had happened, what was happening, between them. Lindsey had pleaded with him to give her, to give them, tonight—even if they were to have nothing else. When he thought at all, he kept his mind focused on that. Mostly, though, he kept his body occupied with feeling. Tomorrow he'd wonder if he were having the same mid-life crisis as his friend Dean. Tomorrow he'd find a name for the strong feeling that was in his heart. Tonight he'd just feel.

At Walker's answer, Lindsey laughed again. "Do you think this is the dress code in Timbuktu?"

Walker grinned as he slipped through the dark kitchen and slid open the patio door. "If it isn't, it ought to be."

The hot and humid night air swept over Lindsey's bare skin, reminding her that there was a real world beyond the idyll she and Walker were living. But she didn't want to be reminded of that. In fact, she refused to be. She concentrated instead on Walker's arms, on his hair-matted chest, on the laughter she heard in his voice. He, too, was living only in the now.

"You know something?" she said, liking his grin, loving his teasing.

"Hmm?" he asked, knowing too well that tomorrow and reality were only frustrating hours away.

"You seem different. I've known you all my life, and suddenly it's as though I've just met you." She smiled. "Does that make sense?"

Walker had been steadily heading for the pool. Slowly, carefully taking the steps, he submerged them to their waists. Cool water, turquoise and refreshing, rose around them like a quiet, untroubled sea.

"Yeah," he answered, understanding exactly what she meant. It was as though they'd met for the first time only hours before. And, in a sense, they had. Lover had only then met lover.

Lowering her, he allowed her body to skim the length of his. The hours they'd spent loving had been in the moonlight-dappled dark. Now the underwater lights illuminated their bodies in a way they had not been before. Lindsey saw the thick pelt covering his chest, the way some of the ebony hair was shaded in silver, the narrowing strip of black that led down his belly and beyond. Walker saw the creamy color of her skin, a smattering of freckles on a single shoulder, the pert fullness of her breasts. He knew the feel of those breasts—the way they filled his hands, the way the nipples tightened when he ran thumb or tongue across them, the way they flattened against him when he held her close. He knew their taste, too. Their sweeter-than-honey taste. Like a greedy man, a starving man, he now indulged himself in their visual beauty.

Lindsey luxuriated in Walker's hunger. She wanted him to look at her, just the way she wanted to look at him. She wanted to see every inch of him, memorize every inch, in case tonight was all she had of him. She wanted memories enough to fill the long, lonely nights that might lay ahead. And she wanted him to remember her. Not as his goddaughter, but as the woman who loved him.

"You are different," Walker whispered, reaching out and touching her love-tossed hair with his fingertips. "So very different."

A tiny smile budded, grew, ripened. "I grew up."

At that, he began to gently twist the blond strands of her hair about his fist. Each roll brought her closer to him until the tips of her breasts brushed against his chest. Her neck was arched, her head angled upward. "Did anyone ever tell you that you grew up in all the right places?" he said, his mouth only milli-inches from hers.

"I've been waiting all these years for you to tell me," she whispered.

He did more than tell her. He showed her. Completing the distance, he dropped his mouth onto hers. He intended the kiss to be gentle and tender, but, when flesh met flesh, his intentions scattered like crisp leaves in a chafing wind. In seconds, the kiss became hot and wet and graphically explicit. Abruptly, Walker jerked his mouth from hers. Just as abruptly, he released her hair, backed away and began to swim brisk laps.

Lindsey let him, even when one lap led into another, then into another, each delivered as though he had a surplus of energy he had to dissipate. She knew, though, that it was more than energy. It was desire. For through all that was happening—his concern, his doubt, his fear of betraying aged friendships—she knew that he desired her. She knew, too, that the extent of that desire startled him. It even frightened him.

Slowly, she began to swim, letting the cool water glide over her damp skin. She was tired. Yet exhilarated. She needed to sleep. Yet sleep was the last thing she'd be able to do. Closing her eyes, she ducked her head beneath the surface, allowing the womblike stillness, the silence, to surround her. When she resurfaced, she saw Walker slowly swimming toward her. He looked as tired, yet as wired, as she.

Using her hands, she smoothed back the wet hair from her face. By placing one hand on each side of her, Walker immediately pinned her to the edge of the pool. Without warning and forcefully, he took her mouth again—one short fierce kiss, as though to prove to himself that he was still in control.

For moments, they didn't speak. They just stared. Finally, Lindsey angled a lock of wet hair from his forehead. "Tired?" she said, her eyes fully on him.

He grinned. "A little. I'm not used to such late nights. We old folks go to bed early."

The grin Lindsey returned was pure deviltry. "You went to bed early."

"Yeah," he answered, the husky delivery of the word sending Lindsey's blood to simmering.

She lazily, sexily drew her finger down his chest. "We could go back to bed . . . and sleep."

"We could."

"Then again," she said, stopping her finger strategically short of his navel, "maybe we could find something better to do."

"I think we'd be talking about one of those miracles you're so fond of believing in. A man has his limits. An old man has even greater limits." He was aware, however, of wanting her even as he spoke of the biological practicality of the male body.

"Ah, yes, you're so old," she said, a spark of teasing lighting her eyes. "You know, I'd be glad to help you put your teeth in a glass or tune your pacemaker."

A grin nipped one corner of his mouth. "Smart aleck."

"No, really. I could push your wheelchair or adjust your hearing aid. I could even rub your bad knee."

"How did you know I had a bad knee?" Walker asked.

"You told me when you were trying to discourage my asking you to dance. But I knew about it, anyway. I know everything about you." She reached down and began to rub his knee. "The game with the Redskins, right? Some defensive back with a bad attitude creamed you on the thirty-sixth yard."

The feel of her hand on his knee was beginning to push all thoughts of football from his mind. In fact, her hand was making him believe in miracles. "I have no idea what yard it was," he said, his voice growing husky.

"It was the thirty-sixth. At least that's what an old newspaper article Mother has said."

"You looked?" he asked, feeling incredibly warm, both by her personal knowledge of him and of the way her fingers were kneading his skin.

"Mmm," she admitted, adding, "How does that feel?"

"Good," he said, his voice having gone from husky to downright thick. "However, it's the wrong knee." His grin was back. "Guess the newspaper didn't mention which knee."

Slowly, Lindsey stopped her massaging. She tried to look vexed, but the grin that kept threatening to turn up the corners of her mouth was seriously interfering. "Why didn't you tell me it was the wrong knee?"

"Why should I? I was enjoying it."

"Were you, now?" Her gray eyes had begun to twinkle, making them glitter like finely cut diamonds.

His eyes twinkled back. "Yeah. I was."

"Well, enjoy this," she said as she unexpectedly splashed a screen of water in his direction and started swimming away.

She caught him totally off guard, but then, he thought as he instinctively started in after her, that was pretty well how she'd caught him in every respect. Not only hadn't he seen her coming, he hadn't had even the smallest glimpse.

Swimming hard, he grabbed her ankle. She squealed, giggled, jerked her foot away. He reached for her again, but all he got was a handful of where she'd been. His heart was already pounding, but its tempo increased dramatically with the sudden need to touch her. How long had it been since he'd touched her? Suddenly it seemed like ten thousand forevers. Their playing took on an element of urgency.

Stretching his arms to their full extent, he kicked harder, encircled her waist with his arm and, to the accompaniment of her laughter, yanked her to him. They both slipped beneath the surface of the water, she fighting him as though he were her mortal enemy. Rolling and tumbling over each other, their bodies in intimate contact, they scrimmaged and fought, teased and played. At last, breathing became imperative. Gasping, they broke from the water.

Beads of water dampened Lindsey's face, clinging like raindrops to her thick tawny eyelashes. The same drops of moisture dewed her parted lips. Her hair, like a veil of gold, hung straight about her shoulders, making her look like a beautiful sea goddess.

Walker was equally wet. His hair streaked onto his forehead, his whisker-shadowed jaws dripped water. Runnels ran through the hair on his chest. He, too, looked like a god rising from the depths of the ocean.

At the sight of Lindsey, Walker's eyes darkened.

At the sight of Walker, Lindsey's breath quickened.

Playtime ended as abruptly as it began.

He hauled her to him, savagely taking her mouth with his. Teeth clashed, tongues probed, body collided with body in warm and wanting ways.

"I want you," she whispered, once more brazenly, truthfully proclaiming her need.

"Then take me," he whispered back, his desire as frenzied as hers.

As he spoke, he drew her legs upward, draping them about his waist even as she folded her arms about his neck. Her breasts cozied next to his chest, while his arms crisscrossed her bare back. She lay open to him, intimately open—her heart, her body. He entered her, driving himself deep. On some plane of thought, he registered the fact that the miracle wasn't that she'd aroused him again, but that each time she did a curious thing happened. Each time, he seemed to grow younger. Each time, his desire for her grew stronger.

This is madness! he thought as his body moved inside hers. A fine and rare and altogether magical madness!

A long while later, each dressed in nothing more than a towel, they lay on the chaise lounge. They were entwined in each other's arms. Overhead, gauzy clouds floated past a full silver moon.

"You're quiet," Walker said, the comment rumbling from his chest. There were only a few hours left before daylight. The night would soon be over. Their night. What would the morrow bring?

As she lay in his arms, a dark thought had crossed Lindsey's mind. She hated herself for letting the thought intrude, but found that she couldn't halt it. Any more than she could stop herself from now bringing up the subject. The pain was still there—sharp, acute, biting her to the quick.

"I wonder if Dad and the girl—pardon me, the woman—from the diner are having a similar evening."

Walker tightened his hold. "Lindsey, don't do this to yourself."

"No, I'm curious. How do men view affairs? Do you think he took her back to his place for a quickie?"

"Lindsey—"

"Or do you think she spent the night?"

"Don't do this."

"Do you think he told her he loved her, or do you think it was clearly understood that everything was just fun and games?"

"I don't think he's doing this for the fun of it. He's trying to prove something to himself."

Lindsey laughed bitterly. "So you think he gritted his teeth and refused to enjoy it?"

"I think there's a difference between temporary pleasure and longtime peace."

Lindsey wasn't placated. "Gee, next you're going to tell me that he thought about Mom the whole time."

"I think that's a real possibility."

"Then you're more naive than I am," Lindsey said, her tone revealing the anger she felt toward her father. The anger that could so easily become bitterness.

"He's been upset by your mother's going on with her life. I think her being able to stand alone took him by surprise. I think it also made him take another look at her. She may not be exactly what, or whom, he thought she was."

Lindsey sat up, sighed, and raked her fingers through her damp hair. "I don't know what to think anymore. Right now, I don't much care. If Dad wants to bed Miss Diner, let him. If he wants to run off to Timbuktu with her, let him. If Mom doesn't want to fight for him, that's her business."

"But you'd fight, right?"

Angling her head, Lindsey looked at the man stretched out beside her. "I don't know," she said honestly. "I used to think I'd fight for what I wanted no matter what, but now I just don't know. If one would rather be turned loose, what's the point of trying to hold on? If holding on is only hurting the one you love, how can you conscionably justify fighting?'' Both knew that the conversation had turned personal. Personal as in their own relationship. Lindsey now asked frankly, ''Do you want me to fight for you? Or do we just chalk this evening up to the kind my father's had?''

At the first of her questions, Walker hadn't known what to answer. Did he want her to fight for him? The second part of the question, however, he had no trouble responding to.

''No!'' he growled, yanking her back down beside him—under him. ''What happened between us is in no way comparable to what happened to your father. And don't you ever say that again! Do you hear me?''

What she heard, what he heard, too, was an answer to the first question. He wanted her to fight for him. He didn't want her to let him walk away. He didn't want her to let him turn his back on what she was offering him.

''I hear,'' she whispered only seconds before his mouth claimed hers.

''...The tropical depression, located two hundred miles southwest of Jamaica, continues to build in intensity, and weather forecasters predict that it will start to organize over the next twenty-four to forty-eight hours. The depression is currently being plotted on a northwest course which may strike the western tip of Cuba. This storm has the potential to be a threat to the Texas and Louisiana Gulf Coast....''

Walker listened to the radio over the sound of sizzling bacon. Beyond that he could hear the shower running. He hadn't slept a wink. Not one. Lindsey had slept precious little more. At a little after five, she'd drifted off to sleep in his arms, cuddling up to him in a way that had stolen his heart. He'd simply held her, wondering what in hell was happening to him, wondering where they went from there.

Still no answer and careful not to wake her, he had crawled from bed at six o'clock. Only minutes before, it had begun to sprinkle, a fact which didn't surprise him in the least because his knee hurt like someone was pounding it with a hammer. Slipping on his jeans and nothing more, he'd quietly taken Lindsey's car keys from her purse and gone out to make sure the car windows were rolled up. On a whim, he'd pulled the car into the garage. He didn't analyze why. He just knew that it had something to do with wanting to keep their night secret from any curious eyes. Returning to the house, he turned on the radio and put on some breakfast. Something—perhaps the radio, perhaps the smell of perking coffee, perhaps his absence—had awakened Lindsey, for shortly thereafter he'd heard the shower.

A thousand thoughts ran through his mind. What would they say to each other? What did he want to say? What did he want her to say? She had said she loved him, but had it only been the madness of the night? Would the same words tumble from her lips by day? And what was he feeling for her? What name should he put to the strong feelings dancing through his heart? Along with these questions came the more practical question of whether or not Dean knew about the possible storm. And what would his best friend say if he knew that he'd spent the night making love to his daughter? He couldn't even begin to fathom an answer to this last one.

Turning the bacon, he opened the refrigerator and removed the juice jar. He poured two glasses, one of which ran over the rim. Wiping up the orange puddle with a wet rag, he then washed the rag out under the faucet. In lieu of a dish towel, he swiped his damp hands down the legs of his jeans. The top button lay unfastened, forming a vee low on his stomach. He'd just reached for a couple of eggs when he heard yet another sound. It was the sound of a brisk knock on the back door seconds before the door flew open.

"Good, you're up," Dean said, storming into the kitchen the way he had a hundred times before over the years.

Walker dropped one of the eggs. It went splat on the kitchen floor.

"Sorry, I didn't mean to startle you," Dean said. He was wearing cutoff shorts, a shirt that needed pressing and sunglasses even though not a sliver of sun peeked through the clouds. In fact, the sprinkling had evolved into a steady drizzle.

Walker said nothing. He simply stared at his friend—and listened to the shower. He did have the presence of mind to put down the other egg before it suffered a fate similar to the first.

Whipping off his sunglasses, Dean grabbed a rag and started to clean up the mess. "I didn't know whether you'd be up." Without giving Walker a chance to comment, he added, "Have you heard about the storm in the Gulf?"

Storm? Walker fought at a hysterical laugh. The storm in the Gulf was nothing compared to the storm about to break in his kitchen!

"Dammit, I hope we don't have to evacuate the platforms," Dean said.

Squatting down as he was, Walker noted, in the idle way that one does the color of the guillotine before the blade falls, that his friend was developing a bald spot to go along with his receding hairline. Dean hadn't tried to cover it up, which maybe was why Walker was noticing it now. It left Dean looking old. Dean also looked tired, as in having been up half the night. He didn't, however, look like a man who'd stayed up having a good time. Instead, he look worried.

Worried?

Walker glanced in the direction of his bedroom. The shower was still running. Thank God! Walker knew, though, that his time was borrowed.

"Look—" Walker began.

"Geez, you're burning the bacon!" Dean said, throwing the egg-stained rag into the sink and yanking the skillet off the fire. Snakelike streams of smoke billowed upward. "Man, what's wrong? You're the one who does mornings, not me."

In the silence, the shower sounded deafening, like a waterfall going over a steep cliff.

As clearly as a spring stream flows, Walker saw realization dawn on his buddy. "Ah, man, I'm sorry. My timing is lousy. It just never crossed my mind that you had a woman here. I had that storm on my mind, and I was up...couldn't sleep...so I thought I'd come on over...."

Walker heard the shower stop. His heart stopped along with it.

"I'll call you later," Walker said, herding his friend toward the door.

"Yeah, sure," Dean said, adding as he nodded toward the bedroom, "Anyone special?"

"Uh...look, let's talk later, huh?" Walker said, opening the back door.

"Right...sure...I gotcha," Dean said, allowing himself to be almost physically ejected from the house.

"We'll talk later. Hey, wait," Dean said, holding on to the door frame, "are you going into the office later?"

Office? What office? Walker had to force himself to think straight. How long did it take a woman to get out of the shower and into her clothes? Or—holy hell!—what if she came in in nothing at all? He wouldn't put it past Lindsey. Not after last night. Walker deliberately positioned himself between Dean and the now crack in the door. "Maybe...maybe not...I don't know."

Dean grinned. "That hot, huh?"

Yeah, Walker thought, but said nothing. "I'll, uh, I'll talk to you later."

Walker closed the door on his friend's muffled "All right" and leaned back. His heart, the one that had stopped earlier, was now pounding a mile a minute, and he'd broken out in a sweat that had nothing to do with the early-morning heat. His legs felt rubbery and useless. Finally, on a deep sigh he pushed from the door. He was midway in the room when the back door was once more flung open.

"My sunglasses!" Dean said, making a hurried dash for the cabinet. He had just picked them up when the world came to an abrupt halt.

"Good morn—Daddy!" Lindsey cried.

It would have been hard to say, Walker thought, which of the two—Dean or Lindsey—looked more startled. Each just stared at the other, as if neither quite believed the other's presence. Walker understood their disbelief. He, too, was bogged down in his own. Surely this wasn't really happening. Surely he was only dreaming. Surely Lindsey couldn't have looked more seductive if she had come into the kitchen totally nude.

She wore one of his shirts, a pastel plaid shirt that he'd had on the day before. The shirt draped her braless breasts in a way that was more than alluring, more than suggestive. The garment then fell to just below her knees, which would have provided adequate cover, had it not been sculpted on the sides, thereby revealing a tantalizing glimpse of her thighs. Her bare feet and the fact that her hair was pulled back in a ponytail once more emphasized her youth. It was a youthfulness instantly negated, however, by the question that raced through Walker's mind: Was she wearing the tiny scrap of lace she called panties? Either way, whether she was or wasn't, played havoc with his masculine senses—even under the harrowing circumstances.

"W-what are you doing here?" Lindsey asked, breaking the silence that ominously hovered over the room. Instinctively, she folded her arms across her chest. The action only emphasized the bare state of her breasts.

"I could ask you that same question," Dean said. When Lindsey made no reply, he added, "Tell me that this isn't what it looks like."

Walker recognized his friend's desperate tone. Dean didn't want to believe what he was seeing and was pleading with them to give him a rational explanation. Forget rational. He'd settle for any explanation. Dark rivers of regret flowed through Walker at the pain he knew he and Lindsey were about to inflict. It was a pain he never wanted to inflict. He tried to imagine the situation reversed. How would he feel if Lindsey were his daughter and he'd found Dean and Lindsey together? But he couldn't. In his wildest imaginings, he couldn't.

Suddenly, Dean raked his fingers through his hair, comically laying the bald spot even more bare. "For God's sake, what's going on here?"

Lindsey looked over at Walker. Walker looked over at Lindsey. Something in her eyes said that she didn't regret a single minute of what had happened between them. That fact gave Walker courage.

"Dean," he said, hesitated, then added, "I swear to God I didn't see this coming."

Dean laughed harshly. "You seduce my daughter and you didn't see it coming!"

"Now, wait a minute," Lindsey said. "If anyone seduced anyone, I seduced him. He didn't want to get involved. I was the one who pushed the issue."

"You don't know what you're saying, honey," Dean said, clearly having trouble seeing his daughter as a seductress. Walker suspected that any father would have the same problem.

"It's true," Lindsey said, looking over at Walker and smiling ruefully. "I shamelessly pursued him. And I don't regret it," she added, transferring her gaze to her father, "even if it means upsetting you."

At her open admission that she didn't regret their loving, a knot formed in Walker's throat. He realized that he wouldn't have been able to withstand it if she had regretted their evening together. The few hours they had spent in each other's arms had become a precious interlude in his life.

"I don't regret it, either," Walker said softly, drawing Lindsey's eyes back to him. The world compressed until it was only the two of them—only him, only her, only the memories they shared. He wanted to take her in his arms. She wanted it, too; he could see her need in her smoky-blue eyes. Reluctantly drawing his gaze away, he once more found his friend. "I knew what I was doing. It might have been Lindsey's idea originally, but I didn't resist too hard."

"I'll just bet," Dean said with a sneer.

Like a beast of a dog, the remark bit Walker, making him bleed from the heart. "I don't deserve that."

"The hell you don't! You seduce my daughter—"

"I told you, he didn't seduce me!"

"Okay, maybe I do deserve it! Hell, I don't know! I've wrestled with this until I don't know anything anymore."

"You sure knew enough to know how to take advantage of Lindsey! How could you do this to me and her mother? We trusted you." The pain of betrayal was obvious.

"I told you he didn't take advantage of me."

Neither man seemed to be listening to her. "I know," Walker said. "I haven't taken any of this lightly. Believe me. I haven't forgotten my friendship with the two of you. I'm just asking you to cut me some slack. The way I'd cut you some. Just give me some time to try to explain—"

"Explain, hell! What's there to explain?"

"Plenty, if you'll just—"

"Will you two stop it?" Lindsey screamed. Into the sudden silence, Lindsey said, "Will you two just stop it?"

Walker let out a long weary sigh as he dragged his hand across his face. Dean held his ground, his position somewhere between hurt and anger. Lindsey tilted her chin a fraction in defiance.

"How dare you barge in here," she said to her father, "and start making accusations and assumptions. Especially since that's what you've been so eager to chastise me about ever since I got home. You've made it more than clear that I have no right to judge you. And now here you are judging me. And Walker."

"It's different," Dean protested.

"It's not different. And, furthermore, I resent your implication that what's gone on between Walker and me is dirty. It isn't. I'm in love with him. I have been for a long while. Walker's the reason I didn't marry Ken."

"My God, this has been going on for a year and a half?"

Lindsey gave a sigh of total exasperation. "Daddy, will you use some common sense? I've been in England. I needed some time to sort out my feelings. I haven't taken this lightly, either. This isn't some wild weekend fling. And you can't blame Walker. He had no idea of my feelings until I returned home."

Dean shook his head. "I don't believe this. You're in love with the man who's practically been a father to you. My God, he *is* your godfather."

"Yes, I'm in love with him," Lindsey said calmly, impressing Walker with her serenity, her maturity.

Dean turned to Walker, who was leaning back against the cabinet as though he needed some support. "And what about you? Are you in love with her?"

"Daddy, that's none of your business—"

"That's all right, Lindsey," Walker said, fully aware that she was trying to keep him from being put on a spot.

He hadn't said he loved her. Not once during the night. In fact, she'd halted him from making any comment after her declaration of love. It was obvious that she'd wanted to give him time. He had needed to give himself that, too. At least, he'd thought he had. But now, when the question was put so bluntly, the answer seemed as obvious as the rain striking the windowpanes.

"Yes," he said as he looked Dean square in the eyes, "I love your daughter. I don't know when it happened. A week ago, last night, a minute ago—I don't know when. I only know that it did. I only know that standing here now, I can honestly say I love her." He glanced up, his eyes finding Lindsey's. Even as he watched, hers glazed with tears. "I know, babe. My timing's lousy."

They stared—each at the other. Walker could see her visibly controlling her tears. He could see her lips trembling with her unsteady breath. He could *feel* her love. God, he wanted her in his arms! He wanted her beneath him! He just wanted her!

Into this emotional warmth, Dean dropped the cool comment, "My God, Walker, have you gone absolutely crazy? She's young enough to be your daughter!"

Slowly, Lindsey turned toward her father. A regal coolness, like a frosty mantle, settled about her. "Let me understand you. It's all right to have an affair with a younger woman, but it's not all right to fall in love with one?"

"I never said it was all right to have an affair—"

"I came by your apartment last night. You weren't alone."

Dean Ellison turned a sickly shade of green. That was quickly eclipsed by a red anger. "How dare you spy on me!"

Quicker than lightning, all the bottled-up anger exploding within her, Lindsey reached out and slapped her father. "How dare you cheat on my mother!" she raged.

Walker saw stunned disbelief cross Dean's face. He saw, too, that Lindsey had startled herself as much as she'd startled her father. This was evinced by her hand, which flew immediately to her mouth. The hand trembled. Instant contrition jumped into her eyes, though no words of apology filled the silence. That was filled only with the echo of her slap. Slowly, suddenly, Dean shoved on his sunglasses and started for the door. He said not a single word.

Neither did Walker.

Or Lindsey.

He simply took her in his arms and held her until her trembling stopped.

Chapter Ten

Walker loved her.

That fact alone got Lindsey through the next twenty-four hours. Walker insisted that they tell her mother about them. Lindsey concurred but, after her father's response, was worried sick at what her mother's reaction would be. In the end, Bunny was shocked, but not unresponsive. She asked them to give her a little time to adjust to the idea. After Walker left, having given Lindsey a slow kiss at the door, Bunny asked her daughter what she and her father had fought about.

"What do you mean?" Lindsey had asked, even more uncomfortable, if that were possible, with this new turn in the conversation. So uncomfortable was she that she stood and walked about the den of her parents' home. She tried to sound nonchalant as she looked here and there at objects that had been familiar since childhood—the small teacup and saucer that had belonged to her maternal grandmother, a cut-crystal vase that had held a fieldful of flowers over the years, a gilt-framed picture of the three of them, she, her mother and her father, smiling.

"I just heard rumblings that you and your father had words."

Lindsey looked away from the photo. Her father's happy face, the one she'd slapped, mocked her. "He wasn't altogether happy with the news about me and Walker." Lindsey laughed brittlely. "Actually, that's putting it mildly."

"Was that all you fought about?"

"Give or take," Lindsey said, hedging.

Bunny, each strand of hair once more in place, her makeup impeccably applied, hesitated only slightly before saying, "Did you fight about the fact that your father's having an affair?"

It had been Lindsey's turn to be shocked, a fact revealed by the widening of her eyes. "You know?"

Nodding her head, Bunny said simply, softly, "Yes."

"But how?"

"A woman just knows. Oh, not that I didn't turn a blind eye in the beginning. I did. But I couldn't run from the fact forever. It hit me hard. I kept thinking that if I'd just done something differently, your father wouldn't have needed another woman." Bunny smiled, a sad curving of her mouth. "If I'd just combed my hair one more time, if I'd just worn a prettier dress, if I'd just served homemade rolls more often."

"That's absurd—"

"Of course it is. And Don helped me to see that. Your father has a problem, Lindsey. He's scared to death at the idea of growing older. I don't know why. He probably doesn't know, either. He just is. But the truth is that I have a problem, too. One of self-image. I've allowed myself to be your father's shadow. I don't want that anymore. I want to find out who Bunny Ellison is. That goal in mind, I've decided to get some counseling."

Lindsey made the mental note that, should she ever meet this illusive Don, she owed him a thank-you. "That's good, Mom. Real good."

"And a divorce, if that's what your father wants. But," she added, "if he comes to his senses, I'm at least willing to talk to him about a future." She smiled. "He's acted like a jerk, but I'm still in love with him. At least that much I know for sure about Bunny Ellison."

The women had parted on a hug—not a mother-daughter hug, but a woman-to-woman hug, which silently said that women, all down through the ages, had been the preservers of relationships. It said, too, that, although Bunny would need time to come to terms with Lindsey and Walker's relationship, she was at least willing to make the effort, that she, as a woman, respected the heart's choice of a mate. However atypical, however imprudent that choice might be.

That conversation had occurred Saturday afternoon. Saturday evening, Walker and Lindsey had dinner at his house. It appeared that their personal lives might have to be shelved for a while.

"...The depression is now officially being called a storm. With winds of growing intensity, the storm is organizing quickly and continuing to move in a southwestern direction. It is believed, as predicted earlier, that it's headed for the tip of Cuba. Should it strike there, it would lose some of its power before streaking on into the Gulf. In either event, whether it strikes Cuba or not, it could mean trouble for the Gulf Coast..."

"What do you think?" Lindsey asked, seeing Walker's frown of concern. They were sitting at the dining room table. The dinner, which they'd prepared together amid laughter and kisses, was finished. Steaming mugs of coffee had replaced it.

"I think it's too early to tell," Walker said, sipping his coffee. "We should know something by morning, though."

"What's the procedure for evacuating a platform?"

"Batten it down as best you can, get the men off and into inland motels. Your father coordinates the on-site evacuation. I take care of inland responsibilities, like lining up motel rooms, renting boats, extra helicopters—whatever's needed."

At the mention of her father, pain crossed Lindsey's face. In an attempt to hide it, she stood, scraped her food scraps onto Walker's plate, and carried both to the kitchen. At the sink, she ran water and began to wash dishes. No sooner had she submerged them than she felt Walker wrap his arms about her waist.

"I know, babe."

Closing her eyes, she leaned back into him. She knew that tears were only a permission away, but she wouldn't give herself that permission.

"I slapped him," she said. "We've hardly even had cross words over the years, and I slapped him. Oh, Walker, did you see the look on his face?"

What he saw was that Lindsey was hurting. Badly. "He'll survive, you'll survive, there'll be a tomorrow for apologies."

"I don't know—"

"I do. He loves you, Lindsey. Don't ever doubt that."

"But I hurt him."

"A parent's love is unconditional. Besides, he hurt you, too."

She turned in his arms, her eyes meeting his. "He hurt you, as well."

"Yeah," Walker said flatly, "but then I hurt him. I guess we'll find out how unconditional a friend's love is."

"I'm sorry," she whispered. "I'm sorry I was the one to come between you two."

Walker brushed back a wisp of hair from her cheek. "Don't be. What you've given me is worth any price I had to pay. Besides, don't you think I'm sorry about coming between you and your father?"

"Don't be," she said, repeating his words. "What you've given me is worth any price I had to pay. Tell me you love me," she said suddenly, as though fearful that she'd only imagined his having said the words. A dozen times over the past twenty-four hours, she'd made a similar request.

With the same indulgent tenderness he always displayed, he brushed her mouth with his. "I love you," he said, saying it over and over, "I love you...I love you...."

He grazed her mouth again, then, moaning, settled his lips firmly against hers. The kiss instantly deepened. Her arms, bubbles of detergent still on her hands, encircled his neck. His hips, clothed in khaki slacks, pressed into hers, pushing her back into the cabinet. His thighs melted into hers. His masculinity, steel-hard against her softness, left little doubt as to what was on his mind.

"Do you really want to wash dishes?" he asked throatily.

"Do you have a better suggestion?" she asked, thinking that, if he didn't, she sure did.

"Oh, yeah," he said, scooping her into his arms and starting for the bedroom. "I've got a suggestion that'll blow washing dishes right out of the water."

In minutes, he had proven his claim. His body, his breath, words of exulted praise flowed over her, making her feel heated, satisfied, complete in a way she'd never felt before. They kissed, caressed, scaled sensual mountains and descended into erotic valleys. They loved. Later, their bodies replete, they cuddled.

"Your idea was definitely better than washing dishes," she purred, lacing her long silken legs with his.

He grinned, entwining his hair-roughed legs with hers. "I thought you'd think so. I also have another excellent idea."

"What?"

"Stay the night."

She grinned. "Why, Mr. Carr, is that a proposition?"

He grinned. "Yeah, and a totally improper one at that." Suddenly, his grin faded as he slipped his hand onto her belly. Her skin felt like velvet, the hair cupping her femininity, like golden fleece. "Lindsey, you know that I'm not taking any precautions against your getting pregnant. I'm assuming neither are you. If you're not, don't you think we should?"

"But I want to have your baby. Okay, maybe not for a while. We'll get used to being husband and wife, then—" She stopped at the streak of pain that darted across his eyes. "Oh, my," she said quietly, hollowly, "have I made a reckless assumption?"

"Lindsey, babe, I..." He hesitated, trying to find a way to explain what he was feeling, thinking. When no words came, he felt her pulling from him. He panicked and held her all the closer. Even so, he knew a part of her had left him. "No, don't go," he pleaded. "Please just listen to me, Lindsey. I want to marry you. I want you to have my baby...."

"...But..." she said, anticipating his next word.

"It wouldn't be fair to you."

"Making me deliriously happy wouldn't be fair?"

"May-December marriages always have a strike against them."

"This would hardly be a May-December marriage. You're not ancient, Walker. Forty-six isn't ancient."

"Forty-seven."

"Excuse me, forty-seven. But that's not exactly over-the-hill, either."

"It may not be over-the-hill, but it's standing on the top looking down." At the argument he saw forming on Lindsey's lips, Lindsey's melon-sweet lips, he said, "Okay, okay. So it wouldn't be May-September. It would still have so few guarantees...."

This time she did pull from him, staring him full in the eyes. "A marriage never has a guarantee. You know that. If you need a case in point, look at my parents. Age-wise, they're compatible and look at the mess they're in."

"I know there are no guarantees, Lindsey, but look at this reasonably. When I'm sixty, you'll be thirty-six. When I'm seventy, you'll be forty-six. I'll be old, Lindsey, and you'll still be in the prime of your life."

"And when you're a hundred and ten, I'll be eighty-six. Okay, say you don't make it to a hundred and ten. Say I don't make it to eighty-six. Couldn't we just be happy we had twenty, thirty, thirty-five years together? With the divorce rate being what it is, that's more than most married couples ever get. And as far as parenting goes, older parents make wonderful parents. They have so much to offer a child."

"Yeah," he said sarcastically. "They can watch someone else pitch balls to their son instead of pitching them themselves."

"That's a crock and you know it. Many men are active into their sixties, even their seventies. You'd have plenty of time to pitch balls. What's the real issue here, Walker? You just don't want to start over with a family again? I mean, I could understand that. You've raised your child. Maybe you don't want—"

"No!" he said so vehemently that it startled Lindsey. "That isn't it. It should be, but it isn't. I've raised my kid, I've paid my dues, and that should be enough, but..." He stopped. When he spoke again, it was with reverence. "I can't think of anything I'd like more than your having my baby."

"Then what is it?" When he said nothing, she said, though it was obviously painful to do so, "You don't love me enough to commit yourself permanently?"

"Dammit, no, that's not it! Haven't you heard anything I've been saying?"

"Yes, but it's not making a whole lot of sense," she said, her voice as angry as his.

"It's simple. I want to be fair to you!"

"You keep saying that, but what does it mean?"

"It means that I have to leave you free." His voice had lowered, as though he were having trouble saying the words when he added, "Free to make changes if you need to."

Lindsey heard the words. She even understood them, but something deep within her rejected them so violently that she had to ask for clarification. "Free to make what changes?"

"Any changes...that you need to." The words had seemed even harder for him to say this second time.

"Changes. Changes like walking away from you when I grow tired of being with you? Changes like moving on to greener pastures when I find them? Changes like leaving you behind when I find a younger man?"

Walker swallowed. "Lindsey, you're so young. You've got so much living ahead of you."

"Were those the kinds of changes you were talking about?" she insisted. When he said nothing, she cried, "Were they?"

"Yes!" For seconds, neither spoke. He simply stared at the way the sheet cupped her breasts. The breathtaking way. She stared at the way the sheet fell away from his chest, a chest that seemed just the width and breadth of her needs. Finally, Walker said, "I'll stay with you for today, for tomorrow, for however long in the future you want."

"But you won't marry me?"

He couldn't imagine the courage it would take to let her walk away from him, but it was a courage he knew he could find if he had to. For her sake. "Lindsey, babe—"

"How dare you belittle what I feel for you," she said, unable to conceal her now full-blown anger. Flinging the sheet from her, she scooted to the edge of the bed. She reached for her blouse and began to scramble into it.

"Lindsey, don't," he said, reaching for her. She shrugged, deflecting his touch, and scooped her panties and jeans from the floor. She thrust her legs into the scrap of lace, adjusted her hips, and tugged them upward. She then tackled the denim.

"You know what it sounds like to me?" she tossed back over her shoulder. "It sounds like you just haven't made a big enough commitment."

"That isn't true—"

"Being in love is like being pregnant. You can't be just a little bit. You either are or you aren't." Standing, she yanked the jeans upward and slipped into her shoes. She turned to face him. The hair that Walker had so thoroughly mussed only a short while before lay scattered about her face. She looked like a fierce lioness. "And when you're in love, Walker, you commit all the way. You take all the chances. You don't compromise. And you damned sure don't leave your partner free to walk away!"

With that, she stormed from the room.

"Lindsey, wait—Lindsey!" Cursing, he fell back against the headboard. A shaft of pain, like a thick stake, pierced his heart. He longed desperately to go back and repeat the scene. Surely he could have handled it better. Surely he could have found more expressive words. Couldn't he have? As the lonely evening wore on, the only thing he knew with certainty was that, even if the scene miraculously could have been repeated, he could not have changed his position.

He had to leave her free.

Because he loved her.

The storm worsened.

To complicate matters, the storm did not conform to meteorologists' expectations. It bypassed Cuba entirely before barging into the Gulf at speeds greater than anticipated. The whole Gulf Coast lay defenseless against its fury, and weathermen went wild trying to forecast where it would strike. Hour by hour, the storm changed direction. That variance necessitated that evacuation procedures be started. No place was safe until the storm had chosen its victim.

The storm at sea, however, couldn't hold a candle to the storm raging in the office of Gal-Tex. Walker, who once more hadn't slept a wink, came in at a little before seven. He felt far older than his forty-seven years, and his knee hurt abominably. The drizzle of the day before, now responding to the approaching storm, had turned into a steady, lightning-laced downpour. From the moment he opened the door to find Lindsey seated behind her desk, the emotional storm had erupted.

"What are you doing here? It's Sunday," Walker said.

At the sight of her, he felt as though his breath had been sucked from his chest. She hadn't slept any better than he. That was obvious from the dark circles beneath her eyes. Ironically, it was her age that was an issue, her age that was the wedge driven between them. If they had many more nights like the last, the age difference might cease to be a problem. She looked as though years—hard years—had been added to her. He fought the urge to say to hell with common sense and ask—no, beg—her to marry him.

He looked awful, Lindsey thought, wanting to rush to him and throw herself into his arms. But she didn't, because in his arms was the only place more painful than not being in his arms. It was painful because it felt wonderful, yet didn't offer the permanence she wanted, needed. She had gone all the way in loving him. He had to go the same distance or there would never be a future for them. Even though it hurt like the devil, she could not, would not, settle for less than his whole.

"I thought you could use some help with the storm moving in. I'm assuming you are evacuating the platforms."

"Yeah," he confirmed. "All four of them. I talked with your father about a half hour ago. He's coming by for a roster of the men aboard each rig and then he's going to begin the evacuation." Walker didn't bring up how strained the conversation had been. The two men had had no choice, however, but to talk. After all, business was business. More importantly, the safety of their employees was involved.

Lindsey steeled herself against the mention of her father. That he was due in any minute set her stomach to doing flip-flops. "Where are the rosters?" she asked, pushing back her chair in preparation to gathering the needed material.

"File cabinet," Walker said, "But I'm not sure how Gerri files them. It might take a miracle to find them." Miracle. Walker idly wondered if Lindsey still believed so freely in miracles. After a few sobering rounds with reality, miracles were never taken for granted.

Walker was uncertain whether or not she'd read his mind, but she responded with a firm, "I'll find them."

And she did after a couple of aborted tries. She had just placed the files on Walker's desk when the door opened. In came a gust of wind and rain. Followed by Dean. He looked as ravaged as the weather, and it came to Lindsey as plain as day that her father wasn't a happy man. Their tiff notwithstanding, he wasn't a happy man. Why had she never noticed that before? Maybe she'd been filled to the brim with her own unhappiness, her own anger, concerning her parents' separation. Maybe there just hadn't been room for her to really see her parents. Something Walker said came back to her, something about pleasure and peace not being the same things. In regard to the affair, maybe her father had been questing after a pleasure that had brought him everything but peace.

Everyone—Walker, Dean, Lindsey—started to speak, but no one got past the first syllable. Everyone waited for someone else to break the ice. In the silence, Walker realized just how much he'd lost. He'd lost the best friend he'd ever had, the best friend he would ever have. That realization saddened him. As for Lindsey, she wanted to apologize to her father for slapping him, but she didn't. She wasn't quite certain why, except that apologies were never easy to make. Then, too, he'd hurt her. Maybe she was holding out for his apology.

Finally, Dean, who'd made no attempt to dress youthfully, said, "I came by for the rosters."

"Here they are," Walker said, passing them to his business partner.

Dean took them, his eyes only fleetingly holding Walker's. He seemed even less capable of looking at his daughter. After initial eye contact, he didn't glance back at Lindsey. Even so, he could not have failed to notice how tired she looked.

"Is everything lined up?" Dean asked, needlessly thumbing through the pages of the first roster.

"Yeah. I've got boats headed for each platform, and I'll make motel arrangements right away."

"Platforms One, Two and Three are less manned," Dean said. "I don't think they have more than about twenty-five men on board each, so I'm heading out to Four. It's got close to forty men."

"That sounds like a good idea."

"You got an ETA for the boats?" Dean asked.

"They should be in position by noon."

"Good. We ought to have everyone on land by nightfall."

"If the storm waits until tomorrow to come ashore, which is what they're predicting, we'll be in good shape."

"Yeah," Dean said. "If."

"Are they still saying that it's traveling more westerly than easterly?"

"That's what they're saying, but you know how it is. Sometimes what you least expect happens."

All three people within the room knew that the conversation had changed direction. All three people knew that he referred to the discovery he'd made the day before.

Walker said nothing.

Lindsey said nothing.

Dean turned to go.

"Daddy?" Lindsey called.

The big-shouldered man turned back, his gaze going to his daughter. Walker was certain that each was going to blurt out an apology, but in the end, neither did. Lindsey said simply, "Be careful."

Her father didn't even say that much. He nodded briskly, abruptly, then walked to the door and disappeared in a squall of rain.

Lindsey wanted to weep.

That desire increased as the morning wore on, for it was obvious that, although Lindsey and Walker were working well together on the surface, below that surface, like electricity hidden within a wire, ran a tension thick and hot. It was in every expression, every gesture, every look each tried not to make, but couldn't help. It was there when Lindsey, on her way back to her desk from the filing cabinet, glanced over at Walker. It was there when Walker chose the same moment to look up at her as he spoke on the telephone.

Their gazes locked.

I want to be in your arms, she seemed to say.

I want you in my arms, he seemed to return.

Then, why are we arguing? Why can't we just love each other and trust in that love to last until tomorrow? Why can't we marry and have babies and—

God, don't you think I want to, but—

"What?" he said suddenly into the receiver. "Oh, yeah. Yeah, that's fine. We'll take the block of thirty rooms." At the hurt he'd seen in Lindsey's eyes, he lowered his. A pain jabbed at his heart, just as a pain stabbed at his knee. He grimaced, thinking that he could at least rub the pain in his knee.

As the hours ticked by, the tension mounted. A hint of lace, the brush of their hands as she passed him a mug of coffee, the gloss of her lips—each left Walker degrees more frustrated, while Lindsey grew increasingly restless with the way spirals of black hair peeked from the vee of his shirt, the way his jeans became creased in all the right places, the way his hair looked rowdy with all the wayward flights of his fingers. She, too, became conscious of Walker's aching knee. Why else would he rub it so consistently? On the other hand, Walker noticed that Lindsey was growing more tired by the hour. Had she really slept as badly as he, which was to say not at all?

And the phone rang constantly, prickling nerves that were already frayed.

"Good God!" Walker barked when the phone rang just as he was hanging up from another call.

"Most of the calls are checking on the men," Lindsey said. "Their loved ones want to know if they're being moved from the rigs."

Walker knew he'd be making the same call if he were in their shoes, but the ringing of the phone was cutting through his skull, making him wonder which hurt the worse, his head or his knee. Searching through his desk, he found two Tylenol and, standing, walked to the water cooler. He downed them in a single gulp.

"...They should be on land by tonight," Lindsey told the caller. "Yes, ma'am," she added, consulting her notes, "he'll be at the Holiday Inn in Beaumont. Yes, ma'am, that number is..." Lindsey gave the number, then hung up. She sighed. "You got two more of whatever you took?"

"Yeah," Walker said, drawing another cup of water, which he handed to her. He then started to his desk for the medicine.

"Does your knee hurt?" Lindsey asked softly.

Walker glanced up. He tossed her the plastic bottle, which she easily caught.

"Yeah," he answered her question. For a fraction of a second, he thought she might ask him if he wanted her to rub it—the way she'd rubbed it Friday night, or maybe it was Saturday morning. The hours had blurred into a single blissful ecstasy. For a fraction of a second, he was afraid. What would he answer if she did ask? Would he have the courage to say no? She didn't ask, however, though it was obvious that her thoughts traveled the same pathway as his.

Lindsey felt the coolness of the water as they'd stood in the swimming pool—naked. She felt the nearness of Walker's body. She heard him saying, a teasing quality to his voice, that she had the wrong knee. She remembered splashing him, the mock fight that had ensued, the erotic ending of that fight.

I want you, she could hear herself saying breathlessly.

Then take me, she could hear him answering back.

She could feel her legs being drawn about his waist. She could feel him entering her—not slowly, but hard and possessively. She could feel...she could feel her body growing hot. She was suddenly aware that he was watching her—as intently as she was watching him.

Walker remembered the coolness of the water, her massaging his knee—the wrong knee—her splashing him with water and then her fleeing from him. Chase. Capture. Carnal reward. He felt his body responding to the erotic memory.

Flinging himself into his desk chair, he growled, "Would you get your father? I need to talk to him."

Five minutes later, Lindsey was patched through to Jim Ramsey, the foreman of Platform Four. It took her only seconds to discover that her father hadn't arrived.

"He isn't there yet," Lindsey relayed to Walker.

He glanced at his watch. It was almost forty-five minutes past the time he'd expected Dean to arrive on site. Even so, he felt no alarm. Obviously, Dean hadn't left when he'd planned to. Picking up the phone, Walker said, "Jim?"

"Yes, sir?"

"Tell Dean to give me a call when he arrives."

"Yes, sir."

"How's the weather?"

"Raining hard with a lot of wind, but so far things aren't too bad."

"We want to get ya'll out before it gets bad."

"Well, you won't get any argument here. The boat arrived at noon and is just about ready to depart."

"Good. What's the condition of the sea?"

"Choppy. Look, me and a couple of others are gonna wait for Mr. Ellison and send the others on inland. There're a few more things we want to fasten down here on the rig."

"Okay. Dean should be there any minute."

"Right. I'll have him call."

But he didn't call. Not in a few minutes. Not in thirty of them. Not in forty-five.

"Do you think he's all right?" Lindsey asked.

"Oh, yeah," Walker said. "In this weather the flight's probably taking longer than usual. And we don't even know that he left on time. Or maybe he decided to fly to another platform first, after all. He's okay."

Walker hoped he sounded believable and, in truth, he did believe what he was saying. It was just that he couldn't shake this funny feeling he had. Exactly an hour later, he could deny the feeling no longer. He called Jim Ramsey again. With repetitive results. Dean hadn't arrived on the island.

"Maybe we should call and see if he left on time," Lindsey said, clearly worried, though trying to minimize it. Even to herself. Mostly to herself.

"Let's give him another thirty minutes," Walker said.

Tacitly, Lindsey agreed. And tried to busy herself with the work on her desk. Surely her father was all right. He'd flown dozens of these trips. In fact, he'd flown far riskier missions in Vietnam, or so she'd been told. The war was only history to her. The fact was that her father was a cool flyer and more than competent. And she was just trying to find something to worry about!

Standing, she said, "I'll be in the bathroom a minute."

Walker nodded, thinking she looked even more tired, if that were possible, and that that funny little feeling, the one that insisted on worrying about Dean, was dying away. For heaven's sake, Dean was one of the best pilots he'd ever known! And the weather wasn't that bad yet. If the two of them weren't at loggerheads, Walker would tell Dean, when he finally called, about his concern, and Dean would feign anger that Walker had even doubted his abilities for the shortest of seconds. Under the circumstances, Walker probably wouldn't tell him...or maybe he would. Hell, maybe it was the light note they needed to begin dissipating some of the darkness of the last few hours.

When the phone rang, Walker was feeling brighter, more hopeful, than he had in a while. "Gal-Tex," he said, leaning back and peering out the window into the late-summer rain. The brightness tarnished in the wake of the words he heard.

Lindsey walked back into the room just as Walker was replacing the phone. She knew that something was wrong the moment she saw Walker's face. Her heart dropped at her feet.

"What is it?"

Walker hesitated, then said, "Your father." He hesitated again. It was only for seconds, but Lindsey thought it might well have been the passage of days. "His helicopter's missing."

Chapter Eleven

Rain, driven by the rising wind, slanted downward from a scowling sky. Occasionally lightning zigzagged, illuminating the stormy darkness as though it were a stage to be spotlighted for an eager audience. Huddled in a rain slicker that some kind soul at the airport had handed her, Lindsey, a player on that stage, walked toward the helicopter that stood waiting for flight. Already the copter blades whipped and whirled, while the lights, like the eyes of a keen-sighted bird, stared ahead. His hair soaking wet, Walker stood talking—shouting, really, to be heard over the wind—to a man by the side of the aircraft. Inside the helicopter, the charter pilot got a last-minute briefing on the weather.

Her father was missing.

Over the last hour, ever since they'd been notified that her father's helicopter was missing, Lindsey had thought of little else. And yet, for all of that, the four words, the simple four words, would not compute. It wasn't that she didn't understand the words. She did. She just couldn't understand them in terms of her father. There had never been a time in her life when she didn't know where her father was. There had never been a time when he wasn't, at worst, a phone call away. But now she had no idea where he was . . . or if he was even alive. Walker had said that there would be a tomorrow for her to apologize to her father for slapping him. It had never crossed her mind that tomorrow was such a fragile thing. These last thoughts—the possibility that her father might not be alive, the possibility that she might never get the chance to apologize to him—congealed her blood, making her ice-cold and chilled to the bone.

At her approach, Walker glanced up. He hadn't wanted her to come to the airport to see him off, but he hadn't been able to stop her. After the shock had settled in, she'd become coolly efficient, almost frighteningly efficient. She hadn't shed a tear. Not one. She'd simply garnered what information she could, then had gone by her parents' house to tell her mother. She had promised to be at the airport before Walker left. Even now, as she walked toward him, she looked calm. Below the calmness, however, Walker suspected that she was nothing more than raw, jangled nerves. He longed to pull her into his arms and never let go. He longed to have her never let go of him because, for the first time in his life, he was scared. Scared half out of his mind.

"Yeah, thanks," he said to the Coast Guard representative.

"Let's keep each other informed," the tall, lean man said.

"Right," Walker said, but his gaze was once more on Lindsey. "You shouldn't be out in this," he said when she stood before him. Fat, moist raindrops hurled themselves against her cheeks and into her hair, making the latter frizz and curl like corkscrews, making her look—as she often did—youthful and in need of protection.

"I'm all right. How about you?"

"Okay," he lied, adding, "I have the coordinates where they think the copter went down."

Up until now, the situation hadn't been summed up so bluntly. Missing was one thing, gone down was another, although one certainly implied the other. All this Lindsey thought out rationally before tipping her chin with courage. "Do they know for a fact that it went down?" The "they" she referred to was the Coast Guard.

"No, but it's a fair assumption. They know the flight plan he filed. They know his time of departure. They know the last radio contact they had with him. Those facts set up a rough set of coordinates. The Coast Guard has a vessel headed in that direction right now."

"I see. So what are you going to do?"

The wind carried this last away, and Walker was forced to shout, "What?"

She turned her face upward, so that the words would better reach his ears. Her eyes, their lashes dewed like the grass on a spring morn, squinted against the rain. "What are you going to do?" she repeated.

Die if I don't kiss you, he thought, but said, "Go out and see if we can see anything. Wreckage can be seen better from the air than from the sea."

Wreckage. A grim scene of helicopter parts floating on the wind-tortured sea captured her mind. "Do you think—"

"Yes," Walker said, anticipating her question by the stark look on her face. It was the question she'd wanted to ask ever since hearing the distressing news. "He's alive." The same funny feeling that had told him that something was wrong, the funny feeling he'd tried to ignore, now told him that his friend was alive. Walker hoped to God he could trust the funny feeling. "There's no reason he shouldn't be. Even if he went down, he had a life jacket, a raft, flares. Your father's not stupid. Plus, he's had survival training. He's all right."

Something in the grit of Walker's jaw told Lindsey that he wanted to believe what he was saying so much that he was going to make himself believe it. Since she had to believe it as strongly as he, she, too, would make herself.

"Bring him back," she whispered. The words found their mark—they wove themselves through and through and then about Walker's heart.

"I will!" he said gruffly. "I will!"

Each wanted to say more, but what? There were still no answers to their personal problems. Lindsey still wanted commitment in the form of marriage, Walker still felt that he couldn't ask her to make that kind of sacrifice. Not for the rest of her life. Her young life.

At the revving of the engine, Walker looked toward the pilot, who gave a let's go sign. Walker waved an okay.

"I've got to go," he said to Lindsey.

She nodded. "I'll, uh, I'll be with Mother. When you learn anything—"

"I'll let you know immediately," he interjected.

She nodded again. Took a reluctant step backward. Followed by another. Then she turned and started running for the building. Suddenly, she stopped. Cold. On a dime.

"Walker?" she hollered.

The sound of his name caught up with him just as he opened the helicopter door. He looked back at Lindsey.

"Be careful! Please!"

Like she, he nodded . . . and watched as once more she turned and started for the airport terminal.

"Lindsey?" he called after her.

She whirled, and waited. One second. Two seconds. For him to say something. Which he never did. Instead, he slammed the helicopter door and started toward her at a clipped run. Without preamble, with a strength that startled even him, he pulled her to him. His lips slammed hard against hers. Her lips were wet from the rain. So were his. Wet and slippery and wonderfully soft, wonderfully hard, each wonderfully hungry for the other. The kiss lasted only seconds. On a groan, Walker tore his mouth from hers. He stared, saying nothing. Yet he didn't have to. Lindsey heard the silent words.

He loved her.

She had accused him of not loving her enough, but she saw that he did love her...every bit as much as she loved him.

Finally, he said, "Believe in miracles."

And then he was gone, racing back toward the waiting helicopter. She watched as he disappeared inside. In seconds the engine whined and the craft began to rise from the ground. The motion created a frenzy of wind, causing the slicker to lap about her body. She held her head downward. The pose was prayerful. In that moment she prayed for a miracle. For a miracle that somehow she and Walker would be able to work out their differences. She prayed, too, that he'd bring her father back to her. So that she could apologize, so that she could feel his arms again, so that she could tell him she loved him.

In spite of how he'd hurt her, she still loved him.

In spite of how he'd hurt her mother, her mother still loved him.

It dawned on Lindsey that maybe she'd just learned a valuable lesson, a lesson that only maturity could teach.

Below the helicopter, the iron-gray sea roiled in anger. Pitching, churning, it sent waves crashing high and wide. Walker's stomach similarly pitched and churned in fear. Even if Dean had managed to survive the impact of a crash, he couldn't last long in this sea, not when the beast was foaming at the mouth so madly, not when the beast was swallowing everything in sight.

"Pretty choppy!" the pilot shouted over the sound of the whining wind and wild rain. He indicated the water below.

"That's an understatement!" Walker hollered back, not for a second taking his eyes off the convulsing gray canvas before him. He was searching for a dot, any dot, that looked out of the ordinary—copter, debris of copter, man.

"The storm's worse than I expected!"

"Yeah," Walker said, glad now that he'd sent word for Ramsey and the last of the crew to abandon the platform. He didn't like the looks of the way the weather was shaping up. All of the other men had been accounted for, their names meticulously checked against the rosters as they'd boarded the boats. "Let's stay in this area," Walker said as he consulted the map, the approximated coordinates of the crash marked in red.

"Right," the pilot said, and set the helicopter on its course. The course consisted roughly of a two-mile area, some ten miles from Platform Four, some sixty miles from shore.

After ten minutes, the pilot shouted, "Hell, you couldn't see a whore dressed in red in this!"

Walker had already arrived at this discouraging conclusion...and had rejected it completely. "I can see!" he growled.

The pilot said nothing, and Walker instantly regretted the snap in his voice.

Another ten minutes passed. Silent minutes. Minutes in which the pilot flew as close to the sea as he dared. Minutes in which Walker thought—he couldn't confirm it with visibility as poor as it was—he saw a Coast Guard boat in the far distance. Then again, maybe he saw nothing. Weary, frightened, he closed his eyes for a moment, giving in to the tension headache that throbbed behind his eyes. One second of rest was all he'd allow himself, however, and he began searching, scanning again. Please, please! he prayed.

"Could we make another run in this area?"

The pilot nodded. Walker knew that the pilot thought that it wouldn't do any good—it hadn't the dozen times they'd already done it—but he was at least willing to indulge him for a while longer. Walker knew, though, that their time was fast running out. The wind was becoming unmanageable, making the craft increasingly hard to handle. Walker could tell this by the way the pilot fought the controls.

"There!" Walker cried suddenly, squinting through the driving rain.

"Where?"

"There! At three o'clock!" Walker's heart sprinted into a hurting rhythm. He told himself not to get his hopes up, but that's precisely what he did. In fact, his hopes soared.

The helicopter angled, banked, lowered as the pilot brought it down as low as he safely could. Beneath the craft's whirring blades, the water swirled in a circular motion. In the center of the circle bobbed part of the hull of a helicopter.

Walker's hopes plummeted. Not only hadn't he located Dean, but he'd irrefutably documented that his helicopter had gone down.

"I'm sor—" the pilot began, only to be cut off with, "Let's make the run again. He's got to be out there."

Walker was keenly aware of what the pilot was thinking, which was that Dean was out there all right—in the belly of the beast. He knew, too, that holding the helicopter on course was growing harder minute by minute. This last was confirmed by the way the wind jostled the craft, as though the chopper were made of straw.

"Damn!" the pilot said, fighting with the collective stick in an attempt to maintain balance. For a second, the sea looked dangerously near. Then the helicopter righted itself. The pilot looked over at Walker, "It's getting bad out here—"

"I know, I know, but let's make the run again!"

Walker knew that he'd given the man no option. But then, if the circumstances had been reversed, would Dean have given the man an option? Hell, no! Walker thought. Dean would have screamed, hollered, demanded and commanded. In short, he would have made a royal pain in the butt of himself. Which was exactly what Walker intended to make of himself. He wasn't going back without Dean. Come hell or high water, come the devil or the salty sea, he was bringing Dean back home with him!

"Make the run again!"

"I'll make more coffee," Bunny said as she reached for the coffeepot.

"No more for me, Mom. I've had enough."

"What about a sandwich? I could fix you a sand—"

"I'm not hungry. Really. Why don't you come sit down?"

"I don't want to sit down. I can't sit down." With this, Bunny stood and took the dirty coffeepot to the sink, where she immediately began to clean it. The cups and saucers followed. Prior to washing the coffeepot, she'd scrubbed the cabinet, watered the hanging basket of ivy and put a load of clothes in the washing machine. "The psychologist I'm seeing says that I control life through activity. As long as I'm busy, doing the things I'm comfortable with, doing the things that comprise a normal life, then nothing bad will happen to me. I mean, I know it can, but I've chosen to believe that it can't."

Despite the worry nibbling at her stomach, Lindsey smiled. "We all play games, Mom. They help to get us through life."

Games. Was she playing games by holding on to the hope that she and Walker could yet be a couple, games like close your eyes to reality, games like pretend and it'll happen? Did she love him so much that she just couldn't envision life without him as her husband, as the father of her children?

"Walker won't marry me," she heard herself saying. At the look her mother sent her, she said, "He thinks it wouldn't be fair to me."

"Is he right?"

In some far corner of her mind, Lindsey realized how odd the question was and not at all what she'd expected as her mother's response. The simple query demanded that she search deeper into her heart. Had Walker simply presented a reality that she chose to ignore? Was she playing another game with herself? Was she so young that she couldn't conceive that time would alter her feelings for him? Would the age difference, which even now was not inconsequential, become even a greater barrier as time wore on? She thought of her life five years, ten years, twenty-five years down the road. Could she imagine her life without Walker?

"No!" she said, in defiance to the barren life stretching before her, to the question her mother had asked. "He isn't right."

Bunny crossed the room and reseated herself. She took her daughter's hand. "Love isn't always perfect," she said. "You don't always get it the way you want it. Sometimes you take it the way you can get it."

"Is that what you're willing to do? Take Dad any way you can get him?"

"Right now, Lindsey, all I want is to see him again. Right now all I want to know is that he's alive." Except for a slight quaver, Bunny's voice was strong, the voice of a woman who'd reduced life to its lowest common denominator. That simplification had strengthened Bunny, as, indeed, had the events of the past weeks.

Seeing her father again was all Lindsey wanted, too. Glancing outside, she realized that night was only hours away. The thought of her father lost at sea, at night, in the midst of a storm, caused an arrow of panic to shoot through her. Was he afraid? Was he, too, sorry that he and his daughter had had words? Would he give anything he owned to apologize? She refused to entertain the notion that he might not be alive.

Where was her father?

Where was Walker?

When would this nightmare end?

"God," Lindsey cried abruptly, pulling her hand from her mother's and standing. She paced back and forth across the kitchen floor. "I wish Walker would call! I wish *anyone* would call!"

"I know," her mother said softly, one hand folded in the other, so that she wouldn't straighten the sugar bowl and creamer. "I know."

But no one did call. Hour blended into hour. Dead time, Lindsey thought. Time in which you didn't really exist. Time in which you simply survived. As though it were a shrine, Lindsey watched the clock above the stove. "Ticktock...ticktock...ticktock," it said, but it whispered, "Dead time...dead time...dead time...."

Dean was dead.

The realization crept into Walker's heart even though he did everything to keep it out. It was the only logical explanation. He and the pilot had searched the sea, as best they could in the inclement weather, and had seen nothing. Except for the one chunk of helicopter debris, there had been not even a remote hint of anything floating on the water. Not that one could see anything with night coming on. Not that one could see anything with the sea heaving and tossing and heaving again. Not even the wreckage of the hull was left in sight. Long ago, it had been sucked under, towed down to the nether world of the hydrous gods.

As had Dean?

The thought sickened Walker, breaking him out in a cold sweat that was incongruous with the hot, humid heat of the evening. Death was one thing. Losing a loved one to a watery grave was yet another. He swallowed hard, wondering if he himself would have met death as valiantly as Dean. And there was no doubt in his mind that, whatever the end, Dean had met it courageously. He was just that kind of guy.

God! Walker thought, he was never going to get to tell him how much he'd always admired him. He was never going to get to explain about Lindsey. He was never going to get to say how sorry he was that the two of them—he and Dean—had had words.

"Mr. Carr?"

Fighting the moisture in his eyes, Walker glanced over at the pilot.

"I can't hold the craft steady much longer. The wind is growing—"

"I know," Walker said. He was no longer angry with the suggestion to call a halt to the search. It was the only prudent thing left to do. It was the only safe thing left to do. He'd promised Lindsey that he'd bring her father back but, obviously, miracles were running in short supply. "Make one more sweep. And then we'll head back."

The pilot, sympathetic to the situation, started the helicopter on its final patrol. The harsh wind, like the palm of a huge hand, shoved the copter, while rain, needle-like, struck the cockpit with such force that it sounded like bullets exploding.

Straining to see through the impending night, Walker stared out the window as the helicopter flew as low to the water as it could, far lower than it should have. The sea sped by, dark, menacing, mocking. The wind whispered a dirge, a deadly melody that played over and over in Walker's mind in a mournful symphony.

It's over... over... you're going to go back without him... the sea has been victorious....

Victory! Hell, yeah, we're going to beat the pants off the Wolverines! Their defense ain't worth dirt compared to ours!... Phyllis? You and Phyllis are gonna get married? Congratulations, though what she wants with a jerk like you I can't imagine... Yeah, we'll be in Nam at the same time. Those Vietcong won't have a chance!...Baby? Phyllis is going to have a baby? That's great, man. Great!...Of course, Bunny's pregnant. You didn't think we'd let you two get ahead of us, did you?...Godfather. We want you to be Lindsey's godfather...Oh, God, man, what can I say? Phyllis shouldn't have died. You know we're there for you. We'll always be there for you... Tell me that this isn't what it looks like. You've betrayed me, betrayed our friendship. Betrayed...betrayed... betrayed...

"I'm sorry, Mr. Carr," the pilot said quietly.

"Yeah," Walker said, his throat so full he could hardly speak.

Silently, the pilot began to turn the helicopter, bringing it in a wide circle and starting back toward the mainland. Walker knew that he was leaving a part of him behind. Maybe one of the best parts of him.

He knew, too, that he was trembling. Fine tremors raced through his hands, making them unsteady. Pain gouged his heart. He closed his eyes, fighting the tears that begged to be shed. It wasn't supposed to end like this. It wasn't supposed to end now. Not when there was so much left to be said.

"What's that?" the pilot asked some ten minutes and several miles later. They were well outside the proposed coordinates.

Walker sat with his chin buried in his hand, staring out the window. "What's what?" he asked, visually following where the pilot led.

"Over there. At one o'clock. I thought I saw a flash of something."

Flare! The word jumped to Walker's mind, bringing with it a resurgence of hope. Sweet, sweet, nothing-sweeter hope!

"Could it have been a flare?"

"That's exactly what I was thinking. Let's have a closer look."

The pilot brought the helicopter lower and lower, closer and closer until, even though encroaching night had spun a black veil about the world, something was visible within the ocean. A dark shape. A bulky shape. A shape that bore a resemblance to a man.

"It's him!" the pilot shouted, and gave a war whoop.

Walker said nothing. He couldn't. Instead, he pondered how strange it was that in the most traumatic times words were hopelessly useless. At least verbally. Internally, he prayed a prayer of thanks to a god that was still in the business of manufacturing miracles. Still without saying a word, Walker unfastened his seat belt and started to the back of the craft.

"Throw down the rope!" the pilot shouted. "But make it quick. We're running low on fuel."

Walker needed no prodding. He was already sliding open the copter door and readying the rope—a kind of harness device—for tossing overboard. Which wasn't going to be an overly easy feat. The wind tore violently at him, forcing him to grip the door opening for balance. Beneath him, he could see the water churning in a near whirlpool fashion as the wind from the helicopter blades battered the sea. He could also seen Dean. A speck in a big, big ocean.

"Hang on, buddy," Walker whispered, leaning forward and dropping the rope. Saberlike rain cut him in the face, while the wind practically ripped his hair from the roots. His breath came hard and fast and hurtfully, and he could feel his clothes being plastered to him.

The rope danced in the air, becoming nothing more than a puppet dashed about by the wind. It also stopped short of reaching Dean. He saw Dean make the effort to grasp it, but failed to do so. Even if the rope had been longer, Dean had been weakened from hours in the sea. The rope was going to have to be handed to him on a silver platter.

Walker cursed, then shouted to the pilot, "Lower!"

"I can't go much lower!"

"We've got to!"

Contrary to what he said he could do, the pilot did inch the craft lower. The rope swung, arched, struck Dean. Dean grappled for it but, again, the lifeline, manipulated by the wind, eluded him.

Walker could feel his friend's frustration. It mirrored his own. "C'mon, Dean," he coaxed. "One more time."

The next time the rope came Dean's way, he didn't even try to grasp it. Exhaustion had set in. He simply bobbed with the pitching sea, as though saving his energy for one last attempt.

"All right, buddy, this is it," Walker crooned, trying to direct the rope once more toward his friend. "We're gonna do it this time, or I'm gonna kick ass." Slowly, slowly—no, back some!—Walker fought to control a flaxen line that clearly owed its allegiance to the wind. "Okay, okay, a little more…just a little more…now grab it, Dean!"

Dean, of course, hadn't heard a word, though perhaps he'd felt the heart-guided instructions. In any event he did grab the rope, fumbled it, then grabbed it again. Walker felt the pressure of his friend on the other end of the line and thought that nothing had ever felt so wonderful. It tugged clean through to his heart.

"Can he get the harness on?" the pilot shouted.

"He'll get it on," Walker said assuringly.

In due time, after a couple of aborted attempts, Dean did fit the harness about him, after fighting to get it over his orange life preserver. He then gave a thumbs-up—or an exhausted something that passed for it.

"I'm bringing him up," Walker called as he started the hydraulic lift.

With a crank and a whine, the rope began to tighten. In seconds, Dean was being drawn from the sea. Dangling, his head angled to one side, he looked like a hanged man. Even through the pummeling rain, Walker could tell that Dean's eyes were closed. Was he, too, praying? Was he, too, regretting all that had been said between them?

Less than a minute later, when Dean came even with the open door, their gazes met and held before Walker shouted, "Hang on! I'll pull you in!"

Walker reached for Dean even as Dean reached for Walker. Both missed. Walker tried again and this time threw his arm about his buddy's waist. Wet and tired, Dean weighed a ton. On a grunt, Walker hauled him inside the aircraft. Both men tumbled to the floor. Emotionally and physically exhausted, they simply lay there.

"Got him?" the pilot shouted.

"Yeah!" Walker called back as he somehow managed to slide the door shut behind him. "Let's go!"

Dean, lying precisely where he'd been dragged on board, and Walker, edging himself to lean against a wall, studied each other. Dean's hair was plastered to his head, as were his clothes to his body. His lips had begun to turn a pale blue, while his skin looked as pallid as new-fallen snow. One of his shoes had disappeared, leaving nothing but a soggy sock to protect his foot. A vine of seaweed, dark green and slimy looking, draped about his other shoe. All in all, he would have passed for a bedraggled puppy.

But then, Walker suspected that he looked little better. He, too, was drenched from head to foot. His heart pounded so loud in his chest that he would have sworn that it was audible. Curiously, it was pounding harder now than when his friend had been missing. It was as though, now that it was over, now that he saw the visible proof of what he'd almost lost, a vial of adrenaline had been shot directly into his veins. He suddenly felt weak-kneed and as listless as the puppy Dean looked like. He also hurt in every joint and muscle of his body. On the flip side, he'd never felt more exhilarated.

"W-what in hell took you so long?" Dean asked finally.

"Why in hell didn't you go down where you were supposed to have?"

"D-didn't want to make it easy."

"Yeah, well, you didn't," Walker said. On some plane he noted that the pilot was heading for home. He also heard the pilot on the radio, reporting that they'd found Dean and to call his family. A vision of Lindsey came to mind. Life. Death. The passage between the two was short, the journey sometimes so unexpected. Hadn't he learned that from Phyllis's untimely death? Did it take nearly losing Dean to once more remind him of this? And when it was all said and done, wasn't loving the only thing that mattered?

Say you don't make it to a hundred and ten. Say I don't make it to eighty-six. Couldn't we just be happy we had twenty, thirty, thirty-five years together?

I want to be fair to you. I have to leave you free.

Being in love is like being pregnant. You can't be just a little bit. You either are or you aren't. And when you're in love, Walker, you commit all the way. You take all the chances. You don't compromise. And you damned sure don't leave your partner free to walk away!

"The engine . . . it just gave out. . . ."

Walker brought his attention back to his friend.

" . . . p-pitched the copter into the s-sea. Totaled. The c-copter's totaled."

"That's what we pay insurance for."

"D-do you have . . . water?"

Walker glanced around, spying the thermos from which he and the pilot had fortified their flagging spirits a couple of times. "How about some coffee?"

"Anything . . . wet."

Uncapping the thermos, Walker poured out a half cup of black coffee. He handed it to Dean. It was then that he noticed how badly Dean was shaking. "Here," Walker said, helping Dean to raise his head and holding the cup to his mouth. He drank slowly, but greedily.

"'Water, water everywhere, but not a d-drop to d-drink,'" Dean quoted the famous poem, a lopsided smile on his face.

Cold.

Dean was as cold as death.

Walker could feel the numbing chill in his hands and face as he held the cup to his friend's lips.

Laying the thermos aside, Walker grabbed a blanket. "Put this around you," he ordered, pulling Dean to him as though he were a baby and draping the blanket about him. Gently he leaned him back—this time against the wall—and gathered the woolen blanket about his neck.

He had just started to remove his hands when Dean abruptly reached for him. He caught Walker's wrist. The power behind his clasp belied his exhaustion. The two men stared. Brawny Dean. Agile Walker. Friends for a thousand years.

"You son of a bitch," Walker whispered at last, "you scared the hell out of me!"

Dean said nothing, though his eyes glazed with tears. And then Walker pulled him back to him. He held him. Tightly. Unashamedly. As his own eyes filled with tears.

Chapter Twelve

"I've screwed everything up," Dean said as he peered into the thermos cup full of coffee, as though there might be answers there that he could find nowhere else.

The helicopter was only miles away from the mainland. Though still wet, Dean had stopped shivering, possibly due to the added coffee Walker had insisted he drink. After their emotional exchange, nothing more had been said. Nothing more needed to be. They might be friends who were at odds with one another, but nonetheless they remained friends. Death's tapping at the door had put their friendship into perspective. Apparently, it had other things, as well.

When Walker, who leaned negligently against the far wall, said nothing, Dean glanced up and over at him. "How can you work all your life building relationships, then flush them down the toilet?" Before Walker could comment, Dean added, "I spent twenty-something years loving Bunny and being loved by her, then whoosh—'' he swiped his hand through the air ''—I throw all that away.''

''Did you?'' Walker asked frankly. At Dean's look of incomprehension, he clarified, ''Did you throw it all away?''

Dean laughed rich notes of sarcasm. ''I'd say I came as close as any man ever did.''

''Close isn't the same thing as actually doing it.''

''I've cheated on my wife, I've asked for a divorce, which she's probably more than happy to grant me and I've alienated my daughter. All in all, I'd say I've come closer than close.''

''Both are worried sick about you.''

The look in Dean's eyes said that he longed to believe that were true, but then he dropped his eyes as though to say that, even if it were, he didn't deserve their concern.

''Don't be so hard on yourself,'' Walker said. ''Growing older isn't easy for any of us. You panicked. There's no shame in fear.''

Fear. It dawned on Walker that maybe that was the basis of his refusal to marry Lindsey. Maybe the reason wasn't nearly as noble as he'd like to believe. Maybe he wasn't nearly as concerned about leaving her free to walk away as he was afraid of what would happen to him should she choose to leave him in the future. Maybe he wasn't nearly as concerned about being fair to her as he was about protecting himself. And maybe that fear rested in the fact that he saw himself growing older—older and unable to hang on to someone as young and beautiful as she. Maybe he and Dean shared the same fear after all, each merely seeking different routes of expression.

''You wouldn't have panicked,'' Dean said.

''Don't be too sure.''

Dean half smiled. "You know what the real kicker is? When I was bobbing around out there on the ocean, it struck me like a ton of bricks that I wasn't afraid to die. I didn't want to, but I wasn't afraid to. What kind of sense does it make not to fear death, but to fear growing older? Which is what growing older is really all about, isn't it?"

"In the main, yes, but you were afraid that life was passing you by."

"Yeah, and so I reached for something that didn't matter and in so doing turned loose of everything that did."

"Lindsey still loves you. Nothing's ever going to change that. She's sick about what happened between the two of you."

At the mention of the fight between him and his daughter, pain streaked across Dean's face. "She and I had never even had words, not any real words," he said, repeating almost exactly what Lindsey had said. "You know, the ironic thing was that I decided the night before not to see Michele again. I really had," he said as though he thought Walker might doubt this eleventh-hour decision.

"I believe you," Walker said, and he did.

"I think I only saw her Friday night because I knew Bunny was with this Don person. Even before, I knew what I was doing was wrong. Not only to Bunny, but to Michele, too. Michele kept saying everything was in the name of a good time, no strings attached, but I sensed that she was getting involved. I didn't want to hurt the kid. I was afraid that she was going to want something from me that I just couldn't give. The truth is that I like her, but I don't love her. I love..." He stopped, as though he no longer had the right to say what he'd been about to. Instead, he said, "I don't love Michele."

Dean downed the last of the hot coffee, stoppered the thermos, and leaned back. The approaching storm buffeted the copter back and forth. Both men were aware that another subject, as stormy as the weather, had yet to be broached.

"Dean..." Walker stopped, searching for the right words, then decided that there were none. "How I feel about Lindsey isn't going to change. I love her. It's that simple, but I want you to understand that I didn't start out knowing this would happen. No one could have been more startled than I was. No one could have fought it any harder than I did."

Dean started to speak, but Walker halted him.

"No, I want to say this. Of course I understand how you feel. Don't you think I'm well aware of what a strain this puts on our friendship? Don't you think I know that I have some responsibility to you and Bunny? Don't you think I've asked myself how I'd feel if the situation were reversed, if you were in love with my daughter? I have. God, I have! A dozen times!"

This time Dean said nothing, and Walker wished that he would—anything to fill the silence that now loomed before them. In the stillness, Walker heard the rain splattering against the helicopter, the chop, chop, chopping of the blades, the pounding of his heart. Say something, dammit! But Dean didn't, and Walker heard himself speaking again. He wanted so desperately for Dean to understand.

"After Phyllis died, I just went through the motions of living. I got up, I did what was expected of me, I went to bed. Only the time I spent with Adam mattered. Only then did I feel...I don't know, alive. But he grew up, left home, and found his own way in the world. Life seemed lonelier after that. The motions got harder to go through. And then came Lindsey. She had—has—a vitality that I'd long ago lost. She's sweet and honest and so filled with life. She makes me feel...young. Ah, hell," Walker said, scrambling his fingers through his hair. "Maybe I'm just having the same mid-life crisis you are. Maybe I'm just trying to hang on to my youth."

"No," Dean said quietly.

So quietly that Walker glanced over at him.

"I could tell Saturday morning that what you had with Lindsey was different than what I had with Michele. Mind you, I didn't much like what I was seeing, but I could tell that it was different. When Lindsey brought up Michele, I just felt . . . dirty. Even through my shock and anger at finding you two together, I could tell that you didn't feel that way about what had happened between you and Lindsey."

"No," Walker said, "that may be the only thing I haven't felt. Confused, elated, disbelieving, concerned, but not dirty. Never that."

The two men heard the pilot asking for clearance to land, which meant that the airport was near. Soon the world, life, would once more intrude.

"I—" Dean began.

"You—" Walker said.

Both stopped, hesitated, waited for the other.

Finally, Dean said, "I haven't grown use to the idea of you and Lindsey, but I promise you that I'll try."

"You may not have to," Walker said, a shadow now fallen over his heart.

"What do you mean?"

"I don't know what our future holds," he said without going into any detail. He noted, though, that he was no longer completely rejecting the idea of marriage. Too much had happened within the last few hours to hold too tightly to old beliefs. Maybe the basic truth was that life was just too short to spend it away from people you loved.

"If you love her," Dean said quietly, "don't let her go." Suddenly, Dean grinned, a slow, simple curving of his mouth. "Did I just say what I thought I did?"

The same smile at Walker's lips, he said, "It must be the acoustics in here."

Ten minutes later the helicopter landed. As Walker was helping Dean from the craft, he saw Lindsey step from the terminal. Totally oblivious to the rain, she began to walk toward the two men. Slowly. Then not so slowly. Finally, she began to run. Walker stepped back, allowing her to sail into her father's outstretched arms.

"Daddy!" she cried as she buried her head in his shoulder.

"I'm okay," Dean whispered as her tears fell. "There's no need to cry. I'm okay."

"I thought—"

"Shh," he said, pulling her tighter, "everything's okay."

For long moments, despite the rain, despite the howling wind, they just held each other. Walker watched, feeling a bright glow warm his heart.

"I'm sorry I slapped—" Lindsey began, but again her father quieted her.

"No apologies, baby. Now or ever. You're my girl. That's all that matters."

Thunder crashed. Lightning flashed. Still they held to one another.

"Dean?"

The voice was soft, sweet, and barely audible in the stormy night. Nonetheless, Dean heard the calling of his name. He glanced up. Lindsey, too, had heard and turned in her father's arms.

"Bunny?" he called, obviously uncertain whether his eyes were deceiving him or not.

Bunny stood only feet away. The rain had doused her hair and was tunneling through her makeup, neither of which she seemed the slightest bit mindful of. The uncertainty in her husband's voice was mirrored in her face. It was clear that she didn't know how her presence would be received. Even so, she stood tall, unbowed, capable of dealing with whatever happened. She was substance and no longer shadow.

Unhurriedly, Dean released his daughter and stepped toward his wife. She, too, started for him, symbolically meeting him halfway. Without a word, she tumbled into his arms.

Walker saw tears of happiness rush to Lindsey's eyes and watched as she swiped them away. When she turned her eyes on him, everything that had ever been wrong in the world was suddenly righted, everything that had ever been cold was suddenly warm. Heart-warm.

"See, I told you," she whispered. "If you believe in miracles, they happen."

The only miracle Walker believed in at that moment was the miracle of love. On a groan, he pulled Lindsey into his arms. As he held her, his heart made a decision. Right or wrong, fair or unfair, he'd just decided their future.

Later that night, all Gal-Tex rigs evacuated, the storm announced its intentions. As unpredictable as ever, it turned toward Mexico, hitting land near Matamoros. No one yet knew the full extent of the devastation, but early reports indicated that property damage far outweighed loss of life. If so, their Mexican neighbors had been lucky, Walker thought as he stood peering out his bedroom window into the rain-damp night. The last few hours had reminded him of the preciousness of life. Nothing else really matter.

Walker grinned inwardly, thinking that he always managed to wax philosophical at a quarter to one in the morning. Taking a sip of cold beer from the can in his hand, he thought that he was also managing to be lonely. Damned lonely. At the airport, he and Lindsey had had time only for a heartfelt embrace. Though it had been one of the hardest things he'd ever done, he'd turned loose of her with nothing more than the brushing of her lips with his. Dean had been exhausted to the point of near collapse, and Lindsey had been needed to drive both him and her mother home. To the house they'd shared together, Bunny had insisted. Walker had done some insisting of his own. He'd insisted that Lindsey stay with them. They needed to be a family again. He had told her that there would be time for the two of them later.

He wished now that he hadn't been so generous, particularly since his heart was so full of feeling, particularly since there were so many things that he wanted to say to her.

Checking his watch, he saw that the minute hand had moved only slightly. It was now twelve minutes until one o'clock. As though to mark the hour, lightning bolted through the sky, a golden thread erratically woven into the blackest of velvet. On a sigh, he took another drink of beer and wondered what Lindsey was doing. He also wondered if he should crawl into the unmade bed behind him and try to get some sleep. This last produced a quiet laugh deep in his bare chest. Sleep was farther away than Lindsey's Timbuktu.

Lindsey.

How he longed to hold her, kiss her, make love to her. How he longed to just be with her. But he wasn't, and that was that, and he had the remainder of a long night before him. Tomorrow. He'd see her tomorrow and—

The pealing of the doorbell startled Walker, causing him to jerk his head in the direction of the front room. A frown on his face, he moved silently from the bedroom to the source of the sound. Which was once more invading the stillness of the house. Whoever was ringing the doorbell was obviously impatient. Impatient. As impatient as he? A thought—actually a wish—crossed his mind. Was it even remotely possible that he knew who was standing at his front door?

"What took you so long?" Lindsey asked the minute Walker opened the door. She was cocked against the doorjamb, a pretty, come-hither smile crooking her moist lips. Flagrantly, like the vixen she could be, she ran her eyes up and down the man dressed only in jeans. She particularly admired his chest, which rippled with muscles. Nothing in her appearance said that earlier in the day they'd been at emotional odds. Nothing in her appearance said that the night before she'd angrily fled his bed after accusing him of not being totally committed.

A slow sexy smile sauntered across Walker's lips. "What's a lady doing ringing a man's doorbell in the middle of the night?"

"Could be the lady just misses the man," she said softly, and without a trace of the smile.

Quicksilver. She was like quicksilver, going from sexy to serious in heartbeats. His own smile faded. "Gee, what a coincidence. The man was just missing the lady."

"Was he?"

"Uh-huh."

"Enough to invite her in?"

"For the night?" he asked, his heart beginning to pound, his temperature rising.

Lindsey's heart began to pound as well, and she could feel her body growing warm and pliable. She had thought the drive to his house would last forever. Each mile traveled, each block passed seemed to take her farther away instead of closer. In fact, the night had dragged as no night in her life ever had. When it became apparent that it was never going to end, when it was obvious that her parents were so absorbed in each other that they wouldn't miss her, she'd slipped from the house. She had to talk to Walker. Now. Tonight. She had to tell him that she would stay in his life, "For however long you want," she heard herself say in answer to his question.

Behind her, rain fell in a now slow sheet, pummeling the roof, the concrete, with a steady drizzling rhythm. The beat of the rain, combined with Walker's shallow breathing and Lindsey's steamy look, produced syncopated notes that sounded like jazz. A lover's jazz.

Walker didn't know whether he pulled her into the house. Lindsey didn't know whether she stepped in of her own volition. Whichever, Lindsey found herself pressed against the closed door with Walker's mouth devouring hers. His hands, one still holding the beer can, were braced against the door, while his body urged itself into hers. He could feel her rain-damp clothes—jeans, cotton blouse, even the lacy undergarments she wore beneath. Lindsey could feel his bare chest, his tight pants, the desire he couldn't hide and which she didn't want him to.

They kissed over and over and over—warmly, wetly, wildly. Their mouths nipped and bit, sipped and supped. Just when one seemed ready to end the kiss, the other would begin it all over again. Gasping, both finally came up for air, though, even then, they didn't pull their mouths from each other. They simply rested bruised mouth against bruised mouth.

"I think your beer is going to my head," Lindsey whispered.

Walker grinned, providing a whole new set of tactile stimuli for Lindsey. "That's exactly where I like it going. God, I've missed you!" he added, as though just remembering the loneliness of minutes before.

"I've missed you," she said. "God, I hate fighting with you!"

"Then, let's not fight." He started to kiss her again, but Lindsey wriggled free.

"No," she said, "I want to talk before you completely intoxicate me."

"Okay," he said, feeling a little drunk himself—drunk with the nearness of the woman he loved.

She had stepped away from him, knowing that there had to be some distance between them if she was to think straight. "I came here to tell you something, and I want to say it now."

Walker saw her uncertainty. The cocksureness she'd arrived with had vanished entirely. "Then say it."

Now that the moment had come, she wasn't sure where to begin. She'd rehearsed her speech a dozen times, but now could remember only fragments of what she'd planned. In the car coming over, it had all seemed so simple—just say what she was feeling. Suddenly, with her future—their future—on the line, simple had become complex. "I, uh, I think that Mother and Dad are going to try to work things out."

It wasn't what Walker had expected her to say, though he wasn't certain what that was. Even so, the news was welcome. "I'm glad."

"Dad told Mother about the... about the affair. And Mother told him that she already knew about it. He told her that he'd gone crazy for a while, but that he thought he was over it and that, if she wanted to, he wanted them to stay together, to try to work things out."

"And what did your mother say?"

"She's taking him back, though she's insisting on his getting counseling with her. She's also determined to go on to school as planned." Lindsey smiled. "I think he's a little fascinated by this new woman he finds in Mother. Alongside the familiar woman who depended on him, loved, cooked and cleaned for him is now a woman who wants to belong to herself, as well."

"I can understand the fascination of the two," Walker said. With her hair pulled back in a ponytail, with the topic of her parents on her lips, Lindsey looked young again, though only seconds before she'd kissed him like a mature woman. This duality had once troubled him. He now just let himself enjoy it. "I can understand," Walker repeated.

"Anyway, this isn't what I wanted to talk to you about," Lindsey said abruptly, obviously nervous about how to proceed.

"It isn't?"

"No," she said, looking him square in the eyes. "I mean, it is and it isn't." She sighed. "I'm doing a terrible job of saying this."

"No, you're not. Just say it." At her hesitation, he repeated, "Just say it, Lindsey."

"While we were waiting to hear about Dad," she said, "Mother and I had a talk, which was the whole point of bringing up Mother and Dad, I guess. She told me that love wasn't always perfect, that you couldn't always get it the way you wanted it, that sometimes... that sometimes you settled for what you could get." What hadn't been said, but what Lindsey had heard her mother silently saying was that women were the preservers of relationships. She still heard the words singing in her heart.

Confused up until this point, Walker thought he finally saw the purpose of the conversation. "I see. And what are you willing to settle for, Lindsey?"

Lindsey licked her suddenly dry lips, swallowed, then said bluntly, "I'll take you any way I can get you. If you don't want to marry me, that's fine. I can live with that. What I can't live without..." Her voice lowered to a breathless whisper. "What I can't live without is you."

The words humbled Walker as he could never remember being humbled before. Setting down the beer can, he stepped toward her and cupped her cheek with his palm. He stared deep into her silver-blue eyes. "You'd do that? Stay with me under those conditions?"

"Yes," she said frankly, feeling the coolness of his hand, the warmth of his body.

"You'd give up wanting marriage?"

"I wouldn't give up wanting it, or trying to persuade you, but I'd accept whatever you were willing to give me."

"What about children?"

She shrugged. "I'll do what you want."

"And what do you want?" he asked huskily.

"To have your baby."

"Even if we're not married?"

"I don't care," she said, looking him square in the eyes. "People who aren't married have babies all the time."

"And you'd do that?"

"Yes," she said unflinchingly.

"Ah, Lindsey," he whispered, lowering his head and kissing her gently.

He then pulled her into his arms and held her. He knew that as long as he lived he would remember the unselfishness he'd witnessed this night. If possible, it had made him love Lindsey more. It had certainly awakened him to just how lucky he was. It also convinced him beyond a doubt that earlier that night he'd made the right decision.

"Lindsey?" he whispered.

"Mmm?" she asked dreamily, content only to be in the arms she'd so sorely missed.

"We need to talk."

"We just did."

"Oh, no, babe," he said as he swung her into his arms and started for the bedroom, "we've only just begun."

Epilogue

"Would you let me do that?" Walker said a year later as he and his wife were putting the finishing touches to the bedroom they'd converted into a nursery.

Like a mirror image, there was two of everything in the room—two cribs, two chests, two hanging hampers stacked high with diapers. There was also an assortment of woolly teddy bears, all waiting expectantly for the twins the doctor said Lindsey was carrying. Twins. A boy and a girl, if sonography could be trusted. At first, Walker had been shocked at the news, but then wondered why he had been. Lindsey never did anything by half measure. Besides, she herself was so full of life that it seemed only logical that she'd bear it in abundance.

"I'm not helpless. I'm just pregnant," Lindsey said, trying to wedge her huge belly close enough to a crib to hang a brightly colored mobile. When she couldn't, she tried a new angle. This one didn't work any better.

"Yeah, very pregnant," he said as he took the mobile from her hand. He stole a quick kiss as he did so.

Lindsey loved the feel of his mouth on hers. A year's worth of kisses had only made her need them more, had only made her love him more. That she was his wife, which he'd insisted upon her being the night she'd gone to him willing to sacrifice whatever she had to to be a part of his life, always gave her pause, always gave her the purest pleasure. She felt as if she were living a fairy tale, a bona fide, happy-ever-after fairy tale.

"So what do you think?" he asked, propping his hands on his hips and standing back to view his handiwork.

Instead of checking out the mobile, she gave her husband a thorough going-over. A pair of glasses perched upon the end of his nose, and he could still predict weather with his arthritic knee, which he gave in to on occasion and let Lindsey rub. Those things considered, however, he'd never looked younger or better to her. Or more relaxed and at ease with life. Even so, he swore that his hair was grayer, the result of trying to keep up with his young wife. She swore that she had trouble keeping up with him.

"I think I love you," she said.

At the sudden seriousness in her voice, he turned. And was once more struck by the child-woman quality his wife possessed. Wearing jeans and one of his long-sleeved white shirts, with socks and tennis shoes on her feet and her hair sleeked back into a ponytail and caught with a scarlet ribbon, she looked like a bright-eyed child. The enormity of her belly belied that youthfulness, however, and Walker knew for a fact that she made love, and loved, like a full-fledged woman. His woman.

Stepping to her, he took her into his arms and, peering through the lenses of his glasses, he found her eyes. They looked like sparkling diamonds. "Let me get this straight," he said. "You're nine months pregnant with a man's child—"

"Children," Lindsey corrected.

". . . children and you *think* you love him?"

Lindsey could feel his hand at the small of her back—the aching small of her back—urging her belly as flush against his as it would go. She could also hear the teasing in his voice. Encircling his neck with her arms, she tilted her head to one side and playfully said, "Well, it could be that if you kissed me I'd know for sure."

Walker fought a grin. "You think that would do it?"

She shrugged coquettishly. "Maybe."

Lowering his head, he kissed her forehead in a fashion that could only be called fatherly.

"You're going to have to do better than that," she said.

"How about this?" he asked, kissing the tip of her nose.

"Not much better," she said, twitching said nose like a bunny rabbit.

"This?" he asked, dipping his head and nipping the side of her neck. His tongue made little circles on her flesh, producing hot, tingly feelings that skipped across her body.

"Now we're getting somewhere."

He nipped the other side of her neck. Bit gently. Then worried the lobe of her ear with the same eager teeth. "Ah, yeah, now we're cooking, although—"

Before she could say another word, Walker's mouth slid onto hers, silencing her to all but a slow moan. Tightening her arms, she leaned into him. At the same time, she parted her lips, encouraging his tongue to do the deliciously wicked things it always did. His tongue did not disappoint her. It darted, dove, delved. In seconds, both were breathing hard, so hard that Walker wrestled his mouth away and rested his forehead against hers. Their breath commingled.

His response to her never ceased to amaze him, just as her response to him never ceased to amaze him. Hers was always so honest, so open, so freely given. He could never remember—or rather chose not to remember—a time when she wasn't in his life. He could, however, remember the loneliness that predated her. Because of that, he could never take her for granted. Their marriage, simple and sweet, marked the beginning of a new life for him. He would always be grateful that Dean had given her away, symbolically saying that he accepted his daughter's choice of a husband. In the end, he'd been willing to live by the creed he'd once espoused; namely, that no third party could stand in judgment of what two other people felt in their hearts. Both Bunny and Adam had had no problem with the marriage. Adam even teasingly called Lindsey "Mom" on occasion.

"I love you," Walker said seriously.

"I love you," she answered back in kind. Suddenly, unexpectedly, delightfully, she laughed. "I steamed your glasses."

"You steam a lot more than my glasses," he answered on a growl, and pulled her to him to prove his point.

"You're just saying that because I'm such a dowdy little creature these days."

"You're fishing for compliments."

"You would, too, if you were the size of a football stadium."

"You're gorgeous, from your curly little head right down to your curly little toes."

"I don't have toes. I don't have feet. At least, I haven't seen them in weeks."

"You have toes. You have feet. Trust me. I know. I put socks and tennis shoes on them this morning."

"You're just saying that."

"I'm not."

"I'll have to give up my ballet career."

"You never had a ballet career."

"Oh, well, how fortunate, because I'd only have to give it up."

Walker grinned.

Lindsey grinned. Her grin gave in, however, to a slight wince.

"Your back?"

"Mmm."

"Does it hurt worse?"

"Not worse. It just hurts." For days there had been a mild ache that the doctor had deemed normal. With the last twenty-four hours, however, the ache had increased.

"You don't think—"

"Walker, you ask me every ten minutes if it's time. You're worse than Adam was waiting for Grace to deliver. I'll let you know when it's time. Besides, it's day and you said yourself that babies only come at night."

Lindsey's suitcase had sat by the front door for days, not that that would do any good when the time came, Lindsey thought, because Walker probably wouldn't even be able to find the front door. Let alone his pants, car keys or wallet. He'd been such a worrywart that he'd almost gotten kicked out of the birthing classes.

"Maybe we should call the doctor," Walker said.

"Maybe we shouldn't."

"I think we definitely should stay in tonight."

"It's Dad's birthday and Mom's gone to all the trouble of throwing a surprise party."

"They'd understand," Walker said, thinking how glad he was that Bunny and Dean were working out their problems. In fact, they seemed happier than they ever had. He knew that it hadn't been easy for Bunny to turn her eyes away from the hurt he'd caused her. Divorce would have been easier, but Walker, like Dean, had learned that Bunny Ellison was a gutsy lady. As for Dean, Walker knew that he lived daily with guilt, knowing the heartache he'd caused. Walker knew, too, that his friend was determined to make it up to his wife. As a token of good faith, he'd sold the sports car, saying that he was too damned old for such nonsense.

"I know they would understand, but I want to be there."

"Okay. But only if you lie down and rest this afternoon."

"Will you lie down with me?"

"That suggestion, as I recall, led to the state you're in," Walker said, running his hands over her stomach.

"Yeah," she said on a purr.

She remembered vividly the rain-splattered afternoon in question, the afternoon they'd drunk champagne and eaten strawberries and made repeated love. It had been a lovely way to begin a family. But then, everything about being married to Walker had been lovely, from the wedding, to the honeymoon in London—they'd save Timbuktu for later, he'd promised—to moving into his house. That he'd once shared the house with another woman in no way disturbed Lindsey. It was a house that had known love. What better place to begin a new life? Besides, she'd brought her collection of teddy bears and a bevy of other possessions that had soon turned the house comfortably into hers. At present, her Winnie the Pooh books lay cribside. She'd also found the book that Walker had once read to her. Soon he'd once more read about kings and queens and simpler things.

True to his word, Walker forced her to rest. An hour later, both lay on the bed, she spooned against him, he gently rubbing her stomach. They had drifted in and out of sleep, in and out of tender and not-so-tender kisses.

"Walker?" she whispered at long last.

"Mmm?" he mumbled.

"Are you afraid?"

He knew she was talking about labor, about becoming parents. "Are you?"

"Not afraid," she answered. "Just a little apprehensive. I'm not sure what to expect."

"Everything'll be fine, Lindsey. I swear it. I'll be right with you." He stopped rubbing her stomach and turned his attention to the small of her back when she grew restless.

Pressing her back against his hand, so he could find the right spot, she said, "I know you will. And I'm really not afraid."

Walker smiled. "Yeah, well, I guess I am a little bit. Being an older father is nice—it comes at a time when you can appreciate things more. But I'm not blind to the problems it creates. Subscribing to *Modern Maturity* and *Parents Magazine* at the same time is a little weird."

"We don't subscribe to either."

"You know the point I'm making."

She did. Of course, she did. And she didn't want to be flippant about his concerns. She rolled toward him and raked back a swath of silver-tinted hair that had fallen across his forehead. "You're vital. You're healthy. You'll be around when they need you most. You'll be around to teach your son to play football and to screen your daughter's dates—or vice versa. And as good a father as you were the first time round, you'll be twice as good the second. They'll adore their daddy.... Just like I do." Suddenly, she grinned, once more her playful impish self. "Look on the bright side. We can have their weddings catered by Meals On Wheels."

Walker laughed and pulled her to him. It was then that she first noticed the little niggling pains that shot through her lower stomach. She said nothing, though, thinking that they would pass. And they did.

"You okay?" he asked minutes later.

"Yeah," she said, struggling to sit on the edge of the bed. "I've got to shower, though, if we're going to Dad's party."

"Want some help?" Walker said, displaying his best leer.

At the ringing of the phone, Lindsey said as she stood and waddled toward the bathroom, "I'll hold the thought."

Reaching for the phone, Walker said, "Hello? Oh, hi, Bunny. Yeah, getting ready now. Yeah, sure, we'll bring our camera. No, no prob—" He stopped when he saw Lindsey, who'd disappeared for a moment inside the bathroom, standing once more in the doorway. A patch of clear liquid moistened the front of her jeans and ran down one pants leg. She was also clutching her stomach.

"I, uh, I think we're going to miss the party, after all," she said softly.

The next thirteen hours were a blur to Walker—a happy, scary, wonderful blur. They were filled with holding his wife's hand, of wiping perspiration from her forehead, of telling her to push just one more time. He hadn't been present at Adam's birth and, although he'd always known birth to be a miracle, he'd had no idea of its magnitude. Nothing, except Lindsey's love, had ever touched him so deeply. At exactly eight minutes apart, a sassy girl first, a bouncing boy second, the twins were born.

Bunny cried.

Dean beamed with pride.

Adam and Grace cheered.

And Walker...

Well, if ever Walker had questioned his decision of wedding a woman so young, of fathering a family at his age, those doubts were forever removed the moment he saw Lindsey's radiant face, the moment he held his healthy, squirming children. With a certainty that defied logic, he knew that he'd made the right choices. Lindsey had turned out to be his lover, his friend, heart of his heart. She had turned out to be the sweetest surprise of his life.

*   *   *   *   *

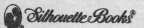

Silhouette Special Edition

presents

SONNY'S GIRLS

by Emilie Richards, Celeste Hamilton and Erica Spindler

They had been Sonny's girls, irresistibly drawn to the charismatic high school football hero. Ten years later, none could forget the night that changed their lives forever.

In July—
ALL THOSE YEARS AGO by Emilie Richards (SSE #684)
Meredith Robbins had left town in shame. Could she ever banish the past and reach for love again?

In August—
DON'T LOOK BACK by Celeste Hamilton (SSE #690)
Cyndi Saint was Sonny's steady. Ten years later, she remembered only his hurtful parting words....

In September—
LONGER THAN... by Erica Spindler (SSE #696)
Bubbly Jennifer Joyce was everybody's friend. But nobody knew the secret longings she felt for bad boy Ryder Hayes....

Take 4 bestselling love stories FREE
Plus get a FREE surprise gift!

Coming Soon

Fashion A Whole New You.
Win a sensual adventurous
trip for two to Hawaii via
American Airlines®, a
brand-new Ford Explorer
4 × 4 and a $2,000
Fashion Allowance.

Plus, special free gifts* are yours to
Fashion A Whole New You.

From September through November, you can take part in
this exciting opportunity from Silhouette.

Watch for details in September.

* with proofs-of-purchase, plus postage and handling